SHADY
RATCHETNESS
To GLORY

SHADY RATCHETNESS To GLORY

Roslyn O'Flaherty-Isaacs

SHADY RATCHETNESS To GLORY

iUniverse books may be ordered through booksellers or by contacting:

iUniverse
1663 Liberty Drive
Bloomington, IN 47403
www.iuniverse.com
844-349-9409

ISBN: 978-1-6632-2577-1 (sc)
ISBN: 978-1-6632-2578-8 (e)

Print information available on the last page.

iUniverse rev. date: 07/15/2021

CONTENTS

SHADY RATCHETNESS TO GLORY... By Roslyn Oflaherty... Hopes to enrich your mind. We all have a duty to not let anyone assonate our character or lower our standards. By conforming to a persecutor; or a supremacy that's confused. Which only makes it hard to distinguished; political belief, relationship or responsibility.

> Bible- KJV 1ˢᵗ Corinthians 1 verse 27 says But God hath
> chosen the foolish things of the world to confound the wise;
> and God hath chosen the weak things of the world to confound
> the things which are mighty.
> KJV-Hebrews 11 verse 1 says; Now faith is the substance
> Of things hoped for, the Evidence of things not seen.

This book is ready to introduce you to its controversial. Inner most vicious cycles of life. Yet it was not written to agitate anyone with vulnerabilities. That may be visible in struggles. Presented in gutter butt fiction. With deception through one's wrongs. Which may need peace or forgiveness!

Hey people let's take a trip. With blood terrorized, endangered individuals. Suffering from jaw dropping hysteria. Which may come from and inner fears or being fearless.

SHADY RATCHETNESS TO GLORY... Hopes to help anyone avoid repeated mistakes. First you must own up to your $ht. Described in one's observation of truth. Which may or may not be from life's wretched settings.

PARENTAL GUIDANCE EXPLICIT CONTENTS...

SHADY RATCHETNESS TO GLORY!

By Roslyn Oflaherty

Fiction describe details, names, characters and places are products of author's imaginations. All books written by Roslyn Oflaherty are written to describe a point. Do not relate fiction events. To any person living or officially pronounced dead. It is entirely coincidental. Parental guidance is advised due to a mature subject that may not be appropriate. Make your own purchase decision! Some parts of this book contain mature adult, contents that are not suitable for children! This book is a fiction artistic expression from the author's imagination. The conflicts of thoughts can be good or bad. You will have the option to keep your intellect rational. The Author Roslyn Oflaherty writes to liberate people. Roslyn is not looking for a spirit of disagreement or manipulation. You must believe that the church is in you. This book was not written for religious discrepancy or radical faith. This book was not written to take the place of the Bible. There are references in this book. Many references were found on the internet. This book is written from the author Roslyn Oflaherty's imagination to help people grow. It is not written to discriminate against anyone. But to put you on a mission to inspiration. For those people that find this book cringeworthy. It may be that the cringe is real. We as a people must do ministry. Especially for guidance for our youth

This book does not take the place of the

HOLY BIBLE KJV

Matthews ~ Chapter 6 Holy Bible KJV

Take heed that ye do not your aims before men, to be seen of them: otherwise ye have no reward of your Father which is in heaven.

Therefore, when thou doest thine aims, do not sound the trumpet before thee, as the hypocrites do in the synagogues and in the streets, that they may have glory of men. Verily I say unto you, they have their rewards.

3 But when thou doest aims, let not thy left hand know what the right hand doeth:

4 That thine aims may be in secret: and thy Father which seeth in secret himself shall reward thee openly.

5 And when thou prayest, thou shalt not be as the hypocrites are: for

they love to pray standing in the synagogues and in the corners of the streets, that they be seen of men. Verily I say unto you, they have their reward.

6 But thou, when thou prayest, enter into thy closet, and when thou hast shut thy door, pray to thy Father which is in secret; and thy Father which seeth in secret shall reward thee openly 2 Kings 4:33

7 But when ye pray, use not vain repetitions, as the heathen do: for they think that they shall be heard for their much speaking. 1 King 18:26

8 Be not ye therefore like unto them: for your Father knoweth what things ye have of, before ye ask him.

9 After this manner therefore pray ye: Our Father which art in heaven Hallowed be the name. Luke 11:2

10 Thy kingdom come. Thy will be done in earth as it is in heaven.

11 Give us this day our daily bread Job 23:12

12 And forgive us our debts, as we forgive our debtors Matt. 18:21

13 And lead us not into temptation, but deliver us from evil: For thine is the kingdom, and the power, and the glory, forever. A'-men

1 Chron. 29:11

14 For if ye forgive men their trespasses, your heavenly Father will also forgive you: Mark 11:25 Col. 3:13

15 But if he forgives not men their trespasses, neither will your Father forgive your trespasses   Matt 18:35

16 Moreover when ye fast, be not, as the hypocrites, of a sad countenance: for they disfigure their faces that they may appear unto men to fast. Verily I say unto you. They have their reward.   Isa.58:5

17 But thou, when thou fastest, anoint thine head, and wash thy face;

18 That thou appear not unto men to fast, but unto thy Father which is in secret: and thy Father, which seeth in secret, shall reward thee openly.

19 Lay not up for yourselves treasures upon earth, where moth and rust doth corrupt, and where thieves break through and steal: Prov. 23:4 James 5:1

20 But lay up for yourselves treasure in heaven, where neither moth nor rust doth corrupt, and where thieves do not break through nor steal:

Matt. 19:21: 1 Tim. 6:19

21 For where your treasure is, there will your heart be also.

22 The light of the body is the eye: if therefore thine eye be single; thy whole body shall be full of light.

23 But if thine eye be evil; thy whole body shall be full of darkness. If there-fore the light that is in thee be dark-ness how great is that darkness!

24 No man can serve two masters: for either he will hate the one, and love the other; or else he will hold to the one, and despise the other, Ye cannot serve God and mammon.

25 Therefore I say unto you, take no thought for your life, what yeshall eat, or what ye shall drink; nor yet for your body, what yeshall put on. Is not the life more than meat, and the body than raiment?   Ps. 55:22

26 Behold the fowl of the air: for they sow not, neither do they reap, nor gather into barns; yet your heavenly Father feedeth them. Are ye not much better than they?   Job 38:41

27 Which of you by taking thought can add one cubit into his stature?

28 And why take ye thought for rai-ment? Consider the lilies of the field, how they grow; they toil not, neither do they spin:

29 And yet I say unto you, that even Sol'-o-mon in all his glory was not arrayed like one of these.

30 Where, if God so clothe the grass of the field, which today is, and to-morrow is cast into the oven, shall he not much more clothe you, O ye of little faith?

31 Therefore take no thought, saying, what shall we eat? or, what shall we drink? or, Wherewithal shall we be clothed?

32 (For after all these things do the Gen'-tiles seeks:) for your heavenly Father knoweth that ye have need of all these things.

33 But seek ye first the kingdom of God, and his righteousness; and all these things shall be added unto you.

34 Take therefore no thought for the morrow: for the morrow shall take thought for the things of itself. Sufficient unto the day is the evil thereof.

DEDICATION

By Roslyn OFlaherty

Is dedicated to the following families. Flaherty/Oflaherty - Jackson - Isaacs - Brown - Dabaze -Antwi - Irish Jr. - Pettiford - Thomas - Davis - Baker - Lalande

Georgianna, Jamal, James,
Wendy, Robert, James, Lucy, Austin
Teya, Tanetta, Porcha,
Laniya, Kenny, Leah,
Jcyona, Quantavious,
Khaliah, Teon, Amadre
Mouse, Jay Jr, Buzz / Kenny
Selma, Dale, Kelvin, Diane,
James, Wanda, William, Shiasia, Angel, Lamont, Author Rody-Ro, and Mama Glo.

Thank you everyone for your support. A Special Blessing to my readers. God thank you for this experience. Writing this book was an awesome challenge. I felt like my mother put this artistic experience in my heart. Which allowed me to write this book. As a true creative person. While not put Father God in a box...

This acknowledgement of SHADY RATCHETNESS TO GLORY BY ROSLYN OFLAHERTY thank you for the experience of unconditional love with no limitations. It has been greatly appreciated while executing my future endeavors.

Special thanks again to you Father God, please watch over me. I know you're not finished with me yet… Please lookout for me as I learn to covert to your direction. I pray people don't put you in a box God. Stuck in their judgement zone. For it is you God and Lord Jesus that makes me believe there is miracles all over the world.

We must pray for one another as we try to live through our imperfections. Amen! Much love and respect.

Roslyn OFLAHERTY would like to wish everyone positive inspiration and happiness. Unidentified uncertainties can play a major role in your future. In life it would be necessary to have a well-thought-out strategy. For high living in obtaining success with your dreams. At the end of the day you must believe in yourself, even though problems negative or positive. You're the only one responsible for making your dreams materialize. Work at it every day. Obtaining picture-perfect order in your life's journey, it may not always exist as fast as you wish. If you believe in it keep an eye on your vision with bravery. SHADY RATCHNESS TO GLORY does exist. It can be saved by glory. {"Gods speed!!!"} It would help if we as people, as a whole understand that we must keep; the word from the bible as well as religion from becoming extinct. As we try to acknowledge it to the best of our ability. Someone's significance or faults should not give anyone the right to condemn them because of their interpretation of the lord word. We should all be concentrating on achieving greatness in sustaining success. Procrastination should never be an issue in our life. We must have harmony amongst life as we try to hold on to our serenity. Think smart and stay safe and always remember the mischievous spirits flees for a season.

Roslyn O'Flaherty

1

INTRODUCTION

Your Hostess Roslyn OFlaherty invites you to read. Her gutter butt stinking thinking in life fiction short stories; SHADY RATCHETNESS TO GLORY You will read circumstances in life that some undergo and believe this is because of overconfident or trouble minded people. While they live guarded and cautious lives as one's individualism crises unfold.

Misplaced feelings and ideas have been traumatized inside of their lives with life's midst of controversy and collateral obligations that have been damaged. They look inside themselves knowing they must demand freedom for themselves and worrying who will protect humanity. They live in danger of potential problems caused by the government. Wishing the government would talk their language and not law terminology, as they back pedal on jargon that is not the commandments of God's government.

They know and believe their integrity is valuable. Their moral worth must not be crushed. Life makes us look for personal independence modifications to the formats of obey. One-persons mishap can cause a domino effect that changes the life of others. From which they have been predestined by.

Visualize yourself conforming to the concept of gentrification in America with no poor or middle class. While you comply with the commands of the existing mentality, which now has you hostage. It simulates you into cultures and relationships that cause barriers of life, which make you obey the traditions.

Why should we be a sufferer from reverse guilt and criticism of associates in business affairs-society and controlling nonsense? The systems administrations officials who is talking about you is often playing both sides of the fence. They can be a treacherous individual. With the purpose of terminating your goals. As they have the legal right to call the shots in your life, with no moral structure. Consequently, you had no choice, but to sign your life's purpose over to them. Losing the control to manage your life's expectation. Their main single-mindedness is to become an annoyance.

Years are spent holding on to the controversy of the constitution of right and wrong. Will this render you capable of holding responsibility to do incredible thing? You must hold on to your peacefulness. Your faith and courage are tested all the time. Which can become in infuriating… This should be the moment in time, in life challenges to stop obeying guidelines of institutionalized thinking. Which is destroying the energy of your concentration to justify your purpose in life.

Business associates are acting shady. To be a victim due to poor judgment of others is not healthy. Always remember what we do with our minds matter. Some people are ratchet and evil imprisoned with their own insecurity. They don't have any influence that controls emotions or a lack of empathy. I wonder have they lost the aptitude to perceive that they have psychologically checked out, even though they are highly intelligent. Do they comprehend how aggressive they can be, as they live in an angry place in their mind? Making their fate go downhill.

To watch the ratchetness in the silent majority. The minute they don't get their way, it makes her for them to stay hushed they often feel persecuted by any conduct. Surviving is not enough when you are looking for a future without distress. They disregard a lot of individuals through intimidation because they won't give them the time of day. Stop looking for people to validate you. It's time to know the purity of your heart, without misery. Let go of the need to have approval of others. Hold on to your self-respect.

You can't travel in the same circle with some individual's negative mentality. Your dreams and aspiration may be on a spiritual level, which everyone won't understand. Take the burdens from your heart. Why should people demoralize your confidence in order to crush your dreams? They are not making any optimistic traditional values on making an input to better your existence or theirs. They are not the ones financing your dreams.

The unpleasantness is making you fall from confidence. Don't be side tracked by your enemies. You must understand that God looks at your heart. People can cause your brainpower and body to over load with stress. The influence they have over your self-esteem, doesn't give you the ability to faithfully believe in yourself. Watch out for the haters, questioning your ability to become successful. While they throw shade intentionally to cause you not to ever get back on your feet.

After all the heart aches and setbacks in your life. Stay prayed up and stay in faith, the wickedness is truly not an act of kindness over your life. Hold your head up and walk in faith. So, the evil spirits do not take your souls peace. Whatever it is you want out of life. You better speak it into existence! Don't bury that seed which bring you Glory. Even though your way of life on this earth is not the {norm} vision of your ancestors.

By not obeying the standards of life in society your existence shouldn't be compromised. To fault find and have judgments that dignifies other masses opinions has internalized in your mind. You feel you must forgive other in order to believe in yourself. Not understanding where their common sense is. You refuse to comply with the feelings in your heart. They continue speaking of you in a derogatory way. This is only being done to cover up their strategies of manipulation.

A person character should not be spoken over with a mischievous manipulating spirit. Society does not want you to intercede for others in the spirit. It's a spiritual warfare, not cardinal. Many people are fighting their own demons. And have not tapped into the fact that the Holy Spirits lives inside you.

We are taught that we must have power over our impulses. Practicing patience will enable us to sit still and understand your blessing is coming. The journey over your life experiences should not leave you with constant worry and fear. You don't want to miss your blessings! A non-inspirational attitude has been forced upon you with deception. Dragging you into danger while exploring alternatives to learn what your existence is really about.

Don't live for other people who are not essential to your life. You did not come out of your mother's womb, born carrying nonsense. That baggage of unconstructiveness, they continue to carry does not belong to you. Your existence in life is not to correct their mess… It's time to live stress free and continue to be blessed. Don't let your heart stay wrecked.

Is life draining your mentality with feelings of discouragement that has become the norm? Is it right to act unsophisticated to others on purpose? Because they have become a needy individual. That doesn't give a dam; about anyone but themselves. Don't put yourself around people who constantly portray to be needier than you. There are plenty of individuals that you can motivate, that won't take your kindness for weakness. Be careful of the wicked mentalities you might endure. There are individuals that play the victim card. I feel we should call a spade a spade.

Compassion and stability are now giving you support. Help is sometimes needed to disregard people; who are uttering nasty remarks that could cause emotional pain. People can only steal your contentment if you let them. The secrets about what you should know about this. Is that all the negativity. In your life might kill you. It's not feeding you spiritually.

2

LIFE STYLE WITH A TESTIMONY

By Roslyn OFlaherty

A life style with a testimony, can you hear me Lord? Blessed, oh Lord in thee I pray. For I have been singled out by the devil. The devil has been on my shoulders long enough. Yet! I was living in a state of being an act of destruction. Lord I've tried freedom and justice the American Way City, State and Federal legislation it doesn't comfort me.

I've lost confidence in the constitution. I have pledged allegiance to the flag of my government and converted to the National Anthem. I was raised to think we lived in the land of the free and the home of the brave. Yet the laws of the land felt strange to my demeanor.

I knew the disrespect of freedom of peace became part of reality. In life's future towards Americanisms chauvinistic, rational and honorable values. I grew up thinking, I had inherited this character of reality at birth. I wondered if this came from the principle of my struggles. The universe of liberty was full of injustice and political enemies.

Recognition of violence brought on by humanity being mistreated, causing suffering souls in this nation. The opportunities of our falling hero tribute to their families sacrifice recognition was not appropriately given. Some family had individuals that were given the Purple Heart. They were isolated left with the consciousness of depression and poverty on a fixed budget. One foot in the door of their homes and the other foot could carry them to rootlessness through gentrification glitches.

When I played by the rules, intensity fighting poverty. Uneasiness reached into my soul as I try to hold on to my innocence. I was living off of thug love. Lord I am not being blessed from hanging in the hood. Now I lift my head in humiliation. For I forgot how to pray!

Prophesying over myself with a divine inspiration. People were taking my kindness for weakness. I aided everyone but myself. Oh God comfort me as I bring the confusion that I have made and put it in your hands. I was lost in life's tragedies. I turned out to be a physically abused house wife. Lost my babies daddy to the next female. She started out being his side piece. The ratchetness became act of awareness to his bitchology and the drugs not knowing, enough was adequate. My husband perverted my view of men. There was interference, from in-laws which made me insignificant in my marriage. They were partial to one situation. "Their child an individual with a sense of entitlement".

It's a challenge to conceive this psychological image of family. In-laws not of blood existence. This was a conflict of interest. Unquestionably disturbing to my beliefs of my marriage vows. While I suffer oppressed elements of abuse. I tried forgiving people but forgiveness became irrational.

My hearts tired of being on the defense. The final destination is not all gravy. When you're being treated in a condescending way. A marriage of lies, power - manipulation and control. Forced to live the unknown. An emotional impact with reference to negative characteristics. Living through events of theory for reasoning.

How could this go on without anyone detecting my pain and suffering? I have stolen to feed my kids. I forgot how to praise them and tell them I love them. Recreation drugs were used to medicate myself; so, I could save my concentration on my new lifecycle. To me my neighborhood had prearranged plans for the public's drug addictions; which destroyed or killed many individuals. I lost my identity because of my man's, drugs-sexual misconduct and my stupidity.

My married name meant nothing; credibility gone spiritually causing me to be bankrupt with no purpose in life. I let people determine my destination. As I looked for love from my spouse who could not look past his ego. Love caused the loss of life rejected as an embryo. Born to suffering a damaged soul. Now I have to realize I had an imaginary husband in an unstable marriage.

Lord, what I can't comprehend is what gives a child the right to say you never did nothing for them??? I did what I felt best in my emotional characteristic of surviving. Really, what if I became an absent parent - of blood relation. I was living a life that I felt abandon in. For I was not emotionally prepared for being a single parent or understanding parent abuse. Yet I stayed and was put through manipulation to the highest level of abuse from their opinion of me. Why couldn't they have lived in my shoes that got them where they are today??? It takes a village to raise a child and the village was belittled also. SOOO, you want to know what I did for you time and time again. "I OPENED MY DOOR…" My self-distinction, as I retraced my steps. "I got kicked in my Ass…" All I wanted to do was hold the family together. It became toxic enough to make me feel frustration as, I opened my emotions time and time again… I don't want negative vibes in my quality of life. I am never going to feel guilty about anything in my life again. I became my own best teacher on my human weakness. I learnt that I was abused my whole life and that's all I knew. That why it was so easy to take abuse, from my abusers in life. I spent my whole life looking for love in abusive situations. God, I know now it was you that was helping me live past many forms of pain stalking abuse. I learned the hard way and lived the hard way even harder. I have to live in peace with my desires and unconditional acceptance. So now I travel through life guarding my heart and soul as I try to live in love. I allowed people to get close to my soul, but now they can't touch my spirit. Now I have strength in faith, as I try to learn the Word. I will never travel down these roads again. Physical and spiritual warfare was fighting that came from being blind by peoples carnal (fleshly, destructive) cravings. This dysfunction has nothing to do peace or glory. There are people that can carry their dysfunctions to the misunderstood compensations of death. My self-discrepancies let me know, somethings and people you just have to let go of. With no emotions of hate. Having to let folks go makes you question. If this is a new form of affection? Well I am thankful to be able to recognize now. Through the transgression of parenting good, bad or indifferent; temperaments. I am not a victim of shame. Father God did not leave me or forsake me! Favor and deliverance have entered my life placing seeds around my necessities, hallelujah. There are lost souls, I wish to touch mentally. I have been a healer to many people my whole life. I will continue to intercede for others in the spirit. The miracles will come from the Lord.

Discharged from the work force. Put out to pasture with ill health. I lost my mind living, to survive in a system with no true advocates. My diverse corrupt, disorientated mind needs healing. As I live in my immoral incomplete cycle of life. Which was out of my comfort zone. I lost comprehension of the Lords' word. I was now a product of the streets negative environment scarcely able to survive. My empathy to understand others became draining as I listened to their cry for help. Along with me saying I needed help. Development now is looked, for from sowing improvement in an original spiritual seed. Which comes from Gods message of the word.

I prayed for progress beyond the life I lived. I needed unconditional life for my endeavors with respect. I know now man cannot help me. I must not rely on man. I can only rely on God. I sold my soul to the devil and bit the bullet of deception. This is irrelevant to, the love of God? Truthfully Lord, I was confused between religion traditions, spiritual therapy and the word, because of many people's interpretation. I wondered if the only place people would find goodness was in death… This was because I heard many people say, I want to die. Was this good for the people they are leaving behind. Along with a bereavement period of suffering. Did they really understand the wages of death and dying? Lord is their beauty in death? Or was this the way they felt they could escape to go to heaven. I was a lost soul and still am. Looking for the feeling of heaven on earth.

My prognosis is it time to rise up and engage, in the house of the Lord. Even though I don't believe in religion and only believe in God's Word. I say again; I am truly still a lost soul. I personally stand before Jesus son of God and ask you to advise me. Will the truth inspire me to take responsibility for my actions? What I have learned in life, I learned from my physical and mental suffering…

Lord lift me up from the illness I have endured. Heal me from my troubles. Tension is ascending. Put me on my feet. So, I can endure my distress and misfortunes. My ideology of life deteriorates from my personality. It has made me less than a full human being. I now continue to live angry and upset. A whole complete cycle of action, living on the edge. I want to stop living a cautious life.

I must be free from drama. Lift this burden in which I carry. Keep me from perpetuating feelings that causes problems. Bring closure, Lord

Jesus to my altercations. For slippage always keeps me from my dreams. Support me as I put trust in you.

I am tired of straddling the fence when it comes to you Lord. I pray for a safe space, for you to assist me in seeking your ministry. I must be free in God's family. So, I pray to the almighty God to delivers me from lusting in life's mischievous temptations. Give me strength and faith to be able to forgive others. Give me the powers to regain my compassion to help people through their misfortunes. For I am prepared to pray! I want to learn how represent the Lord Jesus.

Patterns of my past did not allow me to serve God. God, I need to be the boss of my life for now; it's time for me to return to my roots. As I look for a healthy environment without ratchet people expectation of who I am. I know I still must walk in love. My values must be my top priorities, along with the faith of God's word. I have taken into consideration. That the streets were waiting for me. Drama was unfolded in my life. I want to come in control of my fears. Making my life valuable and rewarding in a full circle of life that will keep me from acting out of distress. I want full control of myself. My wings are ruined and it's time for me to soar. I need a state of mind to walk in love with individuals that are morally wrong, like I am at times.

A rational bond between me and Jesus is needed. So, he can teach me the simplicity of living freedom from complexity. I must not be an idol in my own mind. I'm trying to live a stress-free life. Restricted from pain and everyone's nonsense. My life is just an unpredictable roller coaster. I was at the mercy of my difficulties. Life won't kill me Lord. I'm tired of living in a vicious life cycle!

God, I know you're listening. God I'm glad you're still working on me, till I get it right. So, I say, thank you Lord, for letting me lay my burdens before you as I live through my mistakes. God, I believe that I could be blessed through lost souls. I have forgiven myself after my wrong doings. Please wash away my sins in the blood of Jesus. I will

leave it up to you God, to say if I am prepared for this blessing. I will continue to attempt to humble myself through life.

I appreciate the favor that I have endured in my life. It has taught me to keep the faith, you have stowed upon me. But Father God actions of maturation sometimes makes me back slide from you. God please help me stay in prayer and stand in faith in your word. Amen… I want you to know my sins do not define me. Conversely I understand you are worthy to be praised." Thank you, God, for letting me know I am a testimony waiting to materialize…

God, I feel all I need is Grace and your laws in order to get to my Glory. I have determined that it is sad to say. I am truly still stagnant as a lost soul… Sometimes even though I love you God. I still live in the flesh. I believe in you God. I don't believe in Religion or Doctrine. Some people interpretations of the Word worry me. I have faith that I have been delivered from my life of abuse. Coping by way of detestation is not what I want in my life. I have not been raised in the church. Nor have I ever been part of a church family.

Father God is it a normal part of life. Building trust after being neglected for years. Should the Holy Word make you feel like you are going to depart from this natural life? As you stray away from love in mortal imperfection and tolerating life's obstructions. I am learning that it's me that has to love me. Can you imagine feeling you have been casted out of unconditional love? I have listened to the arrogant remarks. That comes from people's mouths that is supposed to be consumed heartfelt.

Lack of integrity to myself. Sometimes comes from people. Who can't inspire me? I am a lost soul. Even though I know, I was born to be a Queen. I must stop living a cautious life. So, I can be free to face my adversities. God I am worth loving. I have to find out. Where I belong in my life. The Church is a hospital and I believe; the community is the church. I have learned that there will always be a trail, battle or something to overcome. I really feel like I've done those kids into adulthood. So, I have always said just let me impart; the knowledge my Mother and Father has given me too. I have been able to share words of wisdom to many. I lived enough to know there is nothing that God won't help you through. And if you're tested. You better believe that God has the okay to test you. He allows you to be tested because he knows you have everything. You need to pass the test to be victorious! You just have to remember to use it. God I must be better; than I am. So, I can be saved with the power and the glory. In the name of thy Son Amen. Thank you, Jesus we serve, an awesome God.

SHADY RATCHETNESS TO GLORY!
By Roslyn OFlaherty

Staring

Makayla

Pervasive language
Sex - drugs – crimes
And
Dangerous Weapons

3

YOU'RE READY

Roslyn O Flaherty

You're ready to bring yourself to a whole different moral in life. You took a deep breath while a smirk appears continuously your face. Happiness here you come. You're eager to unleash the innovative reality of yourself. That was a belief hidden inside you all along. This new change over you feels like a sensation of knowing; you could no longer compromise what you felt in your heart. You're positive, you can control your temperament with isolation from nonsense. No one will misguide your personal judgement to your new vision of life with critical thinking. You have come to a decision to let God into your life. So, you start looking for a house of worship that would help you keep heavenly thoughts.

You're ready to let mismanaged worldliness out of your soul. In hope that your mind goes in an encouraging direction. You open the entrance to the house of the Lord. You are greeted with admiration as you sit down you pray to yourself. God please lend a hand so, you don't compromise your true self behind doubt of religious conviction. While accepting motives for being in the house of worship are, for a good purpose. You were ready to tap into yourself spiritually. Although you are surrounded in favor, it was time to keep the faith. That through God you are truly loved. For now, it was time to learn the Bible. Convinced now that – "God's kingdom is Gods Government that rules the earth" ...

Roslyn O'Flaherty-Isaacs

"The Holy Bible"
King James Version, REVISED 1987

Act 1 verse 8 says -But ye shall receive power, after that the Holy Ghost is come upon you: and ye shall be witness unto me both in Je-ru-sal-em, and in all Ju-dae-a, and in Sa-ma'-ri-a and unto the utter most part of earth.

Act 5 verse 42 says - And daily in the temple, and in every house, they ceased not to teach and preach Je'-sus Christ.

Luke 21 verse 7 says - And they asked him, saying, Master, but when shall these things be? And what sign will there be when these things shall come to pass?

Luke 21 verse 10 says -Then said unto them, Nations shall rise against nation, and kingdom against kingdom:

Luke 21 verse 28 says - And when these things begin to come to pass, then look up, your heads; for your redemption drawe'th nigh.

Luke 21 verse 25 says - And there shall be signs in the sun, and in the moon, and in the stars; and upon the earth distress of nations with perplexity; the sea and the waves roaring;

Luke 21 verse 31 says - So likewise Ye when Ye see things come to pass, know Ye that the kingdom of God is nigh at hand.

Daniel 2 verse 44 says - And in the days if these Kings shall the Gods of heaven set up a kingdom, which shall never be destroyed: and the kingdom shall not be left to other people, but it shall break in pieces and consume all these kingdoms, and it shall stand for ever.

Luke 8 verse 1 says - And it came to pass afterward, that he went throughout every city and village, preaching an shewing the glad tidings of the kingdom of God: and the twelve were him.

Mathews 6 verse 9 say - After this manner therefore pray ye: Our Father Hallow be thy name.

Mathews 6 verse 10 says - Thy kingdom come. Thy will be done in earth, as it is in heaven.

Mathew 24 verse 3 says - And as he sat upon the Mount of Olives, the

Disciples came unto him privately saying, tell us, when shall these things be? And what shall be the sign of thy coming, and of the world?

Mathews 24 verse 14 says - And this gospel of the kingdom shall be preached in all the world for a witness unto all nations; an then shall the end come.

Mathews 24 verse 12 says - And because iniquity shall bound, the love of many shall wax cold.

Mathews 24 verse 22 says - And except those days should be shortened, there should no flesh be saved: but for the elect's sake those days shall be shortened.

Mathews 18 verse 18 says - Verily I say unto you. Whatsoever ye shall

bind on earth shall be bound in heaven and what so ever ye shall loose on earth shall be loosed in heaven.

Mathews 18 verse 19 says - Again I say unto you. That if two of you shall agree as touching anything that they shall ask, it shall be done for them of my father which art in heaven.

Mathews 18 verse 20 says - For where two or three are gathered together in my name, there am I in the midst of them.

1st John 5 verse 9 says - And we know that we are of God, and the whole lieth in wickedness.

Genesis 2 verse 17 says - But of the tree of the knowledge of good and evil, thou shalt not eat of it: for in the day that thou eatest thereof thou shalt surely die.

Genesis 3 verse 1 says - Now the serpent was more subtil than any beast of the field which the lord God has made, and he said unto the woman yea, hath God said. Ye shall not eat from the tree of the garden?

Genesis 3 verse 2 says - And the woman said unto the serpent. We may not eat of the tree of the garden:

Genesis 3 verse 3 says - But of the fruit of the tree which is in mist of the Garden. God hath said, ye shall not eat of it neither. Shall ye touch it lest ye shall die.

Genesis 3 verse 5 says - For God doth know that in the day ye eat thereof, then your eyes shall be as gods knowing good and evil.

Mathew 24 verse 21 says - For then shall be great tribulation, such as was not since the beginning of the world to this time, no nor ever shall be.

Mathew 28 verse 18 says - And Jesus came and spake unto them, saying all power is given unto me haven and in earth.

Mathew 28 verse 19 says - Go ye therefore, and teach all nations, baptizing them in the name of the Father and of the son, and of the Holy Ghost.

Mathew 28 verse 20 says - Teach them to observe all things whatsoever I have commanded you: and, lo, I am with you always, even unto end the world A-men.

1 Corinthians 8 verse 5 says - For though there be that are called gods. Whether in heaven or in earth. (As there be gods many, and lords many.

Roman 5 verse 11 says - And not only so, but we also joy in God through our Lord Jesus Christ, by who we have now received atonement.

Roman 5 verse 12 says - Wherefore, as by one-man sin entered into the world, and death by sin; and so, death passed upon all men, for that all have sinned;

Roman 5 verse 13 says - (For until the law sin was in the world: but sin is not imputed when there is no law.

John 17 verse 3 says - And this is life eternal, that they might know thee the only true God and Jesus Christ, whom thou hast sent.

Revelations 1 verse 5 says - And from Je-sus Christ, who is the faithful witness, and the first begotten of the dead, and the prince the kings on earth. Unto him that loved us. And washed us from our sins in his blood.

Act 5 verse 27 say - Saying, did not we straitly command you that ye should not teach in this name? And, behold ye have filled Jeru-sa-lem with your doctrine, an intend to bring this man's blood upon us.

Gate and broad is the way that leadeth to destruction, and many there be which go in threat:

Mathew 7 verse 14 says - Because strait is the gate, and narrow is the way which leadeth unto life, and few there be that find it.

Mathew 7 verse 21 says - Not everyone that saith unto me. Lord Lord, shall enter into the kingdom of heaven; but he that doeth the will of my father which is in heaven.

Mathew 7 verse 22 says - Many will say to me in that day Lord Lord, have we not prophesied in the name? And in thy name have cast out devils? And in thy name done much wonderful work?

Hope you enjoyed the Bible Verses from the holy Bible. KJV

GOD IS THE UNIVERSAL RULER
THIS IS GOD'S GOVERNMENT
SOME WICKED INDIVIDUALS. THINK THEY RULE
THE WORLD. WITHOUT A GODLY LIFE.

STOP HATING -WITH-SHADY RATCHNESS...
TRY GRACE-GLORY PRAYER
Finding strength of love,
TO BE BLESSED
DON'T BE OPPRESSED
YOU ARE NOT ALONE OR HOPELESS...

4

TEMPLE OF PRAISE

Roslyn OFlaherty

You were craving the hunger from the church so bad. Eager to learn about church it was like therapy for you spiritually and emotionally. It was soothing the soul authenticity bringing tranquility. This was refreshing to your intellect. Despite that fact you were not cultured on how to fellowship. It did not bother you because now you sensed, you were surrounded by the love of God. You want to be taught how-to walk-in faith with God, so you could be blessed and be able to bless others. The church was a comfortable place of worship that was considered to you as testimonial identity for all folks.

Now deciding to make the TEMPLE OF PRAISE your church home. There was no excuse not to attend. It offers a place of respect and serenity. Church service were on Sundays and Wednesday nights, they also had Bible Studies. On the weekend you became emotionally involved in a woman's workshops. Although you are a spiritual person you believed; that the Holy Spirit was an active force from God to create the universe.

Church gave you the implements you needed to boost yourself esteem. You now had a church family. They taught you how to dress appropriately for church. You always dress in tight slacks with a cleavage blouses to church. Your clothes were always clean. That was what you thought was appropriate for church; since you believed God said, come as you are. You could not entertain the thought of keeping the churches dress code. In your mind you did not think clothes were going to take you to heaven. Yet you thought it was important to go along with the churches dress code for now. The house of worship showed a powerful and debatable outlook on life, when it came to sinners in the outside world. Even thou most of them had reckless and ratchet characters. It was alright for their ego because they were forswearing in the house of the lord. All their hidden morals were righteous in their hearts blessed faith. You stayed under cover with your thoughts. You did not always show your true emotions.

The TEMPLE OF PRAISE was full stories of motivation and wisdom that touched situations you were living in the outside world. The Bible put in plain words that certain battles in life did not belong to you. You knew you were born into a world of death and sin. You were taught that Jesus accepts you with open arms. You believed favor was spoken into your life. You read the book of PROVERBS, in the BIBLE every day.

Insightful that your life's beliefs had church, growth goals that contradicted your personal stresses. God had a plan for your existence. This thought made you accept the fact it was time to let God control your destiny. So, you stayed in confidence. The congregation of "THE TEMPLE OF PRAISE" was influencing you to pray to God. He was your father in heaven. You were hoping one day to give bible studies and workshops.

Your new the church family always visited other churches for bible discussions. After learning entirely all bible studies the churches had to offer. You thought you were on a mission from God. Did you really have the calling from God? Nevertheless, the fact, that you were claiming that you were familiar with the consensuses of the Bible. You started bible studies in your home. Prophesying over individuals from the congregation at the church you attended.

Believing you could make things perfect and save people from their sins. You taught them about God, Jesus Christ and the Devil the fallen Angel. You believed in Jesus but wonder if he was at the rich people's mercy? Did he come to save the poor? While the devil tried to thrust them out of their comfort zone. You wanted to know more about Priest and Synagogues! Were the people taken advantage of by the priest? Did Jesus have power without his Fathers approval? Were the Priest scared of Jesus? You wanted to know more about Apostles, Disciples and Prophets.

You knew you did not know much about Gods Laws or how to teach about his kingdom; Jesus Christ. Yet you encourage the group at your bible study through your personal beliefs, to let you lay hands on them. As the rest of the group prayed, you informed them that "THE SINNERS PRAYER" would offer them a closer relationship with the Lord.

You knew Jesus was the 1st created and God's son was created as a spirit. Then he was recognized with flesh as God's son on earth. The people were confused because they never heard of THE SINNERS PRAYER was being used to let Christ into their life.

They started screaming questions while in the bible study. Why do people have to be baptized? Does the Bible say ashes to ashes, dusts to dust? Does this mean you would be resurrected from the grave? If you are cremated would they make it to this place you call heaven? When you are cremated and you become ashes, does your spirit stay in heaven after cremation? Are you resurrected from the dead? You became confused your head was spinning. They were asking too many questions at one time. So, you made the people chant with you because you didn't know the whole truth of your new religion. You were chanting and speaking in tongues as you preached your version of God's word from the Bible?

The Bible Study Group was still confused! What was the true way to praise Father God? One lady from the group would not let you lay hands on her. She said Jesus Christ is my Lord and Savior. Please explain why you are laying hands on the church group and placing them on the floor? She said you have no right, to say you are anointing them! The church members continued chanting while praying at the same time.

Who are you the woman asked? You said you are representing Jesus Christ. Are you truly here on behalf of the Lord? The members started to think you were doing all this for self-gratification. With the notion you were superior to everybody. Now your integrity is at stake! Your spiritual family is looking for answers. They believed God knew their heart and they were fine with that. To be called to your house for bible study. They began to get worried that you took, the circumstances pertaining to Bible study a little too far.

This form of teaching the Bible did not make anyone recognize the word. This was not effective studying of the Bible. This bible study technique was not serving the purpose of growing in confidence spiritually.

They were looking for a more solid foundation while praying to the Lord. Some members, knew they needed more than that to take them to God. At this moment in time you gained self-confidence that they collectively could learn how to stay in faith and on the right pathway.

5

LET US PRAY

Roslyn OFlaherty

Let us all pray and give hope to the people who live in disastrous conditions. Floods, hurricanes, tornadoes, fires and volcano eruptions; make it unbearable for some to return home. The social system fails to make accessible, expected help. Preparing for volcano eruption catastrophes is not adequate all the time. Disaster insurance is needed to live in certain areas. Poverty stricken while living under the pressure of feeling condemned in what some call a recession. Basic needs are not being met, citizens are in need of food, shelter and clothing.

Neighborhoods are filled with dope, medical cannabis and prescription drug that are leaving people drug induced. They are being sold to take care of the deficit and recreational use. Many individuals inquire about drug programs and mental institutions opposed to incarceration. Once they are caught unlawfully obtaining or using a chemical substance. Drug programs offer job training and a chance to get a good job. The homeless sometimes are blessed with apartments. People are losing hope in themselves, scared to reenter into society. Even though they were given a chance to work the drug program to obtain their needs. They are in need of knowledge without wishful thinking.

Prayers are needed to stop brutality and people living on the streets panhandling which exist right under our noses. The gentrification going on around us will make many individuals homeless and jobless.

Men -Women and children are in need of a habitat for support after being cleared from foster care, hospitals, shelters, jails, drug programs, mental institutions, SRO etc. Gentrification is a big problem that needs to be addressed. What help can be given to those people whose lives have been disturbed from housing fees rising. People are sleeping on the streets in tents. (Side walk sleeping.) Some parents that are incarcerated are forced to sign Temporary Custody Papers to family member. So, their children don't fall in the foster care system. (Temporary Custody Papers allow inmates to get their child back, when they reenter back into society.) Parenting classes are available during their time in jail. Advocates will be needed for family structure.

Let us pray for new born babies that are incarcerated after birth once their mamma leaves the hospital. Mother and child are placed in a facility with a jail nursery unit. This is the child's residency for at least one year. Some children can stay longer depending on facility. This is where mothers learn how to bond behind bars with their infant. As they prepare for freedom in life after incarceration. These parents should be given respect. For not running from the wisdom and opportunities to family values as they live in survival mode.

Man-Woman-and Child, family, genetically, respect, values, patience, Favor, provider, school, affirmative action shootings, education religion, holiday, civil rights, president, election, 14th amendment, race, freedom, champion, blessed, proud, discrimination, hung, jury, social rights, constitutional, acceptance, grace, home owners, affordable housing, joy, ghettoization, gentrification, genocide, homeless, facts, approved, heartless, America, labor, crops, again, poor, middle class, rich, influence, impeachment, outrage, immigration, taxes, lies, deception, arbitration, citizenship papers, passports, approval, segregation, elderly, social security, circumstances, loyalty, hunger, FDA, food, voucher, shelters, poverty stricken, incarcerated, lawyer, unlawfulness, bail bondsmen, time, denial, sexual scandal, buying, testify, prosecutor, mercy, death, penalty, mistrial, public defender, dying, mourn, murdering, color, guilty, condemnation, corporate status, survivalist, sickness, welfare, confusion, business, laptop, digital, copy machine, entrepreneurship, sacrifice, interference, direction, honor, power, job employment, military recruiting office, modified, faith, homeless, foster care, Jail, group homes, crises center, psychiatrist, therapist, attitude, mental institution, counselor, doctors, nurses, cops, judicial, system, unsafe, DWI, integrity, right, wrong, identification, democracy, catastrophe, busted, disgusted, prison, death penalty, suffering, public-defender, prosecutor, life, victimized, job training, adult education, proud, scholarship, amazing, schools, student loans, annual credit report, business loan, bank, wisdom, wrong, meaningless, fight, wisdom, mortgage, debt, tittle struck, identity thief, pity, betrayal, lies, child support, head of estate, opinion, divorce decree, mental health, disability, grief, crime, white-collar crime, blue-collar crime, history-case, deposition, collusion, scandal, FBI, United Nations, politicians, congress Attorney General, Inspector General, Uncle Sam, legion, War, brave men and woman, social-media, cell phones, campaign, deception, money, folks, malpractice suet's, rape, child abduction, slavery, inappropriate, victim, deposition, societal, direction emancipation, courage, apartheid, historical, disable, veterans, revolution / evolution, politics, enemy's, constitutional, understanding, deformation, sadness, Will the United States be wiped off the map? Atomic science/ nuclear warfare, dooms-day, treason, petrified, incompetence, extortion, felony, destruction, hell, dependability, justice, trust, honor, election, mistrial, irrelevant, prison, fraud, stop-n-frisk, time, diligence, religion, church, tithes and offerings, victory, heaven, help, sorrow, suffering, gun shooting, man slaughter, assassination during church service, Is death inevitable, investigator, chance, change, friends, lovers, marriage, adultery, shacking-up, intercourse, absurd, condemn, abortion, healing journey, – bank loans, public-aid, tears, money, checks, cash, credit card, education, scholarships, fundamental, parole, probation, juvenile deliquescent, violence, bullies, ethnic group, LGBT, frightening, Dementia, ultima's disease, consequences, virus, fungus, transplants, kidney, liver, heart, brain, tumor, Family life, liberating, foundations, kids, hoodies, killing kids, leadership, angry, gun control, drug circulation, altercations, demonstrations, accountability, hushed, laws, choices, tears, cry, blood-sweat, courage, peace, heart, caring, lives, Love, Trust, Hope, Peace, Glory, Grace, Respect, Confidence, Life, Humble, Wisdom, Smile, Righteousness, Mercy, Joy, Favor…

PRAY ON YOUR KNEES…
And
SPEAK THE WORD…

Gay men and women beaten, terrorized. This is due to people's judgement and lack of common sense. More information about GLBT community is needed. Our hero's sexuality in the closet as they fight in the military, bound to the war's destruction clock. As they honor our country, many people forget they are war heroes. Race and genders are often misunderstood in the armed forces. We are taught this is the land of the free. The land of the brave. Our world's murder rate is climbing.

Men and women are on the corner inebriated. Dope fiends on the nod. Parents are active in the civil rights movement. Churches hold rallies they are also protesting in marches. Stop the violence (Homicides) Demanding better condition. For their privileges to freedom and to end the murders that occur in society. While trying to understand how people could shoot up a house of worship. Some church members are frightening to walk the street and fellowship. Yet they will collect money in front of the church. Taking cash from the same lost souls at church bake sales.

The church congregations should be sympathetic to the needs of God lost children. Some of Gods children are unsure of themselves. When it comes to going, to church and climbing under neath the Lord and seeking Father Gods word. The Lost Souls... Need to understand religious instruction and how to be prayed up, while they learn what a blessing is. They do not need to be discriminated against by the clicks that exist in the Lord's house. The shepherd of the congregation needs to lead Gods people. Their role for leadership should be greatly respected. All members must learn how to pay tithes - Malachi 3:10... Young teenagers are looking for guidance and a foundation for growth. The church can help by obtaining bibles for the less fortunate teens. Job/Scholarships for educational grants. Opposed to bank loans for a good education. Re-entry back into society for military soldiers and their families. Help is needed with getting military benefits and health care. Church should have military days each one teaches one..., Shelter victims should be exposed to methods on how to obtain the food. (Food pantry or obtaining an EBT program etc.) prison victims and the lost Souls, Youth, elderly etc. Should be taught to obtain birth certificates, social security cards and voter's registration card at a public function. Applications should be provided for them with stamps envelopes and a legal advocate. Job fair Applications will be filled out for them if necessary. God's houses of worships do exist for the good of others. Let teach them how to write a resume and dress accordingly for interviews. Everybody is important and so are their needs. Church folks must learn how to own land and their own homes. As well as their own business. We must be taught how to grow our own food. Pursue a good religious foundation. Look for one that is realistic to our needs. We must obtain the actual knowledge of God and obtain a true relationship with Christ. It is time to acknowledge the community is the church.

Domestic violence is on a rise. Cultures disconnected from people's souls. As they look for leadership and a connection to justice in this land of opportunity. Children are being disowned by their parents. Our kids are experiencing child imprisonment. Individual held against their will because people don't know their rights legally. Everyone is due respect and should be treated with common decency.

The reality of slavery has been thrust upon us once again. Bullying and suicide has to stop! Our children are being gunned down in broad day light by; friends, strangers and police etc. Street drugs and prescription drugs are becoming the norm to get high. Some Individuals think it's lit. Psychotropic for mental illness can be obtained in treatment centers or in a hospital. Human beings are working for half the normal wages on a full-time job. Children are being abuse on social media, as well as in their household, foster care homes and detention centers etc.

Kids are on the news for murdering their parents. There are individuals waiting to take what's yours! Identity thief is at an all-time high. Imagine someone scamming you out of your life savings. Through one telephone call or access to your computer. Cruel law enforcement and violence present death to the general public. Rape and robberies haunt our neighborhoods. (DWI) – driving while intoxicated and with cell phones are causing accidents which kill and cripple citizens. Death by guns has a power over society that is out of control. Safety is needed for our formative years in households and on our streets.

The dollar assets value is eroding. The representation of the dollar that is in circulation may change and have a new distribution of currency that some call the ditch dollar. This will be used in order to wreck the world. Economics is crippling us. Why doesn't what we call our government communication exercise our human rights? As we try to correct a heritage of self-destruction. Trying to figure out if we would be living in what some declare to being White America for the next generations to come. We look to humanitarians for relief. God will empower our self-determination!

Some people believe that discernment won't make their heart strong. Others welcome aid or they are willing to be of assistance to other as they acquire how to survive. People have misplaced their sense of direction and existence. They don't have anything to accept as true and tolerate the life they have been given. Not knowing how to be in high spirits or communicate in this world. Many couples continue living, functioning in depression or thug love relationship. God knows where we came from and what we can endure. There is no time to be living backwards!

Domestic violence and jail time have become the norm for some adults. Parent abuse affects the children in some households. The family stays together and doesn't even realize they are living in a dysfunctional house hold. Everything seems perfect. Love with doubts is a fixation of a livelihood in their mind. Women calling men whore dogs as they give reference to women as that Bia-tch. Which may cause individuals an unproductive life day after day.

On a regular basis they sit on the bench or stoop in front of the building. There is a life past this which some call a plantation mentality. Living from their neighborhood stoop to the store and to the bench and back in the house. They manage to take the kids occasionally to the park. Where the neighborhood kids are introduced to drugs and violence in some communities. Gun shootings in church and in our schools. Should religious instruction be put back in the school system?

Abductions into gang's and kiddy prostitution. Kids snatched from the park forced to ride the subway all day with their adolescent pimp. They are taken to motels in hours of darkness force to perform sex acts on grown folks. Individuals losing their lives killed so their organs can be sold. Our children's photograph was being passed around on a milk carton saying they were missing. Society launches programs to help search for lost families love ones. Children are now seen on missing posters in department stores and post office etc.

The parks are where the children become skilled at sell drugs. A continued cycle of alcohol, guns and death comes with this learning experience. Have these children ever seen the Statue of Liberty or rode the Staten Island Ferry? Taken a trip to the empire state building? Have they had the chance to explore the Museum of Natural History or the Planetarium? Tourists that don't live in New York City come to experience this. They ride tour buses that passes the famous Apollo Theater and ride through historical neighborhoods. The closest some New Yorker came to a tour bus is NYC transportation or Bee line buses. Some have been fortunate to take an express bus through midtown.

For some a plantation mentality is genocide crippling their minds and their future. This mentality is a way of living and surviving. Many of these individuals are the most intelligent people; you could meet in your life. Some are just stagnated in government assistance. Some people exist as Gods lost children.

The recession has focused on foreclosures and lost wages that have made people homeless. Homes are being destroyed by the droughts. People living without flood insurance are emotional and mentality destroyed as they wait for their government for support. Some people have home insurance that is not worth the paper it is written on. Floods have made people homeless. Leaving them with a mortgage on property that is damaged or destroyed. They are bankrupted and the home insurance only covers certain parts of the property they still own, which is not paid in full. People become desperate selling their homes and land with bank leans, taxes owed and water bills without informing the buyer.

Why is our center of attention on diamonds, and gold, the newest fashions? Prison programs with jails lesson are used to discipline our children. In hopes to shock them and make them fit for the social order. Television and computers are the innovative baby sitters. We have even learned how to worship God from telephones, television or a computer without opening the Bible... This has become the encouragement and love from our hearts to nurture our young children. Will disrespectful rude children be found in the Lords kingdom? Yet they live in our family circle radicle and irrational. God's prayer and the Bible should be implemented into their existence.

It should be a sin to be kept blind. On what is really happening in the world and, the problems that we really needed deliverance from. Know that deliverance brings on love. Turn up your praise and be blessed with heavy favor. Why is college education making our graduation students over qualified for employment? They are forced to flip burgers for a living. In reality the only thing they have obtained is a hefty bill of fifty thousand dollars or better on their college tuition for some, it is referred to as student loan debt. Nonprofessional graduating student or their parents are obligated to pay the bill. Colleges and jails are our billion-dollar industries.

Take a look at our health plans. Most of the general public can't manage to pay to go see their doctor. A visit that has a thirty-five-dollar copay. Their Primary Care Physician send them with a referral to a specialist to get an MRI. Why are people being forced to pay a fifty-dollar copayment? To get a blood test and MRI on a major organ. After receiving blood test and MRI you are escorted around a wall. Where you get to see the specialist, who read the MRI for another Fifty bucks. After they read your MRI you are given an appointment to come back. You were asked to return in 4 weeks. At this appointment you will have a consultation on your condition. You then realize there was no talk about the blood test results. At the 4-week appointment, two doctor specialists collaborate on your major organ. A Discussion about an operation took place between them. Like you were not even in the room. (The 4-week appointment cost another Fifty dollars.) The result was sent to your primary care physician. Who sent you to the specialist in the first place? You had to pay the primary care doctor another thirty-five-dollar copay. Where an explanation was given, about your visit with the two specialists. Nothing has been done in reference to curing your major organ. Just another copayment that continues to remind you that; the public can live by the sword of a copay and die by the sword in health care. You can't continue to pay copayments, so you decide to remain living with your sick body part.

Senior citizens have worked all their lives. At this day and age, they have to pay for their Medicare part B health premium. Many soldiers have served in the military armed forces. Some went A-Wall or have a dishonorable discharge. Others completed their tour or became disable in need of a psychiatrist. They are now on Social Security Disability; hungry with nutritional deficiencies. Our war heroes are denied proper housing and medical care. This effected many military families. Whose love one that were sent home from their military tour of duty? Suffering while waiting to die. For some family members there were no advocates. To get 0them through the bereavement period they faced. While feeling lost and alone with a broken heart.

Clean water has become a devastating crisis. Are our senior citizens and soldiers the lost souls? Indigent people are living from hand to mouth. These individuals and many others won't have access to clean water. Starving of thirst as they suffer from a food shortage. There are folks that take advantage of food pantry's and government assistance. Water bills are being paid by home owners. Should they have to buy bottle water? Just to have fresh water to drink? Human kind is in a water war. Who would ever think the world, could be taken over with water that the Lord provided us with? The filth and pollution are not an unplanned mistake. Man will be drilling for water someday. As we live in the land of the rich and thirsty. The economy is in a financial turmoil. What is the tax coded for the super-rich who hide their money overseas? Wealthy individuals should be willing to pay taxes. Without continuing to the only thing, they should do is invest money to benefit them.

Weather condition are bad (global warning?) as we suffer with climate disruption with emotional distress. People struggle to live through hurricanes and tornado storms, volcano eruptions etc... Their homes are being demolished. Heat waves are killing people. Fires are destroying our land. Is the ozone layer a danger to us? The earth is also being controlled with urban floods. Nations are living in mishap condition that are impacting people's lives. Leaving them in doubt as they live emotionally overwhelmed.

Water Levels are low as we live with water droughts. People are suffering they are thirsty for clean water. Corporations are selling water to the poor. Times are coming where only the rich will, always have fresh water. The rich should remember they can become financially bankrupt.

Mosquitoes are giving humans viruses that kill. Viruses are brought from other continents. Which our government tries to cure and contain so it does get out of control. Cancer and blood diseases as well as Aids. Along with organ are being studied to give better health care. More organs donors are needed.

The flu has killed many people. Hepatitis A, B, C, D; is a sickly virus that is going around. Many Doctors that can't explain what is wrong with you will tell you that you have a virus. Antibiotics are prescribed to patients when not necessary. Communities are suffering with bed bugs in their schools, dwellings and public transportation. An epidemic of rat's roaches and ants are taking over our neighborhoods and public transportation. Dogs and Cats walk the streets hungry. Some are abused and left for dead. Animals are becoming extinct throughout the world.

Our nation fights wars that we don't understand. I Question why we fight the same way in our neighborhoods. We struggle to live in our lost society as we look for world peace. As the enemy rears his ugly head. Our civilization is declining. The Lord is waiting for us to see past our troubles. We have all sinned in one way or another.

God loves us even when we are dirty and stinking just plain old messy. We were born into a journey from God. You must realize it and enjoy becoming the best at it. I hope we can live in a no judgment zone. Where human beings stop sticking their nose up; and turning their heads at other people with problems. Especially if they are called people of God. This will enable god's children to come to church and fellowship with one another. We are all God's children made in his image. We do not need to be the lost souls! We will follow the path that God laid out for us. One day we will dwell in the house of the lord.

"It takes a village to raise a youngster." Should we give our perception on what love, truth and reality are? Yet we speak on how we want to raise child and our youth. What would be the standard of life for the lost souls? That some have casted away from the church. Individuals who are often casted away by some church folks who are fighting with their own demons.

It is of God for a church family to glorify themselves, as they look for self-gratification in Jesus name Amen? I guess some people feel they get glory for that? For they truly stay in the house of the lord and extend a hand to the people no further than the church door.

Church members scared to praise God in their community. There is a life with God outside the church wall that can be offer to many individuals. Seek the word in your heart and you will find it. Pass it on to others. Let God full you and others with his mercy. Is it right to use idolatry while studying religion to destroy others? Don't let our convictions be a dance with a devil and his dictatorship.

The gift of life is in fact forgiveness. Most people find that a level of disrespect. Can continually come in forgiving some people. It's time to go out and get souls. The victory is truly upon us. Walk in faith, you can be a blessing in someone else's life… We must know we will make it in life and God gets the glory for us being delivered, from the penalty of our sins. You are a soldier for Christ Jesus! We must stay in faith and be patient God knows our hearts! Remember to get your praise!

6

BIBLE STUDY

Roslyn OFlaherty

Your Bible study became one big incident that swayed you to think about all the concerns of the members of the church that attended. Although your intentions were good now it was time to tell Pastor what happened. This was the reason that you were so eager to teach some scriptures. You took the bible studying to a whole other level that went overboard.

You attempted to teach your perception of Gods commandments. Your attitude still remained positive as, you told the church members about the Lord. You truly wanted to be more acquainted with the word of God. You knew you needed to comprehend the Bible better and, what it really teaches. You wanted to be a messenger for the place of worship. The word of God was first in your mind. The congregation was less important because you had to work on yourself. Your love was for God and your church family however you felt your bible study was a selfish act.

Your attitude changed and you began preaching to congregation members, like they were in a cult. There was no reason for you not to comprehend the unconventional methods used. With the controversy of your Bible study. Your self-sufficient mind and soul brought you to a Plato. Where people's opinions no longer matter. Then something came over you. You were using some of last week's Sunday praise from the church to benefit yourself and not be a blessing too others. As a result, you apologized to everyone who attended your Bible study. The things that could bring positive productivity from the Word. Was lifted from your psychological state. Your heart needed to be more solid and stationary about getting back on the precise track with the congregation. You were happy for the grace and mercy you believed was from God with the forgiveness from church members.

You were now feeling you were in a content place in your studies. You knew Gods favor made you notice your blessing again. Your life began to give you an inspiration that you, would have to leave some people behind. It was time to regulate the positive self-growth within you. Everyone you fellowshipped with thought you were the expressively strong. Convinced that things did not have an effect on you. This was not true you needed people to lean on just like the next human being.

You were looking for comfort from their hearts; that you did not have to share with anyone else. Waiting for anyone to pay attention and listen to your thoughts for more than just your joy. You realized God was the resource to your new level of favor. It was a miracle. Now you were feeling an energetic love for life. The experience of love was more than you ever faced before.

New strategies and new beginnings were captivating to your mind. Was this truly the destiny to the victory of your soul to unconditional love and grace? Love and faith were revealed to you. The lord was part of your deliverance. You believed you could speak the love of the Lord into existence. Yet you were convinced more than ever, no one would turn your pearl into swine. The word of God and Jesus Christ was everything to you. Why was it crucial for people to start arguments about the word of God? It's not good to debate Doctrine of scriptures. The bible should not be debated about in order to get to their point of observation. You recognized that was not a battle to fight. Particularly because you ascertain with the fact that Satan deceived the whole world.

You believed you were surrounded with the blessings of God. God created the heaven and the earth. Jesus Christ was his master worker. You always said your prayers and asked God to do away with all the reflections of pain and suffering from your life. Since you gave the Bible Study and prayed over the people who attended. Your word of worship made you believed God would let grace and mercy follow you through all your days. You now accepted Gods wisdom and decided that you would be the church to the people.

There was a perfect world that you wanted to enjoy. Now was the time to show the people from the bible study, how to get they're through prayer.

You knew you were the Queen God made you to be. This sensation that came from feeling like a Queen. You vowed to yourself you would not let anyone take this existence away from you again. One day life would give you the experience of preaching a sermon. Yet you knew you were not prepared. "You gave praise to the laws of God's word of righteousness." Your well-thought-out views in your head brought on hard times. Did they really serve a purpose? The only thing you controlled was how you acted towards people.

Procrastination became one of your major problems. So, you reached out and began to associate your time to the church. You also started to feel Gods Angels were watching over you. Feeling now that only the bible could give you an idea about faith and decency. All your life you held God in your heart. Realizing God put you in a better place in life. God brought you and your family, out of hard times. You didn't understand why you were experiencing the evilness of the world. Now you were starting to think could you be speaking this evilness into existence? Even though you realize God had a plan for you all along.

Your life has changed for the better. Praise for your Father God had brought you mercy. KJV

"Philippians Chapter 4 verse 11 and 12"

Verse 11 says- Not that I speak in respect of want: for I have learned, in whatso-ever state I am, therewith to be content.

Verse 12 says- I know both how to be abased, and I know how to abound: everywhere and in all things, I am instructed both to be full and to be hungry, both to abound and to suffer need.

THAT MEANS- I have learned how to be content.

Whether I'm in need

Or

Whether I have plenty.

7

GOD'S PRAYER

Roslyn OFlaherty

Your past didn't make it into your future. Hallelujah… Members of the church felt it was crucial to tell you, God told them to tell you something to do with your life. You looked at them for you knew if God had something to say to you, he would not tell them to tell you. Every week God was relaying a message to them to give to you. You liked to keep things in the right perspective as far as church was concerned. It was best for you to take religion in moderation. You were not ready to get on board with church members. Who wanted to fellowship after church and tell you what God expects you to do?

You knew faith was wonderful. Some of the people in your church worshiped the church. Instead of Jesus Christ their Lord and savior. You were always polite and you would give them a pleasant smile. While the congregation tried to direct your life. Even though they continued to know what God told them to tell you. Your beliefs was that God has a principle for everyone. Values are what some folks have to figure out themselves. You realized everyone went to the Lord for motivation. Your interpretation of the word. Was clarification for your mind and aspirations in life along with Gods love.

You are grateful to be at this point in your life. Your high spiritual energy helped you live, life with gratitude. Praying to live in a no judgments zone where opinions are not really necessary. Nitpicking people placed labels on you. Speaking what you are going to accomplish in life, and you are not going to become… Predicting you defiantly need the favor of the

Lord. They were more in tuned with what; the rest of your life is going to be like. Till your dying day. The truth was they could not find the time figure out their own future.

With Jesus blessing you knew you truly have been given, the gift of appreciation. This gift was changing who you are. Your faith promotes serenity that keeps you in prayer. There was no reason to reevaluate your choice to get involved in church.

The church is having their yearly picnic. You tried to invite some of your family and friends. A feeling of abandonment comes upon you. People have removed themselves from every equation of your life style. Some individuals were getting tired of you preaching to them. You were given the impression that you were bothering them. You were convinced all you were trying to do is bring souls to the Lord.

Your knowledge of the Bible must have worried folks away. Feelings of being forced into the word troubled them. While trying to identify with what they were feeling. This was frustrating… Did you go overboard, like the experience at your Bible study?

The Picnic was nice and the food was delicious. There was lots of sports competitions with prizes. Dance and singing talent contests with no age limits. You really enjoyed yourself spiritually at the church annual picnic. You were a little dissatisfied with the decision. That your family and friends made, not to attend your church gathering. You were not going to disengage yourself from your belief in your Lord and Savior. You knew you had to continue to walk in love.

Your expectation of their presence. Was not going to stop you from knowing you were anointed, with the favor of God. Preordain to live in victory. You would not misplace your way in the faith of the Lord. Going to the house of worship was a must. Sometimes people would treat you unkind about going to church. Calling you out of your name. As they assumed you thought you were better than them. All you were trying to do was see Gods ultimate goal for your life. He made you humble yourself. Now all you needed to learn was how to sit still.

You felt it necessary to express your joy. While knowing in your mind. One day there would come a time. It would become necessary to leave some folks behind because of your beliefs. The crazy thing was that you loved them unconditionally. They were your strength and would always hold a place in your heart. Their life would always bring love to them. You knew one thing that you believed in God... It was time to be grateful for your blessings. Roman chapter 6 verse 16 says- Know ye not, that to whom ye yields yourselves servants to obey, his servants ye are to whom ye obey; whether of sin unto death, or of obedience unto righteousness?

8

CHURCHFOLK?   C

By Rosln OFlaherty

Some men in church lusted for you. They knew it nevertheless they did not verbalize it. They felt the humiliation that took place in their marriage. Counseling was given in church that was supposed to help, give a resolution to marriage concerns. We were all grown-ups. However, some people's egos got in the way. They would never discuss their erotic desires through church counseling. You questioned whether you could stay in a good place in your heart and mind. As male church member desired you sexually. Did the existence of trying to place Gods truth in your life. Only have to do with you? What gives church folks the right to influence this blame of fleshly sin upon your life?

The Followers were prepared to make their so call courageous men actions of sin your reality. Why are they telling you to look for repentance? For issues that have nothing to do with you. Should you go back to this place of worship? Was it time to stand up, for the respect that was due to you? The Pastor did not deal with what was going on with the people attending Sunday worship. He knew about all the affairs. Could he be guilty of the same actions of lust?

It was now clear that everyone, knew what was going on in the house of worship. Was the congregation under a sinful frame of mind influence? Members of the church went to parties on Saturday. Occasionally on Sunday they entered the religious house of worship. Smelling like booze, half-drunk during prayer services.

Woman were always picking out new male church member they wanted to have an affair with. Some of the men that came from broken marriages. Looking for woman that could manipulate into loving them. Really all these men were doing was just being messy. Most of them had children they left behind and never looked back. They were looking to escape this situation. They presumed it was time to establish a new home. The women were thirsty Queens. Looking for a male hoe they could consider their companion of lust. Most of these affairs became respected relationships in the church. With a good passionate venture that manifested into love with pride. Through counseling most of the couples got married with the churches blessing.

You wanted to learn how to bring new members to the church. Why was the collect plate the only thing that was consistent in the church? Pastor wanted to go on a trip. The collection plate was passed for the members to pay for the trip. Always asking the congregation if you can sow eighty dollars please come up and pay your tithes. You were not saying there were not any faithful members. Some of them were sixty, seventy years of age and attend they church since child. They were not interested in bringing the church policy and procedures up to the current era. The church struggle to keep the food pantry full, the church was in need of a new roof. The copy machine was broken down, cleaning products were limited, and the Bibles were raggedy. The church had backed up bills. Pastor claimed we should not worry about the condition of the church or bills. He said we must have faith and wait on God. Always telling us to pray for the churches problem. Now you believed in praying and God. What you didn't believe is God wanting everybody sitting back looking irresponsible waiting on a miracle. You believe God would have wanted the church to help themselves, and consider that a blessing. You knew God knew everybody in the house of worship had two arms two leg and a brain. It was time for everyone in the church to think about more than their me-me-me complex. Some members of the congregation had to learn it was not all about them.

Due to the negative habit of the church. You just didn't consider yourself to be the only one in church. That fell out of faith once in a while. Well you hoped God could forgive you. Due to the condition you thought you had to conform to. Truthfully you believed some church members were not looking for change, just confusion.

To have clicks among church members. Which had nothing to do with you. Should they have the right to take offence to everyone's personality differences? What happened to being able to repenting for your sins? The betrayal that went on by their spouses was the biggest immoralities. That should have been next month's sermon. For in your eyes a sin was a sin. Yet you could not believe that when it came to sin. The church board members really felt that your name. Was the only name to be of blameworthiness? The gossip in the church was only to criticize you. You were looking for a miracle to bring you triumph from Gods word. The church had a lot of sick mined people. Sometimes you though the church was their hospital clinic. You did not want to play in their psychotic performances.

9

EJECTION QUALIFICATIONS

Roslyn OFlaherty

You began to experience a sense of loneliness. Once you tried to stay away from gossiping women of the church. Their association was not of any significance to you. Certain moments of the day. You were just plain impressive to them. Conscious of their negative actions. Equipped to be the holy phony, the church member made you out to be. Your mischievous mind set. Was ready to rear its ugly head. The church folks made you believe. It was alright for you to hurt people. Considering this to be an offensive violation. To all the principals of the house of the Lord. You felt in an uncomfortable and righteous position, as they took your kindness for weakness.

The manipulation process you had them under was not of God. You use them to obtain things for your benefits. The women of the church husbands wined and dined you. Taking care of your bills that you could not take care of. When they came to your home. You used them for manual labor and denied them sex. You were on a mission to keep up this act of flirtation.

Your self-centeredness was out of control. It went on so long that there was no shame to you game. You decided to give everyone a reason to call you trifolin. As you pranced around them displaying your sexy side. You decided to teach the congregation how-to walk-in love. They could not stand your meet and greet. People attending worship felt, regretful that you were part of their church family.

Now that the shoe was on the other foot. The clicks squad could not stand you. This felt good to you because now the church clicks really had something to gossip about as you manipulated and control them. Men escorting you to and from church as you dressed in your sexy clothes. You did not care that your clothes were inappropriate. Your pants were cut extremely low in the back. The men's eyes bulged at the site of your tramp stamp and butt crack showing. Always wearing half your breast out with cleavage being revealed. This standard of living helped you get your life straight. Now you really felt like part of their church family. You knew it killed them when you stepped out of pastor's car on occasion. This upset the gossiping click and their husbands.

Even though you attended church. Folks began to look down on you. Becoming frustrated over your negative actions. During church service you began to yell at the top of your lungs. Tears streamed down your face. Chatting in tongues as heart started beating out of control.

Clarifying your description of the word. Something had taken over you. Feelings of exhilaration had occupied your soul. Your own appropriate glimpse of thoughts. Were displayed through tongues. Praising the true interpretation of the word taught in church. When you screamed the congregation screamed even louder dancing, falling to the floor full of glory.

The pastor ushers lift you from the surface in which you passed out. They removed you out of church service and put you in the clergy's office. Dazed you felt the clergy remove one of your breasts from your cleavage top. He sucks it while he removed his Johnson from his pants. He released himself on your breast and sucked his sperm off the nipple. Yelling like he was speaking in tongues also. Even though you felt wet and discussed. Truthfully it excited you. He fondled you until the service was over. The pastor and his board members had a conversation with you about your behavior during the church service. You were half listening to them. The church now was your treatment center for your fleshly episodes. What you wanted to do at home, would be carried out in your flesh-eating treatment center. The men now would be eating you out and paying your rent on the reg. You were surprise when some of the wife's joined in to hit that spot. You just told them to open wide. You began to like this little store front church. It was the Bodega on the block.

Every Sunday your actions got spiteful. You became argumentative to the whole congregation. They would still go along with your behavior and let you use them. They felt threaten because you knew all their business. They did not wish for you to expose them to rest of the church. So, they did everything you requested. Guest from another church had come to the store front church. To listen to the pastor, speak. Your performance was so unbearable. That the visiting church excused themselves from church service before it was over.

The congregation was praying that undesirable spirit out of the house of worship at the end of the service. You still were not concerned about your actions. You were definitely showing them your true colors. You shamed the church and they still were in disbelief about what had just occurred. There were principles of behavior that applied to all administrative staff. Yet the minister did not know why your behavior was tolerated. He hoped not to see you in service anytime soon. You repeated and persistently violated the rules of the church. They had a behavior contract you refused to follow.

You're conduct and character were not habit essential for spiritual growth. You never join the church and were never baptized. You just called it your church home. You were mad that they got rid of you because you had religious instabilities and too many insecurity issues. All this time you were using church as your personnel reformation for your self-centered position. You left the place of worship with ejection qualifications.

10

CHET TAKES MAKAYLA
TO A MAN'S HOUSE

Roslyn OFlaherty

Your God was a respectable God. Why was it so hard for you to stay in faith? Trouble always seemed to follow you. You were not being blessed. Why; you did not understand. This was not the moment in time for you to give up on fixing your troubled life. For you truly pursued taken your troubles to the Lord. You knew prayer could change you. You became confused why prayer didn't stop all your mess and confusion. You tried to ignore people and not argue with them. How could you aspect God to keep you, when it is tough for you to keep yourself.

You prayed to God, considering him to be your protector. You wanted answers; Lord why me? Your negative battle in which you continued to put yourself through. Told you why not you! Your ideas action and beliefs now had you living out of your comfort zone. As you considered yourself a sufferer of fear. You played the victim card every chance you got. People can be so unkind. You could not believe. The discussion they were having about you, and you're manipulating spirit. They said you practice witch craft and dark magic.

The rumor started because your buddy Chet took you to see a man. When you entered his apartment. You started to speak; the man said shush! Was this man paranoid you wondered? The apartment was dark the curtains were drawn shut. The man's residence had a strange odor that you never smelt in your life. It was not funky or a scent of medication. A strange aroma like it might. Have been uncooked liver blood.

You and Chet were asked to be seated on a bench made of wood. The man singled you out asking; what can I possibly do for you at this moment. You told the man you wanted to become wealthy. He asked what you mean. You wish to become rich. Yes, you replied! I want to be prosperous. I wish to obtain a lump sum of cash. That will make me able to sustain my life with monetary stability. The man left his seat lit some candles around the room and went to another room. You were hoping the man did not start talking about sinful things or worshiping them. You started to get scared. Was this man into spiritual magic? You sat with your friend Chet in silence as, the aroma of the odor in the air thickened.

Something made you feel mistaken about the visit. You wanted to be well-off at any expense. For some reason you could not have a word come from your mouth. It felt like your lips were frozen and the temperature of your body got extremely hot. As you felt a cool breeze come across the room. It was gone in a matter of second. The air filled up in your body and you felt like you wanted to die. You could not talk to anybody and you could not comprehend why. Thoughts came rushing in your mind was this spell craft? Were you cursed with a hex? Was this because of the money you wanted to obtain you, wondered? Would this affect your demeanor? Twenty-five minutes later the man returned from the back room. He told you to stand up and your body went back to normal. He stared at you he was sweating up a storm. You were scared shitless.

You felt strange like the human spirit. Had left your body for a few seconds. You started thinking; could this be some kind of evil black magic? Was this a satanic spell you were under? Now you began to feel different was this man controlling you? The man grabbed your hand, stand up he said! As you tried to lower your body to the bench. You started sweating profusely. From your face to your feet. He placed a medium size plastic bottle. With some blue foam like. Liquid soft slime in the palm of your hand. Go home and take a bath for five days. Add one cap of this solution to your bath water. You went to ask him a question and he said Shush again! Shush do as I say! In a real deep voice, he said that's Two Hundred Dollars. The thought of contemplating being rich made you excited to give the man, Two Hundred Bucks;

When you took your first bath you decided to dispense the whole bottle of blue foam soft slime liquid in the tub. You began to grin, saying I'm going to become so we wealthy. The water in the tub was an aqua blue color. The water had the same smell as the man's house. You soaked in the bathtub for five hours pouring the blue water over your body repeatedly.

Your friend Chet went to church. While fellowshipping he spoke about the blue substance you had bathed in. You knew you did not have a deranged mind. You kept repeating Psalms 27 verse 1 thru 14 over and over in your head. Your spirit did not have a battle between God and evil. You felt there was no reason to be demonized by anyone. You were not pleased with your so-called friend's judgment. Why did you feel this unexpected sensation of terror and anger? Your faith in God was a motivating factor in your life. You took their opinion of you and released it to God and put it on the altar. You prayed God I turn everything over to you Amen…

You sensed that your compassion for others. Was tucked away in an abnormal place. The enemy wanted you to step out of faith. You wanted a happy successful life. Your intentions were to ignore people. The harsh conditions of your past. Would be just that you're former natural life. You would not be discouraged. After all the incidents that occurred in the church. You knew you needed prayer, but were could you go. You felt your spirit needed a cleansing from your soul inside and out.

Knowing you want serenity in your life. So, you started church hopping. In hopes to get into a good Bible Based Church. That would be filling your needs. You were determined to keep your life on the right path. You prayed my Father in heaven. I have arrived at the entrance of this church. Please bring contentment to my existence. Keep me in confidence as I open this door. With the hopes of gaining love, and respect from this valuable new opportunity.

You finally got establish in this accommodation of worship. With good intention of praising the Lord. Wow the day at this place of worship was excellent. You were in a fine state of mentality. About your decision to attend this church. You had learnt not to let the church goers. Rent unnecessary space in your heart or head. The people were pleasant and welcomed you at the door. You were escorting straight to the front of the church. It is good the Lord is always ready. To welcome you into his direction.

When you stepped into the church. Everyone had their Bibles open reading the scriptures. You were ecstatic to see every one participating in the church service. You felt good about God's forgiveness. It was a worthy feeling with compassion. After the church members read certain Bible scriptures. God forgiveness made you feel. You could call on him like a child of God. You now believed the explanation of the creation of the Bible. God has a purpose for all mankind.

Looking around the church you were flabbergasted. There were no cameras, Stages for musical bands to perform on. Wow this church was not on television. There were no books to buy. You were able to put whatever payment of tithes; you could afford in the collection plate. Without feeling pressured. It was just a small old fashion church.

People were clapping and singing you were amazed. There was no teleprompt. To read the word or songs from. The church members and the choir sung beautifully.

You were relaxed and you knew this would be the church you would unite with. A feeling was in your heart and soul which gave you no disbelief. This was where you desired to be. From the greeting at the door. You recognized you had arrived to a church of comfort. The fact the Ministers were of faith was a plus. There was no lust in their souls. Their mannerism was spiritually beautiful. It was a blessing to see love and harmony in this place of worship.

The church made it possible for God to become personal to you. In the Bible you found a passage that made complete sense. You were able to comprehend the logic in the way Pastor preached his sermon. Even though you were destined to be at this church. You encountered the presence of God in your spirit. It felt so good like you truly arrived at your destination with forgiveness.

You identified with the fact it was necessary to go back to your old church. It was time to ask the whole congregation for forgiveness. For your behavior and disrespecting their house of the Lord and thy God. You had no doubt that they would recognize you were sincere. You were able to tell your demeanor had altered. You were no longer skeptic of your ability to respect the members of your old church.

It was time to talk to the Lord. You were not sure why you could not extend your love. Without something being in it for you. Knowing this was a miserable way to be. You would come into a lot of favor in your life and lose everything. The truth was that you lived with no appreciation or thoughtfulness of others. Making you fall short from your blessing.

While observing yourself in the mirror. There was the person some church member saw you as a former church member who spoke wickedness into existence. They have endured what appears to be the horror of negativity in your life. It was also not pleasing because of your deceptive ways! In your mind church folks had become your enemy.

An apology was necessary to move on with your life. This would enable you to keep your composure. While dealing with issues that were important. Your spirit felt good. An acknowledgement that removed some doubt of your bad ways reoccurring. The new church changed your ego. Making you grow in faith with new beliefs. Accepting the fact that all churches was not full of lies and deception.

It was time to dispense your heart to everyone. Being grateful for life again brought on love. Feeling like less than a human being had left your emotions. Honoring Lord Jesus in good time and bad times. Praying Lord Jesus please cleanse my soul. From the inside as well as the outside. Committed to controlling your ways of lust and self-pity. Now self-discipline had become a new way of living.

This experience was real. Now church felt inspirational. Life had done a three-hundred-and-sixty-degree turn. In such a short period of time. Your mind still races from this huge miracle. Causing an obvious existence to your inner self life's intellect of duty. There was no room for defectiveness.

1. One can believe that God is love; you should not put your spiritual trust in man.
2. You will walk in love and God knows your heart.
3. God will guide you into your own spiritual way.
4. There are too many unrealistic expectations of holiness.
5. God should not be put in a box as far as religion.
6. God does not want you to be over whelmed or under whelmed for his love.

7. Repentance is here for us to repent for our sins.
8. Jesus did not die in vain.
9. You must seek your own salvation with the Lord.
10. Who is to say one person's belief in teaching the Bible is right?
11. You wanted to learn the Bible and not get into the religion of others right now. The interpretation of the bible was what you needed mentally.
12. You can have a voice and not hide in man's perception of you.
13. You were now bounded by God's act of kindness and now know it is time for you to learn how to obey his word to enter into a higher spiritual walk. Your misconception of God! Would not take away from him loving you.
14. You recognize that Jesus died for your sins.
15. You thanked God for waiting for you, until you get it right. Amen...

God was no longer out of place in your life. Your bitterness from your past life had prepared dignity and a new heart felt way of living. Was this the time to surrender to The Lord Jesus Christ? You believed yes it was... The answers came to you from the Bible. It was time to do more than feel the love of God and study his word. Mercy and grace were given to you. God is sovereign and you desired to be obedient to his love over you. Self-control was the tools to achieve greatness.

The Bible is law from beginning to end. The word of God is alive. You joined the church and gave your life to the Lord and worshiped psychologically. Leaving your detrimental life style behind. As you represented Jesus Christ. This would allow you to exist while learning how to obey Gods word. You were not surprised you were looking forward to learn from, the calling placed on your life... A peaceful feeling you felt in your heart, mind and soul. Although you were tired of waiting. It was time to have the calling from God... You were ready to do the Lords work with truthfulness. Knowing it would bring on a source of self-pride without hindrance.

This personally made you feeling great value. Even though you lived a past life full of terror and ratchetness. You identified with the fact; you were feeling like a child of God. Based on self-agreement. While bearing in mind it takes all kind of people to make a world. It was your decision to serve the Lord. While praying for all the people in the world. Even before praying for yourself. You honored the decision to do this every morning. Your main concern was to have ever lasting life. With forgiveness of your past. Knowing Jesus was needed so bad. You yearned for his approval. Truly believing he had prepared a nonaggressive place for you. Prayer and truly collaborating on the word worked...

You will be getting baptized on Sunday. This conformation showed that you must obey the Bible. You truly wished you knew how life would unfold. Now understanding the word, with this first-hand relationship with God. While questioning the ability to obey the word. There was no mistake it was time to really consider having the calling from God. However, it was easy to give into the temptation of sin. From the flesh being weak. A manipulating spirit was causing signs of fluctuating previous retaliations. For now, you recognized faith was needed. Jesus Christ gave his life for you.

The battle with convictions was time consuming. To repent for your sins seemed to keep you at ease. You learned discernment in dealing with others. It is Sunday and you realize the seed of greatness. Was taken over your natural life. In view of the fact you were ready to obey. Jesus Christ your Lord and Savior.

The baptism was in order. Everyone that would be baptized that day. Would be placed under water and received the word. You stood in line wearing a white robe. With a black shirt and a tee shirt under it. When it was your turn. You were in a big tub with water. The Pastor said a few words. Then you were placed beneath the water. The water was pouring over your soul. When you came out of the water you felt blessed. A new refreshed essence of cleanliness was in existence.

There was a yearning to serve God. Feelings ran through your head about the baptism and being devoted to God. It was an honor and a privilege. Jesus Christ was now your Lord and Savior. Your relationship with the word in the Bible. Would actually begin blessing you from that moment on. You were always a spiritual person. Did the baptism make you spiritual with a religion? You wanted forever to remain in God's love. God Glory was now your miracle. You believed in Jesus with the firm belief of Gods and his word.

The personal commitment to Gods prayer. Felt like it began almost immediately as you came from under the water. You knew your heart must change. So, you could be in compliant to the commandments. The Good Lord had something for you. What he would ask you to do when the time came. Sit still - Humble yourself, Shush...

11

REFERENCE FROM~ KJV BIBLE

Holman bible publisher – Revised 1981 – Copy right 1998

You were thinking about the commandments that were given to Moses. Deuteronomy 5: 6 -21

6. I am the Lord thy God, which brought thee out of the land of E'-gypt, from the house of bondage.

7. Thou shall have none other God before me.

8. Thou shalt not make thee any graven image, or any likeness of anything that is in heaven above, or that is in the earth beneath, or that is in the water beneath the earth:

9. Thou shalt not bow thyself unto them, nor serve them: for I the lord thy God am a jealous God, visiting the iniquity of the fathers upon the children unto the third and fourth generation of them that hate me.

10. And shewing mercy unto thousands of them that love me and keep my commandments.

11. Thou shalt not take the name of the Lord thy God in vain: for the Lord will not hold him guiltless that taketh his name in vain.

12. Keep the Sabbath day to sanctify it, as the Lord God hath commanded thee.

13. Six days thou shalt labor, and do all thy work:

14. But the seventh day is the Sabbath of the Lord thy God: in it thou shalt not do any work, thou, nor thy son nor thy daughter, nor thy manservant, nor thy maidservant, nor thy ox, nor thine ass, nor any of thy cattle, nor thy stranger that is within thy gates: that thy manservant and thy maid servant may rest as well as thou.

15. And remember that thou was a servant in the land of E-gypt, and that the Lord thy God brought thee out thence through a mighty hand and by stretched out arm: therefore the Lord thy commanded thee to keep the Sabbath day.

16. Honour thy father and the mother, as the Lord thy God hath commanded thee:

17. Thou shalt not kill.

18. Neither shalt thou commit adultery.

19. Neither shalt thou steal.

20. Neither shalt thou bear false witness against thy neighbor.

21. Neither shalt thou desire thy neighbour's wife; neither shalt thou covet thy neighbour's house, his field, or his manservant, or his maid servant, his ox, or his ass or anything that is thy neighbour's.

12

BAPTISIM CERTIFICATE

Roslyn OFlaherty

You are now baptized. The water evidence is the repentance; you were ready for the act of obedience. This was a Baptism in Jesus name and God the Father. You are now on the path to eternal life. You now have a Baptismal Certificate given to you at your new church home. When you received it, you said Lord I am yours mind, body and soul… Amen!

Filled with a feeling of self-importance. That was a huge step in your life. It brought you a sensation of peace. You were no longer quick to being annoyed. You were baptized for six months now. You did not feel the influence of what you called a Demon. You rebuked him in the name of Jesus.

You felt God was worthy of your prey's at church, home an as well at work. Even though you were part of a church, your relatives and friend appreciated you now. Some relatives loved you from a distance. Understanding why, you took it to the Alter for forgiveness. Not knowing if this truly, was the right place to take it. Friends and relatives participated in selling dinners for the church fund raiser. Donating cakes and cookies for the Annual Bake Sale. The money was collected for CHILDREN AIDS ORGANIZATION in the hospital.

The kid's wellbeing was the most important concern at the church. They found scholarship for their educations. Funds were donated for children to go away to, camp in the summer. They were educated on how to play tennis and, chest. This gave them the chance to compete in tournaments. While networking for opportunities to meet opponents from different churches. God is good, he gets the glory. You now accept yourself for who you really are spiritually and mentally. You stayed in faith and stayed prayed up. Jesus Christ cleansed you from unrighteousness circumstances. Forgiving you and your sins. You felt Gods goodness emotionally. Jesus Christ was your Lord and Savior.

You were tired of the bad morale of the world. You were sure the demon's discrepancy of judgments. Would no longer exist in your life. Your faith level made you believe again. That favor was for a life time. At this moment focusing on life's pleasures. Was easy with God guarding your heart.

MAKAYLA welcome back to reality. You are living in what you consider to be proper praise. Always remember that the Devil don't have no new tricks. Stay heedful of your pass. So, you can stay in faith and have a blessed future!!! Amen... What MAKAYLA didn't know was she needed to be praying and focus on her personality. What she need was a body cleansing to release all her stresses. It was time to confess all her sins... She was once poison to herself and others... Makayla truly wanted to thrive under Gods care. She needs to understand who God said she was. And let go of her negative assessment of herself. She needed to understand the obstinate affection, of forgiveness from thy God. Makayla wanted to be his child of greatness.

13

MAKAYLA AND TYREE

By Roslyn OFlaherty

Makayla's existence was on the right course. Her healing and saving had come from Christ. She was thinking like a positive individual walking in love. The acknowledgement of God's love was the only power over her. Makayla was given all the rewards of life's mental picture of confidence. A purpose to live without constant worry. People's approval and animosity was necessarily lifted from Makayla's spirit. Ready to know another life besides fantasy. The baptism was a healing for inspired greatness. No longer under the strain of life's negative attacks. Her conscious was clear from being angry. Recognizing love for her journey towards a positive future. A division of mental aspirations of her beliefs. To share with this new way of life. Makayla always-over thought the information of life and its rules. Makayla kept this Bible verse in her head after the Baptism. Ephesian 2:10 says- For we are Gods masterpiece He has created us a new in Christ Jesus, so we can do the good things he planned for us long ago. Halleluiah...

Makayla met a man in the neighborhood library. The gentlemen walked up to her and said hello. Do you mind if I sit here? He was a good-looking man. He was well dressed and smelling good. Very nice voice and diction... His body language showed confidence. Makayla said sure, you can sit here. She could not stop drooling. As he sat down, he stated his name was Tyree. May I ask what your name is? She looked directly up into his eyes and said my name is Makayla... That is a pretty name. Tyree asked Makayla do you live in the vicinity. Makayla replied, are you writing a book about me. He laughed, Tyree had a smile that made Makayla look twice, as he licked his lips...

Tyree did not need to know her whole government. Yet it seemed like He had calculated a strategy. To control his emotions before sitting down. Makayla kept blushing. He was fine. Oh lord; Makayla thought to herself. This man could be my rib. The more Tyree talked to Makayla. The better he looked especially when he tilted his head. Shifting his eye directly in her direction. He sat back in his chair. She did not want to have lust in her heart. Makayla took a deep breath. She glanced at him showing self-confidence; they hit it off right away and continued to talk. Makayla was now relaxed.

Tyree said I saw you from across the street. When you enter the library. Makayla started concentrating hanging on his every word. Giving him her full interest to the discussion. I watched you go up the steps and through the door. No, I'm not a stalker. Tyree said I never did this before. It's not every day you see a beautiful woman. I just had to meet you. Makayla I am not sure how you feel about me. I really enjoyed your conversation. I must excuse myself. It's time to go back to work. My boss is having a mandatory meeting. Take my cell phone number. Feel free to use it any time. Makayla thought in her mind. Another man with a business card. His job number was the first number she noticed. Tyree said bye and was on his way.

A week later Makayla found Tyree's phone number in her pocket book. She decides to dial the number. He picked up on the second ring. Makayla's heart was beating fast. When he said hello Makayla. How are you? She concentrated on the fact Tyree remembered her name. They chatted for a while. Before he asked Makayla if he could take her to dinner. She agreed and meet him in front of the library.

They settled on meeting at 7:00. This gave Makayla three hours to meet him. When she finished getting dressed. Makayla looked in the mirror and said not bad. She looked respectable and was smelling good. Makayla started out to the library in her Honda. She parked on the side of the library. And walked to the front of the building. Tyree just pulled up in a Mercedes Benz. He jumped out the car and greets her with his attractive smile. Suited down and smelling good. He kept his hands in his pockets. He was fidgety like his nerves, had got them best of him.

Tyree kissed her on the cheek and unlocked the car door. Makayla sat down getting a whiff of the leather in the car. It was brand new. Wow, this car cost is about Thirty thousand dollars. They drove off, Makayla are you comfortable he asked. Makayla whispered yes. Thinking who is this man?

They pulled up in front of a place called Capone. Makayla surely, had never seen such a fine restaurant before. They specialized in seafood. The valet parked the car. They proceeded to go in and sat down. Tyree complimented Makayla on her dress. She whispered thank you. While thinking about how good Tyree smelt.

They order their food from the menu. His mannerisms were absolutely perfect. The entrée was brought to the table and Tyree said grace - Father God we humble ourselves before you as, we take this time to break bread in your name. Thank you for this food you have provided us with. To safeguard our souls with nourishment. Amen!

They started to talk. It was as if the conversation. Was continuing from the library. Makayla excused herself from the table and went to the lady's room. She pulled out Tyree's business card from her purse. This man was a pilot for Santisk Airlines. This Airline had private planes. Makayla looked up and said God, meeting this man has a sign of favor written all over it. Thank you, Lord!

She came back to the table. This time she greeted Tyree with a smile. Their dinner was served. They were very happy. Enjoying each other's company. Talking and laughing like they knew each other for years. Tyree spoke loudly to get Makayla attention. I am having a magnificent time. I find you to be a very intelligent lady. It was nice having a grown-up conversation. Explaining how he had not dated a woman; for about two years.

Tyree winked, tell Makayla he hoped to see her again. They enjoyed dessert together. Then left the restaurant to locate the car. Makayla can I drop you home. The library will be fine. He let her off in front of the library. Makayla waited for him to pull off. She was not ready for Tyree to see her Honda. It had a dent in the front with a taped-up head light. Makayla forgot to provide; Tyree with her telephone number.

14

A PLEASANT SPIRIT TWISTED AROUND

By Roslyn OFlaherty

Makayla could not stop smiling at church. Singing all the hymns with a pleasant spirit. She happened to turn around. Tyree was in the rear of the church. Wow this can't be! She twisted around in her seat again. Not wanting the diagnosis of her imagination to take over. It was him tall, dark and handsome! Was Tyree a stalker? Her heart was pounding fast. Makayla did not know what to think.

Pastor Cameron finished up his sermon on - The Misfortunes That Un-Forgiveness Can Cause! Pastor Cameron was a guest speaker at the church. After seeing Tyree, the sermon sound like Blah, Blah, Blah to Makayla's ears. The Pastor of the church said his last prayer. Blessing the whole congregation. Telling everyone to recognize when it their season. It was time to acknowledge it when it comes. To be able to prosper and have growth. With their Supernatural being as part of their lifecycle.

The church members started leaving to go home. Makayla exited from the side door to avoid seeing Tyree. She turns the corner and he was right there in her face. He said Makayla what are you doing here? She looked at him strange. Know Tyree why are you here? Are you stalking me, she asked? Know I'm not my mother invited me to her church. It is her first day to sing, as part of the choir.

My Mama's name is Mrs. Jenkins. I never told you my full name. My name is Tyree Jenkins. Now it all made sense. Tyree's name was on his business card. She knew he was telling the truth. Pleased to meet you Makayla smiled. If I knew you were attended this church. I would have attended this place; of worship every Sunday. Tyree stated he went to church, over on Wilson Drive. He inched toward her. Inquiring if they could hang out. Makayla said ok without hesitation. I did not bring my car. Do you have yours? She answered yes, I'm parked right here. Makayla pointed to her Honda that she hid from him on their date. Let me tell my mother. That I will see her later.

He climbed in Makayla's car. So how are you doing today? I'm fine, I really thought you were stalking me Tyree. Now Makayla do I really look like a stalker. I am glad you were at church this morning. I won't lie I did think about you. Now that you know my last name. What is yours? My name is Makayla Henderson. That is a pretty name for such a beautiful woman. She was blushing. May I tell you something Makayla? Don't laugh at me but, I know I'm going to marry you. Let me have the pleasure of getting to know you better. I know I can make you happy. You don't have to be devoted to me. Your company is what makes me happy for now. I mean it! I'm going to be your husband. I will always treat you good. Just like a Queen.

Makayla was baffled. For some strange reason she believed him. Her heart was truly into Tyree. Wow she was ready to recognize what he felt. Makayla was looking for friendship. Without being his one-night stand. She was not ready to be attached. Expressing to Tyree that one day in the future. Would be the time to be open. To the idea of marriage. It was surprising Tyree did not have a fear of commitment. Makayla did not want to be devoted to Tyree's willingness to get married. Makayla was looking for faithfulness and respect in a relationship.

They arrived at a coffee shop. Enjoying Danish and coffee as they continued converse sating. When their visit was over. Tyree was taken to the designated area he preferred. Makayla had to work the next day. Tyree was not informed where Makayla worked. Showing up uninvited would definitely identify him as a stalker.

15

BLESS THE FAVOR!

Roslyn OFlaherty

Times were hard for Makayla. While trying to pay an, old student loan. Which was made in order to furnish a new apartment. God had blessed her with an apartment, car and a job. Finally relaxed with less problematic moments around others. There were no longer feelings of self-hatred. Just a new outlook on life. To keep on staying in faith with Jesus Christ. She started reading the KJV Bible every night. Memorizing as many bible verses as possible. Which had developed into an exceptionally, good part of Makayla's church life.

Something was omitted though. Makayla knew it was time to apologize to her parents; Mr. and Mrs. Henderson. For all the viciousness. That was place in their life. Through reverse guilt; always holding them responsible for her short comings. She knew the power of the spoken words. Speaking it against them always in a negative difficulty. She had to find her true happiness with wisdom.

The stubbornness of this experience made her irritated. Even though her parents apologized for hardships. In which she states was Tolerated during her upbringing. They asked God to forgive everyone involved. While asking for closure for the whole family. They were living parent abuse administered by Makayla. They refused to let Makayla hold them hostage to the family's past. Along with her spirit of manipulation. To make them victims to the drama with a dialogue of the crap. Wretchedness was included in her particular DNA. Which was identified as a HENDERSON awful upbringing.

Makayla was not a little girl anymore. She had to be responsible for the hopelessness felt. From living in what some people identified through; her negative spiritual outbreaks. Don't get it twisted now, there was good motivating facts that was acknowledged. It was time to bless the favor. She was an extremely intelligent individual.

Makayla was now a grown woman and her parents were not perfect. Makayla's parents pleaded for God to let her pardon the families misunderstood nonsense. They knew they were not faultless. But would no longer live being tortured. They did not truly understand their daughter. They believed it would cripple Makayla. If she did not live her own life. So, they let go out of love. It was time to leave the nest. They had pulled the cushion from under her behind.

Relying on them all the time was not creating positive recognition. Just secrets with negative validation. Makayla took it like her parents had abandoned her. Really her mom and dad had, moved on with their life. They could no longer baby sit the motives; of Makayla's selfishness and deceitful ways.

Makayla was glad she had a good relationship with God. Along with knowledge, presentations from religious leaders. She would share her faith with others. Jesus was Makayla's structure for emotional support. The Aforementioned concerns that overwhelmed the happiness in her heart were deteriorating. The knowledge of the word was significant to her since the Baptism.

Makayla continued staying in touch with her emotional state. Was all the cruelty, Makayla felt her parents' fault? Was that their mechanism? That made excuses for horrific choices? Makayla had an Omen. Which was an indirect way to have the ability; to be verbally insulting. Makayla capability to justify fault finding. Was unquestionably out of hand by remaining in denial. Did her unethical mind still resonate, reality? On the low!

It was time to discover her wisdom of revitalization. To let God, change who she truly was. The significance was observed by God. Makayla felt no shame in her behavior. On some levels she would confess her guilt. She discerned that to challenge one's imperfections. Was what an arrogant person does. Makayla uses revenge to promote mercy. Was this the qualities of an obnoxious blameworthy sinner or is it a direct disobedience to the Lord.

Was it really necessary to illustrate? A lack of consideration or respect to others. With an attitude of abnormality? Makayla knew there was a significant difference. She detected signs of an awful attitude. There was no human being who did not sin. Makayla felt they did it knowingly. As well as unknowingly at their convenience. Jesus died for their sins. And God was in the business, intended for forgiveness.

Makayla was ignorant with manipulating actions within her mind. Only to be beneficial to herself. Time was needed to work on inappropriate injustice towards her parents. Makayla passing a verdict over their lives. Which was to cover up her own confusion. God didn't bless the chaos. That had become so frustrating.

Makayla was just being shady thinking; she was walking in favor. So, forgiveness was given to both of her parents. Makayla's well thought-out living situations. Was now a heartfelt blessing. An imaged emotional relief within her existence of God! While pray for the chance. To thank Jesus for a change in life.

16

MAKAYLA AND CLARISSA HANG OUT AT DELUXE LOUNGE

By Roslyn OFlaherty

It was a warm summer night. With a nice cool breeze. Makayla decided to go see her cousin Clarissa. She rang the doorbell. Clarissa answered the door, jumping into Makayla's arms. Makayla Yelled surprise! Hey Cuz, what's up, long time no see... You look good girl! I like your shoes Clarissa. So how have you been Makayla? I'm still trying to figure out spiritual side. I don't attend church down town anymore. I changed my church and got baptized girl.

Clarissa, I met a man name Tyree. Let me tell you he is fine. Thick chocolaty brother with a strong back. Well-groomed always smelling good and financially independent. We've hung out three times already. He speaks intelligently with conversations that are breathtaking. I think he is a stalker. Makayla explained how he indicated. Observing her outside the library. They also went on a date at a fancy restaurant. Then he showed up at my Church. That's when I thought Tyree was a stalker. did go out with him after church. Clarissa said that does not sound good. Makayla, he sounds a little scary to me. Tyree told me he's going to marry me! That's enough about this dude Makayla. Makayla knew Clarissa was just hatting...

Makayla, there's this new after hour spot on Gothic Drive. It's called Deluxe Lounge a nice hangout spot. We are going there so you can calm down about this dude Tyree. Let me go and get decent Makayla. I have these new pants. I've been dying to wear at the club. I have a nice sexy top that will go with your skirt. A little make up wouldn't hurt either. I'm down with that Clarissa. They drank a glass of wine before they left. Makayla had not gone clubbing in a while. They drove down to the after-hour spot. They stood on line to get in. Security patted them down and checked their purse. It cost them thirty dollars to get in. The place was packed. With plenty sophisticated gents. The music was nice, oldies but goodies. From the seventies and eighties.

They went to the bar and ordered a bottle of Chardonnay. An older man walked up. Telling the bartender; put whatever their drinks on his tab. Hello would you ladies like to join me at my table. They agreed and followed him to the V.I.P. section. Everyone sat down a bottle of Chardonnay was place down. The gentlemen said my name is Earlton. He was drinking that dark liquor. It was top shelf. The ladies said hi nice to meet you Earlton. My name is Clarissa and this is my cousin Makayla. They talked for a while and Clarissa got up to dance.

Clarissa and Makayla had an understanding. They would leave the premises of Deluxe Lounge together. Earlton moved over closer to Makayla. While ordering her another drink. He had her pushed up in the corner in the booth. She could not budge. It made her feel uncomfortable. After finishing the glass of wine. Makayla excused herself from the table. To go to the lady's room.

She accidently bumped into this man down stairs. She said excuse me sir. Makayla looked up he was eye candy. Damn, a tootsie roll pop. All cover in chocolate. He had a jet-black beard and mustache. Makayla was a sucker for the bad boys. Hey Lady my name is Marshall. Can I have this dance? She went on the dance floor with him. The song turned from a fast song. To a slow song.

Makayla felt a little tipsy from the drinks. She was able to compose herself and act like lady. Marshall pulled her real close. Makayla started breathing hard and pressed against him. Feeling wet like he entered her. This guy was calm and smooth talking at the same time. Makayla answered him yes Daddy. For some reason she felt the need to say that. She dropped into his arms and felt secure. They danced three songs straight. She felt something rising hard between each song. She could No longer identify with a word Marshall was talking about while they danced. Makayla excused herself to go to the lady's room. Clarissa was standing right outside the bathroom. Come with me inside Makayla said. I just danced with a guy three songs straight.

There was something about him Cuz. That I have not figured out so far. Makayla snap out of it we just got here. You're acting like you are in love. Let me introduce you to some of my friends and acquaintances. They left the restroom. Makayla they are sitting over here. Makayla and Clarissa arrived at the table. Marshall was sitting at the end of the table. That was a change from his energetic spirit on the dance floor. Makayla was introduced to everyone at the table. Clarissa went to introduce Marshall. Makayla interrupted her saying. I know him; it's a small world.

Now Makayla felt more relaxed about Marshall's presence. Since her cousin knew him. Marshall kept staring at Makayla there was a sparkle in his eyes. Clarissa was astonished that they claimed to be friends. Marshall was just an associate to her. Marshall excused himself to go shoot some pool. Makayla watched him as he bent over the table. Makayla thought this man was sexy. As she imagined being lifted in the air. He pressing against her breast as Marshall placed her on the pool table.

Makayla caught herself lusting over this man. She knew it was time to go. Her thoughts were taken to another level. She recognized it was inappropriate. Makayla had just been baptized. The club started to get to her. Makayla told Clarissa; she was ready to leave. Before she could finish the sentence. Marshall came back to the table. Can I have this last dance before you leave? Makayla agreed and was undecided whether this was a good move on her part.

It was another slow record. She was back in his arms. She felt good about the dance. Then Marshall gently ran his hand across her butt. Marshall was working her skirt. It slid from one part of her ass to another. It seemed like it happened all in one stroke of his finger. He pulled her closer and she felt an erection. Makayla's thong was wet. She had been celibate for two year. It was time to end this dance. Her desire to do so was not stronger than her will.

Marshall had gotten his way with Makayla. The song finally ended. She ran to the table and was ready to leave. Can I have your number Makayla? I'd like to take you out sometime. Her dumb ass truly believed.

She saw a passion of love in his eyes. Makayla's mind went to her and Marshall in a hotel room having erotic foreplay. She gave Marshall her cell phone number right away. He walked her to the door and kissed her on the cheek good night.

17

ALINA

By Roslyn OFlaherty

Makayla wound up at Clarissa's house. She did not even remember getting in the car. Makayla had a hangover and was glad to be safe. Wow her head began to feel; like it was going to split open. She woke up too late. To attend church service. Well good morning Makayla. I see you got your party on last night. Sure Did… Good morning Clarissa, I had a ball. That chardonnay was effective. I was relaxed at Deluxe Lounge. Just like you said I would be. I did not get a chance to eat any food. I loved the music and the crowd was nice. Makayla If we would have stayed a little longer. I believe you would have; had something to eat!

Marshall's having his hand on your tit was probably good too! Makayla just smiled. That performance you and Marshall had on that dance floor was something else. All you needed was a bed. That skirt was moving better than you. Marshall did everything but touch your twat Girrrl. Makayla there was this woman that was checking you out. Do you remember having a conversation with her? Clarissa stop playing! No I'm serious. You put her number in your pocketbook. I'm telling you Makayla the woman was hitting on you. Well Clarissa, I don't know who you're talking about.

Makayla looked in her purse. There was a number. The woman's name was Alina. That is a beautiful name. Clarissa what does she look like? Don't tell me now you're attracted to women. Makayla snap out of it; lose the number! I would never give you poor advice. You want to be loved by someone that bad. Soon as you meet an individual; radars full of love go off in your brain. Makayla then you manage to incorporate their

70

character into your life. I didn't see you, that much in the party. Did you have a nice time Clarissa? I always have a nice time at Deluxe Lounge. I danced all night. The music was great. I saw some of my friends. That are regulars at the Lounge.

Well Clarissa, I think it is time I started heading home. Makayla left her cousins house. Remembering how she had an unbelievable time. Classy individuals attended the party. The soul food that was catered, looked and smelt really good.

Makayla could not get over the fact that a woman. Was interested in her. What Makayla didn't know was that Alina had a whole agenda planned out for her life. Makayla would be playing scratch and sniff around her ass. While kissing and licking the hole! Alina enjoyed anal sex. Due to her circumcision; she did not have a lot of virginal penetration. The hardship would be to; have to fake orgasms.

This is why Alina really didn't prefer male sex partners. Don't get it twisted now! She would do a brother in a minute if required. She wanted Makayla to give her soft strokes around her nipples. While having a fictional vision. Being booty popped with just one finger. The minute she saw her in deluxe lounge. She knew Makayla would be using a lamb skin dildo on her. Ass eating would be her new sexual category.

Alina considered herself the master of the tongue. Knowing she could twist Makayla clit anyway she wanted. A welcomed arousal from the wetness and a bottle of Henny. Alina knew she could pull this off. Without alarming Makayla of her vagina mutilation. Lickity lick, with plenty of wetness. Stroking that puss ever so gently.

Anxious to have Makayla speaking in tongues. This would be her new sexual dialect. While Alina sprung that cherry. The cat will arrive, Meow. Making her become conscious. Of the taste in the juice from the kitty cat.

Makayla decided to call Alina. She pulled over to the side of the road. Reaching into her purse and retrieved the number. Maybe Clarissa was confused. The woman could not be interested. In potentially meeting a woman in Deluxe Lounge.

Makayla wondered if Alina thought she was Bi curious or a lesbian. As the phone rang. Makayla took a deep breath and started to panic. A woman answered saying hello. Makayla said, hello can I speak to Alina. This is Alina how are you. I'm fine, I found your number in my purse. I remember you Makayla. They talked a while. Alina asked do you mind if we hook up later on. Makayla agreed she would be ready at 3:00 pm. She was easily inducted. From the passion that came from Alina voice.

Makayla was happy to meet with Alina. She was looking for a little companionship. Was not interested in mixing sex with friendship. Makayla met Alina in front of her house. While driving to Alina's dwelling. They spoke a little about Deluxe Lounge. When they entered Alina's place of residence. Makayla had a seat on the couch. The apartment was beautiful and well clean.

Alina served Makayla some wine. Alina was a gorgeous young lady. They talked a while. Alina pulled out a dollar bill. She folded it in half and put some cocaine on it. She put the white powder up her nose. Then she passed it to Makayla to try some. Alina new she could get Makayla to ride. The white horse any time she wanted. If she could teach her how to sniff. So, she passes the bill and the spoon.

It was Makayla's first time. She tried it! When she put it to her nose most of it spilled right back out her nostril. They sipped their wine and conversed for a while. Alina ran her lips across Makayla's mouth. Then started caressing her breast. Placed her hand up Makayla skirt. Ok baby open your legs real wide let me in! So, my hands can play in that thong. Makayla did as she was asked. Alina rubbed her gently, as she got moist. Alina removed her hand and said that smells nice. Makayla knew, Alina played in her shaved pussy. Better than any man she ever had. Could this unexpected feeling. Be coming from her new experience of sniffing Cocaine? She was Caressing Makayla, making her horny as hell.

They continued to party enjoying each other's company. Alina was extremely excited. To see Makayla's horny ass naked. She placed the cocaine on her pussy and sucked it off. Alina got a freeze the coke was good. Makayla spread her legs willingly. Alina started undressing her breast hung firm. Her nipples were in full view. She placed her breast in Makayla's mouth. Makayla sucked and licked her nipples with pleasure. She wanted that nipple hard all over her tongue. Sucking her beautiful breast like she was a new born baby. Bit the nipple just a tiny bit. Alina's screamed with excitement. Her breast stayed wet and moist. Alina moaned as she played with herself. She could not let on about the condition of her clit. She got up turned out the light. She opened her legs wide enough. So, Makayla could imagine. She saw her pussy clearly.

Makayla dry humped Alina. Makayla thought Alina's body was bang-in. Then Alana strapped on a long rubber chocolate penis. With a lamb skin condom. She spread Makayla's legs open real wide. Peeked at that beautiful pink clit. She could tell Makayla didn't get fucked much.

Alina straddled Makayla open wide baby. Let me all the way up in your puss. So, I can penetrate you deeply with my dildo. She played with Makayla's clit with the other hand. Makayla's shit was tight. Her leg was shaking. As she yelled fuck me harder. Don't tease me baby. Ou-oh slide up further inside me.

I'm ready Alina, Makayla started screaming! I'm ready to cum. Cum Makayla I got you. Makayla's clit was no longer sitting on the couch. By the time Alina got through eating her out. Makayla was in shock that another woman. Knew how to hit that spot for her.

She was moaning loud and breathing hard. It was a fantastic feeling. Her twat was being touched ever so gently by Alina. And penetrated better than being with a man. Was this because a woman knows; what another woman wants? Alina was proud to have initiated. Makayla's first sexual experience sucking on a dildo...

Alina truly wanted to try some anal beads. Makayla began to think was she Bi- curious or Bi - ready? Could this sexual episode make Makayla bi- sexual? After all she did enjoy every aspect of having sexual intercourse with Alina.

Alina loved the fact that Makayla had shaved her pussy. She saw Makayla clit; she licked it. Then held it in her mouth keeping it warm and wet for a minute. Then she played with it. Stroking it softly with her tongue. Makayla was moaning loud now. Yes, that's it keep my pussy moist baby! Hit that right their lick it baby, lick it. Alina licked it slow and soft. And sucked that twat good. Till Makayla released all over her lips. She just kept Cumming. Alina stuck the rubber penis. Inside her with a little force. The chocolate penis was drenched in cum. Alina jumped up and let Makayla give her a blow job. Makayla could not believe. She had been turned out by a woman and her new B.O.B!

After Makayla had been pleasured by Alina. They relaxed a little while. Sniffing coke and finishing up their drinks. Makayla said it's getting late

I think; I should go. They showered together. Then Alina took Makayla home. They sat in front of her house and talked for a while. Alina said she enjoyed herself. She kissed Makayla on the cheek and stepped off.

Makayla knew she couldn't tell Clarissa. She would consider her new sexual experience. Sexual exploitation that went on while. Her cozen was drinking and drugging! Discerning Makayla was crazy for sleeping Alina.

Makayla did not know why. She slept with Alina. Clarissa always said, Makayla slept with people. While looking for love. Makayla just believed she had a free spirit. When it came to sexual intercourse with no real value. Looking for excitement to get her hot spot lit. Makayla was baptized and Alina christened her behind!

18

COCAINE

By Roslyn OFlaherty

Makayla enjoyed her involvement with Alina. She continued to see her on a daily basis. Alina set aside cocaine for Makayla every day. Makayla was hooked to the point that her coke habit disgusted Alina. Makayla lost a little weight. She was still thick. Her skin color changed to a dried out ashy black. It just looked ashy even with brand name foundation. Her eyes and cheeks had sunken in a little. Half the time when you saw Makayla. Her hair and nails were disheartening along with her hygiene. Makayla was a coke head. Using cocaine compulsively on the low.

Makayla was still seeing Tyree every now and then. They enjoyed each other's company. He took her out on dates on many occasions. Tyree and Makayla never slept together. Tyree always reminded Makayla that they would be married one day. Tyree was a perfect gentleman he did not believe in having sex without being married.

Makayla was chasing that first hit of cocaine. While stressed with an addiction. Always on the go looking for that high she felt. She was open off, her first sniff of coke. Makayla was on a mission… No matter how much she desired coke. The bill could be filled all the way to the top. That first hit was never in the package. The craving just got stronger and this sickened Makayla. When she remembers the good days. She had on a mission to God…

Makayla force herself to sleep, eat and cleanse her body. She started looking like a night hag. The walking dead with dripping nasal mucus or a bleeding nose. She would instantly want to shit on herself. At the thought of copping. Cocaine was no longer a choice of drug or her recreational stimulant. It had become a way of life. The Chase was on junkie style…

The cocaine consequences had caused element variations in her common sense. Makayla had an emotional dependence. On coke which caused sensitive sorrow at times. Alina turned her out sexually and got her hooked. Alina did not want to take responsibility for any of her actions. So, Makayla did not take responsibility for stealing or selling Alina's personal possessions.

The amount Makayla snorted had increased. The effects of the drug made her angry and paranoid. Her addiction was out of control. Causing moodiness – just hostile. Makayla was a clean individual. Her addiction took over. Cocaine was bringing on confrontation. Makayla was no longer doing the drug. The drug was doing her.

Cocaine had Makayla looking like a bag lady. With black rings around her eyes. Looking filthy and dirty. Makayla had become a beggar bum. All she had to do is see cocaine in tinfoil; and she would literally, shit on herself. Makayla found it extremely difficult to stop using. The drug altered her personality. Makayla still considered herself still functional.

Makayla would sit in her bowel movement until all the coke was gone. She chewed her tongue. While constantly scratching her ass and blowing her booger nose. Makayla could not stand getting nose bleeds. The blood would just pour from Makayla's nose. There was a hole in her nose; up inside the nostril. It was excruciating, to have an ice pack placed. On the top of her nose; to stop it from bleeding.

Makayla's mind, body and soul were sick. However, you couldn't tell Makayla; she wasn't a Diva. The fly girl act was just unbearable. She stopped attending church on a regular basis. Sniffing cocaine had her in a drug war with herself. Makayla looked so repulsive. That you could not figure out. If her age was a number; or was her age a condition. Cocaine had ruined her career. Makayla didn't have no paper coming in. Her money was depleted it had run its course. This woman needed God now more than ever.

Makayla was disgusted with herself. For getting involved with Alina; and the white powder that contained misery. With a negative dispute for everyone in her route. Alina would not sleep with Makayla anymore. Makayla was disgusted the coke had dominated her life. Alina had deceived

Makayla. She had become her drug connect. Makayla's level of addiction was raised to the point. That she had an obsession for cocaine; craving it all the time. She prayed for God to take the cocaine taste out of her mouth. So, she could get off this path of destruction.

Baptized one day and a coke head the next. She could not hide behind the church. She did not want anyone to know about her experimental drug abuse. As she kept Alina as an enabler to her addiction to cocaine. Makayla was embarrassed. And did not want Tyree or Clarissa to observe her appearance. Or her state of mind as a coke head. Alina became exhausted with her behavior. Makayla finally figured out Alina had used her. Alina was a drug dealer!

Alina had not pressured Makayla into sniffing cocaine. Makayla felt she was seduced and had been taken advantage of. Alina was never exposed by police for the drugs. She had stashed in her apartment. The apartment was robbed a couple of times.

Makayla had a lot of unpaid debt. Alina was tired of Makayla pleading all the time for cocaine. I have a friend of mine. I want you to meet Makayla. This man loves helping women manage their lives. He will let you indulge in his product when it is necessary. Makayla didn't know what. Alina was chatting about. Yet she invited the thought of meeting him. Alina explained that she could not keep being her enabler.

My friend will definitely make you a sex slave. Your tab up in here will stay clear. Makayla you have a coke habit. That I just can't fix. Here take this package and come over tomorrow about six o'clock. I will introduce you to him.

The next day Makayla needed a hit so bad. She showed up at Alina's at four thirty. Makayla was thirsty for cocaine and obtained a package on credit. While waiting for Alina's friend to show up. The doorbell rang a big muscular looking gentleman entered. Alina's place of residence. He turned around and Makayla's mouth flew open. It was Marshall from Deluxe Lounge. The man she dances with and permitted him too practically. Seduce her on the dance floor. Alina tried to introduce them however. Makayla said I met him before. It's a small world.

Marshall said; I heard you needed to work. Makayla did not realize Marshall was a pimp. She was set up by Alina and Marshall. They are so ratchet! Makayla thought to herself. They both knew what they wanted to accomplish. Now Makayla would be force to sell her ass. This woman was feeling like a commodity. Cocaine was her new mission in life. While Sniffing and swallowing boogers. Marshall would be renting space between Makayla's legs. She was scared! Hesitant of her functional ability under these circumstances. Her actions to benefit from a drug; was a curse. It made Makayla feel like. It had supernatural powers. A guardianship towards her new accountabilities. Her pimp Marshall and Alina along with her drug cravings. Let Makayla know this was not the time to show. A sign of weakness. Marshall swore he was gold diggers. Selling ass was, his free enterprise.

The cocaine was part of the agenda. The first day she met them at Deluxe Lounge. Alina you are right! I can make a nice prostitute tab off Makayla. They spoke as if Makayla was not there. He handed Makayla some drugs; her eyes lit up. Excepting the white powder that she pleasured from him. Inhaling the coke quickly as Marshall indicated. You're working for me. I'm your pimp baby. I will keep your habit fed.

Makayla finished the package; it gave her the courage she needed. To say I am not working for you. Marshall lifted Makayla into the air by her neck. Her legs were dangling. She felt a feeling of breathlessness as he began slapping her. Consider yourself a hooker Makayla. You're working for me. Every night you will suck and fuck. Bringing the funds, you make to your daddy. Makayla was baffled.

Makayla had been choked and bitch slapped at the same time. With negative communicated instructions bestowed upon her. Like it should have been an honor. Who does Marshall think he is? How could her life change in just a short period of time? Makayla had gone from being baptized at her church. To her new life of prostitution which was part of organized crime. Marshall pushed Makayla to the floor and stepped on her neck, threatening her. You are now one of my prostitutes! Makayla knew this would be an adversity to her life. A disaster was waiting to happen.

Makayla was told to speak of herself. As a correlation escort. Always get your paid-up front. Before you have any sexual acts. Each sexual act had a different price. Wear a condom with all your sex partners. You do as I say, now get up! Alina, I want you and Makayla to strip for me. Alina was an escort and dealer for Marshall. A good fuck for Alina could come from a man or a woman. She was definitely a swallower!

Makayla was mad Marshall didn't know where her spot was. She undressed along with Alina. Marshall ordered both of them to make love to each other. Did you instruct Makayla on what her responsibilities will be? Like I told you to do Alina? I did as you said Marshall. Makayla and Alina were at the mercy of Marshall. They gave him a sex performance. They put coke on each other's tits and ate it off.

Marshall pleasured himself; stroking his dick. Makayla thought the head of his dick was pretty. She thought to herself. If she should ask Marshall if he wanted a blow job. For she knew; she wanted that Johnson. Along with the drug relationship. As he stroked it faster to his climax. Damn Makayla thought she could become hooked on his dick along with the drugs. Marshall was a man who did not have an erectile dysfunction.

The combination of coke and Marshalls big balls. Kept going through Makayla's brain. Imaging tongue action; As if she was playing with both balls in her mouth. But it was Alina tit she was sucking on. Marshall was fine. Makayla knew she could kiss that dick every day. Not wanting to taste his cum; was not even a question. Makayla had the answer to that. She was ready to swallow. Marshall's hard-on was made for her cunt and her cunt only. It was firm the way she preferred it. And she knew Alina had road that boner. Makayla welcomed the thought of getting a turn. She was ready to bring that erection down...

She snapped out of that sexual desire. When she heard Marshall's deep voice. I expect better when it comes to my clients. Alina and Makayla, you better make it happen. Now go take a shower! He threw a baggie full of cocaine on the floor. For his escorts and stepped off.

Makayla now became offended. At the way Marshall had spoken to them. He talked to them. Like they were disgusting foul-smelling hoes. When they got out the shower Marshall was gone. Makayla knew she brought all this upon herself. Along with being a victim of a set-up implemented by Marshall and Alina.

Makayla's actions from her drug of choice. Would now have her turning tricks. Makayla was referring to herself as an escort. She would rather suck Marshall's dick. While screwing him for money and product. She knew he want to penetrate her big ass at Deluxe Lounge. The way he was playing; with her skirt on the dance floor. Marshall knew he could have flipped up the back of her skirt. With his pinky and stick his dick way up. Inside her twat with no problem. For he had dam near tore the thong off her beautiful black ass. Marshall was the man in charge. Makayla was set up by playing. Fuck buddies with Alina the help. Cocaine had made Makayla a slave to all the nonsense. Being a slave to coke. Would make Makayla tired of being sick in tired. Coke up her nose and off goes her clothes.

19

MARSHALL

By Roslyn OFlaherty

Marshall forced Makayla to move in with Alina. They were given new clothes. Taught how to walk and dine with fine manners. Also given the pay scale amounts. For all the expected sexual acts of exploitation. Money that was to be agreed upon. Before any sexual acts occurred. The money was to be paid at that point. Marshall pimped their ass on a reg.

The patrons were older men. That expected physical intimacy. Some men only wanted romance. That was easy money. Alina sexed all the female clients. Makayla and Alina never refused to comply with Marshall's demands. They knew he was treacherous and crazy. They were scared of his cruel and unusual disciplinary actions. Money was the top priority in the escort service. Marshall would co-sign any sexual act. If the money was right.

Cocaine played a big part in their affiliation with Marshall. Makayla never thought, she would be a prostitute. Turning tricks on the street would have really broken Alina and Makayla's spirit. Marshall loved the power that he had over them as call girls. Makayla detected that the white powder had taken over. She was ashamed of herself. Makayla was not interested. In having any kind of sexual relationship with Marshall anymore.

Alina had a crush on Marshall. Even though he treated her like a dog. Marshall was an evil man. Who only preyed on woman's weaknesses? Makayla did as she was told. While trying to detox off the cocaine. This would be the only way. Makayla could break away from Marshall. Cocaine would no longer have power. Makayla truly loved herself.

Makayla pretended to be stupid. No longer willing to justify people's bullshit. Coke became draining to her mind. She was scared her heart would bust. Death would be knocking at her door. The cocaine was messing up her life. It was time to cut back on the amount. Of cocaine she was sniffing. Her body stayed drenched in sweat. While lying in the bed. Shivering balled up in a fetal position. Feeling alone like nobody cared.

Makayla didn't know what was worse. The craving for coke or the withdrawal. Cocaine was her drug of choice. Relying on it to be used for recreational use. Coke dominated her life. Giving her only on option. To pray, for the coke urge to be gone. With the understanding that this miracle. Was for Makayla to stop sniffing. Helping to overcome all negativity in the drug life. With an encouraging effort and no anxiety.

Once Makayla's withdrawal symptoms were over. She was stronger and built up a defense wall. For her new life's worth. Living life on its terms. Lots of crying; feeling sorry for herself. Not sympathetic to others who were still using. Because they had a choice. To leave drugs like she did. There was no each one teach one. In this lesson of don't use drugs.

Emotionally now vulnerable dealing with life's terms. Makayla was exhibiting feelings of being naked; from not drugging. Detoxing had taken the S off her chest. It made people upset her. The drug was in Makayla life to numb her. From that manipulating spirits, and abuse she was experiencing.

Detoxing revealed to Makayla how messy. The people in her life were involved in dangerous intense obstacles. That were causing wasted energy. Only she could shut this down. Having this new drug free life. Could have her found lifeless. By the hands of Marshall.

Makayla had the right to get out of the ratchetness. She was ready to focus. On her will to live. Thoughts of leaving Marshall Escort service. Made it easier not to pay attention, to the cocaine craving. Makayla put aside time. So, her focal point could stay on, departing from Marshall.

The more Makayla stayed off cocaine. The more her mental and physical capabilities got better. Marshall knew he was in control. He was in control. He was conveying ratchetness on a demented level. Makayla was stripped of the advantages; for her humanity. Marshall's mindset came from the gutter.

Makayla knew that the God that she once served. Gave her two arms; two legs and a brain. It was time for her to get to stepping. Thought of beating Marshall at his own game. Kept her heart racing. She was going to establish a strategy to follow. Along with the will to leave and live. This would help Makayla trust the process.

The product she was expected to sniff was sold it to her regular clients. The funds would be used to escape from Marshall. He had no right to dictate Makayla's life…

Makayla's mind was on Tyree, her one and only love. Thinking of taking their relationship to a new level one day. It was tiresome; having to sneak away. To meet up with Tyree. Marshall was very obnoxious and verbally offensive to Alina and Makayla. Working as Marshalls escort service became their ongoing professional hazard with no compassion. Makayla wore a black eye every now and then. The fellas were not ready for drug free Makayla. One guy choked her ass! This was the type of man. That would choke you; and leave you for dead. He was a pervert. She needed to watch her mouth according to him.

The men she escorted were not manly enough for her. Some required pills for an erection. She liked men with big feet coming through the door. A bulge with instant growth in their briefs. She knew if they would cum fast. She could get her paid quicker. Makayla wasn't interested in pillow talk. It had become sickening. To escort men with no intellectual function. Plain old idiots… With a little ass penis. That would keep falling out her puss. While he gets furious! If she did not help him. Put it back in over and over again.

Its disgusted Makayla when men. Wanted crazy stuff performed on them. She could not believe these jack asses wanted to drink urine. Makayla thought they wanted her to go in the bathroom. To pea in a cup. So, they could drink it. While sniffing the coke; she was selling G's. Nah, but these Mr. Mic Nasty's wanted Makayla. To stand over them and piss in their mouth. They would drink her piss. From each other's mouth and gag. They were bugging out. While masturbating one ass hole yelled. That's right baby. Give me that golden shower. As she watched the cum. Run down his Johnson. Makayla couldn't believe it. Yean never seen no one act like this before. This was the high light of an orgy. Peeing on each other in a lustful moment of thirsty drunkenness.

One man had Makayla act like his mother. Wearing an adult pamper sucking on her tit. She held him in her arms. Rocking him and dude starts screaming loudly. Crying like a little Biatch, Makayla was Dunn, Dunn... Where the hell; did Marshall find these fools? This dude was wylin; and drooling all over her. Makayla started yelling back at him. Get the Fuck Off Me... Was Makayla The Simp...?

The killer was one day. When Makayla was being an escort to a pot head. He had the nerve to ask her. If he shits on himself. Would she change him? Baby, I'll pay you good. That's It! Makayla could not believe. Dude wanted her to clean shit off his grown ass. "You bugging out right now Bro" I'll tell you what! I'm let you wipe my ass. She went in the bathroom to shit. Makayla defecated got up off the toilet bent over, and he clean her up. Playing scratch and sniff; as Makayla kept yelling. Ou-oh... That's what you want baby. Isn't it! Yeah wipe it over here. Aha – That's what, I'm talking about... You make a good ass wipe. Dude sat up and examined, the shit. Like he wanted to eat it... So, Makayla made him pay double. She was not fit-in to hop in his pamper. The sad thing about it was; the pot head was smoking roaches. Out the ash tray. He didn't even have a blunt or bud. But he laced his roaches with coke in e-z wide paper. REALLY –for real, for real... That's what he considered smoking that ENDO. He paid for Makayla's shit. Pussy ain't free NA' MEAN; Hmmm...

Makayla had to think. Was she meeting strange men; like this when she was coked up? Had the cocaine and liquor have her so zooted, with a distilled spirit? Makayla thought when she was high. She was more superior to everyone around her. For months her diction even changed. From hanging out with these lost souls. Her opinions had also been altered and she was a lost soul also.

Makayla had a big mouth and got bashed in it all the time. She had to deal with enraged people that were detestable. Makayla was now gully; with no fear in her heart. When dealing with Alina. Marshall would take the majority, of Alina and Makayla's earnings. This retribution was a payment. For protection in the escort service business.

Marshall was a coldblooded killer. A corrupt drug dealer. With no morals or ethics. Living off the profits. He obtained from his prostitutes

and drugs. There was certainly not a lot of safety being an escort. Na'
Makayla had been raped at gun point; and abducted in a van. Where was
the protection, when she was sexually battered? A police report was not
filed. Makayla thought she was going to get murdered. Constantly being
treated like trash. Men took turns with her orally. As they physically
entered every part of her body. They didn't have to take it there. Where
was Marshall her protector? Makayla was dumb tight.

She knew the bullshit shit had to stop. It would not have been
surprising to Makayla. If she found out, Marshall had set her up and got
compensated. All Marshall did for Alina and Makayla was publicize their
souls. They continued to be a steady tax-free income for Marshall. While
living as slaves in the sex and drug industry. Makayla and Alina were out
there jugging their ass. They barely received anything in return. Very
seldom able to serve rich men that smelled good.

The older gentlemen often smelt like some kind of medicine. You
would get a whiff of an ointment for joint pain. Makayla met married men
looking for a threesome. Their wives were invited. To share in their sexual
gratification. This would affect their marriages. If one of them got jealous.

Marshall didn't care if clients were bisexual or heterosexual. As long as
Alina and Makayla made him money. Makayla wanted to get established
away from Marshall. All he did was stifle her. She was going to try to get
away. When she got her finances in order. Makayla was scared for her
safety. She was drug free; this would be the perfect time. For arrangements
of her getaway.

Makayla having sex with different men, was killing her spirit. Marshall
was not sympathetic. To the fact her brain and body was exhausted.
Marshall's sex agenda did not allow. Her to hold a thought on many
occasions. Makayla prayed for a healing. The control factor had become
unbearable. The thought of leaving. Was entrenched in her concentration.

Makayla got dressed and her hand bag was full to capacity. With all
the stuff she might need. Marshall did not allow her to have identification.
Makayla knew this was the perfect opportunity. For departure out of
Marshall's hell hole. Of a life that brought on excruciating pain and
distasteful situations. Her destiny had become top priority. Leaving behind
the cell phone that was a present from Marshall. Not having the phone.

Would make it impossible for Alina or Marshall to control Makayla's existence.

Makayla took a suit case jam-packed with money. She found it stashed in Marshalls. Trap house was full of drugs. She left all the drugs there. That would be sold out of Marshall's ban-do. Makayla was scared when she drove off. She went to the gas station and filled up her hooptie. Once Makayla got on the high-way. She became less nervous and began speaking out loud. Dear Lord, I don't know if I have the right to call your name. For a long time, I have prayed for success and prosperity. My life is lacking respect. I have obtained, what I call wealth.

I feel! I worked for this money through a life style. I should have never been in. I was robbed of my dignity. Through unsafe sexual acts. In the finest elegant hotels and ghetto motels. This money was made from these unfortunate events. A man name Marshall tried to nickel and dime me. Out of my share of the dough. Real talk... Marshall though I was a trashy, sawbuck working hoe. I would never work for ten dollars a person. Marshall is going to try to retrieve the stolen money. Even if he has to put someone in a body bag. I admit... I was thirsty... Well what's done is done! I was being extra. I know what it is to face adversity. It's time for Mama to live!!!

The suit case full of money. That I have Lord. I want to ask you is this, the level of achievement for my life. My spirit is broken... I need you now more than ever Lord. I believe me thieving this suit case. Will cause me to lose my life. This decision, I have made to steal Lord. Came from the mentality. I have at this present moment.

Lord was my life's external appearance one of desperation? Lord do you think. I will leave this experience alive? Lord I ask you please watch over me. So, there are no triggers. That will make me relive old routines of my past. I stopped attending AGAPE CHURCH OF WISDOM OF FAITH. I strayed from you lord after attending DELUXE LOUNGE. That all I remember. After my mental and spiritual down fall. Well Lord, thanks for listening to me. It means a lot to me. Lord I want you to know. I will be praying for forgiveness. When I find a place to live. I know I have sinned. Lord am I truly a work in progress? Thanks again for listening Makayla. Amen

20

DEFENSELESS

By Roslyn OFlaherty

Marshall had a client for Makayla. He kept ringing her cell phone. Wondering why there was no answer. This was a high paying client. That requested to see Makayla. The clients escort services were paid for in advance. Marshall got in his vehicle; he was furious. Makayla had fell from total inconsistency. Concerning the expectations of Marshall. Especially his number one rule. Answer your cell phone at all times.

That coke head Makayla won't answer the phone. Who does she think she is? Marshall reached the building. Where he ran his business out of. Alina was in the living room. He saw her as he came through the entrance. He yelled where the hell is Makayla? I don't know, she was not here when I woke up. I thought she was with you. What do you mean Alina? You don't know where Makayla is?

Marshall started kicking and beaten Alina. Stomping her more viciously as her body hit floor. Alina's eye was puffy. Instantly swollen shut. It turned a dark bluish purple. Alina was torture by Marshall. Totally defenseless her arm had become dislocated from the shoulder. Speaking in a timid voice. Alina continued to say. I don't know where Makayla is. The more she spoke. Of not knowing where Makayla was. The more Marshall thrashed Alina like the sex slave. He truly though she was. Marshall dragged her by her hair shouting. Get up from the floor! Alina cried praying under her breathe. Lord please help me. I need your assistance. This man is going to kill me. I never asked you. To do anything for me before. I can no longer endure the pain. From this brutal beating. Marshall was the pimp with Guap. Why did Alina always have to keep tabs on Makayla? Alina was getting too old for this babysitting gig. Marshall needed Makayla to be an escort. For one of his well-paying customers. Who was willing to pay a substantial amount of money an hour? Marshall wanted the coins. Makayla would keep the man as a steady customer. He paid to have anal sex. Marshall knew this dude was into strange sexual behavior. Makayla was supposed to sell her ass. With no safeguard from anyone.

Where was Makayla, this was the question in Marshall and Alina's mind? Marshal kept on screaming. That girl is messing up my business. Marshall's vicious ugliness resurfaced. There is money that needs to be made. I'll kill her! Marshall was still fucking Alina up brutally. She was terrified. Was Marshall's money the root of all evil; or was not having your own money the root to all evil? Could it just be this son of a bitch Marshall; knew he would not have power over Makayla ass again?

21

CLARISSA

Roslyn OFlaherty

Marshall entered Deluxe Lounge and found Makayla's cousin Clarissa. Where is she, he yelled at her? Where is who? I'm looking for your cousin Makayla. I have not seen Makayla in months. This dude grabbed Clarissa. By her arm real hard. Snatching her up out of her chair. Marshall took her outside and started threatening her. Clarissa, I think it would be in your best interest. To find your cousin. Makayla better get in touch with me. She needs, to make this money for me. Makayla will be sorry if she crosses me. What Money Clarissa asked? My money! Marshall pulled out a gun and shoved it in her face. Sending a message of cruelty, because Makayla was deceitful. Get in the car Marshall yelled. With a temperament causing affliction.

He took Clarissa to a secluded place. Marshall was totally aggressive. While ripping her thong off. As he brutally raped her. He stuck the gun up in her vagina. Please don't shoot me. She had to give him oral sex. As he choked Clarissa. She could hardly breathe as he bent her over. Clarissa cried as he entered her naked body. Marshall was forceful as he laid her over his car.

Suck me off again he yelled. Clarissa was in panic mode. Feeling like she was going to pass out. Clarissa placed her hands around his Johnson, trembling. Jerk it he yelled! After two strokes. He tossed her over and entered her rectum. It was tight and Marshall moaned. Feeling the skin stretch over his erection. Imagining that it would be easy for him. To have a sexual affection; with her on a reg.

Clarissa screamed it seemed to turn him on. He moaned as he humped her rougher and faster. Dam you feel good Clarissa! He slap her ass in a violent manner. Frightening her even more. She could feel the crap; coming out of rectum. Clarissa could smell it! It seemed to turn Marshall on. As he rubbed it all over her back repeatedly. He turned her over climbed on top of her. Discharging sperm all over her face. Clarissa was cruelly raped. She thought Marshall was going to leave; her for dead, or kidnap her.

Now tell Makayla if she does not come back and get this money for me. Every time I see you Clarissa. I'm going to make you pay; by pleasuring me with your body. Marshall made her put on her ragged clothes. He dropped her in the back of Deluxe Lounge.

Clarissa was to hurt and embarrassed. She walked wobbly and climbed in her car. Clarissa drove off smelling like shit. She watched Marshall walk back in Deluxe Lounge. With his chest poked out. Look at this self-righteous bitch. His irrational behavior wasn't acceptable in today's society. Marshall was a sociopath. Clarissa had to live this unforgettable, ruthless journey. That caused suffering with stress. A consequence that came from Makayla's betrayal. That was set against Marshall.

Clarissa started thinking, what had Makayla got herself into this time? Marshall was a sex fanatic as, far as she was concerned. Clarissa cried and could not stop trembling. Clarissa body was in excruciating pain. From the inside out. Her skin was bruised, with black and blue marks. Even though this was a police matter. Clarissa was petrified!

Clarissa started screaming out of control. Makayla drama just follows you universally. What have I become involved in? Every time Makayla deals with a man. It turns into chaos. Her life must be out of control. Makayla is living with a; I don't give a damn approach. Makayla must have stopped going to church. She needs to see a psychiatrist before someone one winds up dead behind her dumb ass.

Clarissa knew she would have to hide out. Until she could locate Makayla. Marshall had definitely lost his fucking mind. He was addicted to his erotic previsions. Makayla had a way. Of making men go senseless. Then she was through with them. Was Marshall just greedy for money? The confusion continued with no genuine repentance. Makayla always pulled the victim card. Everything was always all about her. The behavior pattern was truly psychotic. Makayla always got into circumstances. That always affected the stability of others.

Clarissa began shaking and crying. She was injured badly and her body was unbearably sore. Where could Makayla be? Crying all the way home. When entering the shower. All you could hear is screaming. While Clarissa cried hysterically. Scrubbing her skin for a half an hour till it was raw. She could still smell a scent of foul shit. Imagining Marshall's hands and gun all over her body. Clarissa felt dirty and annoyed. Just disgusted with fuckin Makayla and Marshall.

Makayla must be at Uncle Pete's. That was their much-loved Uncle. Clarissa left home with a packed suit case. Still feeling weak, dragging herself body in the vehicle. Clarissa made sure no one was following her. Driving for three hours sickened. Before she made it to Uncle Pete's house. Makayla's car was parked out front.

Clarissa knocked on the door. When Uncle Pete opened the door Clarissa weak fragile beaten body. Fell instantly into his arms. She explained to Uncle Pete and Makayla. What had occurred sexually. While she was tormented. Remembering how Marshall kept yelling! Tell Makayla come make this money. Makayla started crying telling them how. Marshall forced her to become a prostitute. Explaining how she was set up. By Alina becoming strung out on cocaine. Clarissa started spazzing out. You serious, Makayla! I told you not to fuck. With that bitch Alina! Makayla was dead-ass, with no voice.

Uncle Pete said in a loud voice. I'm going to kill that bastard. Marshalls buggin! He grabbed his gun. Telling Clarissa and Makayla to lock the door. Stay off your cell phones. Makayla was glad; she did not have the cell phone. Marshall had given to her. I'll be back! Slamming the house door. Uncle Pete then took off in his car. He knew who Marshall was. They had grown up in the same neighborhood. Marshall was his wing man in the clubs. He knew Marshall was an unbalanced, intimidating motherfucker. A born Psychopathic killer unable to feel. What he does to people.

Uncle Pete waited in his car down the block. From Marshall recreational drug house. Ready to seek out revenge. When Marshall showed up Uncle Pete followed him. Face to face; Uncle Pete shot him and left him for dead. No questions asked! Marshall fell behind the bushes. The shrubbery covered his body. Marshall did not survive. His appearance from the neck up. Had the most damaged. When they found Marshalls body rig amorist had set in. Marshall was found because of the stench smell. That came from his body.

Makayla and Clarissa saw it on the news. Marshall was in a body bag. The detectives and law evidence officers, examined the scene. When Uncle Pete returned home four days later. He packed some of his personal belongings. To stayed a motel out of town. In case he needed an alibi. Marshall was dead! Now Makayla, Clarissa and Uncle Pete had a bond. Which involved that dead mother fuckin, crazy Marshall. It was their new family secret.

Makayla waited for time to pass. Making an anonymous phone call to the police station. She told the detectives that she witnessed. Alina point a gun at Marshall in front of his building. Makayla explained Alina's connection to Marshall. Informing the detective's about things. Only the shooter would have information of. Makayla gave incriminating evidence. On the murder weapon and crime scene that was not public knowledge.

The detectives had collected enough evidence. That would place Alina at the scene of the crime. The evidence they gathered caused Alina to look guilty. Makayla new it was a matter of time. Before Alina was picked up and convicted of Marshall's Murder. Makayla never told anyone about the suit case full of money. That she took from Marshall. As far as Makayla was concerned. She was paid in full.

22

MAKAYLA

By Roslyn OFlaherty

Makayla learned her thoughtless deranged; irrational behavior. From her ex-pimp Marshall. He had been her best negative mentor. She was trained on how to survive on the streets. The suffering that Makayla had to tolerate. Made her former clients think. She liked a little deception in her life. Makayla prayed to the Lord. That she would never be seen. By her Johns again in life. Makayla's dumb ass was not willing. To take any responsibility. For her schizophrenic problems or the brutal. Beaten. Clarissa had endured. Makayla was not about to let anyone judge her. The thought of living in shame about her pass never entered her mind.

Marshall raped and beat Clarissa. She lost her inner peace. Marshall ruined her self-esteem. His self-centered ass did not care. After he abused her. The next day Makayla had the nerve to tell Clarissa. That she ready to return, back to church. That was her place of support. Which kept her disowning the participation? She played in her cousin's rape. Clarissa was sick of Makayla. She didn't even try to console her. Clarissa was waiting to see if Makayla. Would be apologetic for what happened to her with Marshall.

Clarissa could barely walk. Had Makayla turned heartless? Marshall seemed like the devil. The devil was the falling angel. Can he get insider your heart and mind? All she said was Clarissa you were courageous. Clarissa has been lying in the bed. Three months of taking pain killers for intense discomfort. Uncle Pete was not sure. If Makayla understood everything that happened.

Was Uncle Pete and Clarissa living feelings of torture? The penalties of Makayla's bad decisions. He was concerned about Makayla. For it was like, she had a wall up. When it came to discussing. Everything that was going wrong in Clarissa life.

How did Makayla get involved with Marshall and Alina? Uncle Pete felt he should have been given. An explanation about how this happening to Clarissa. After all Uncle Pete; felt like a ruthless killer. When it came to Marshall's death. There was more to this story. An Uncle Pete knew it. He heard Makayla tell Clarissa. She was ready to go back to church. What was she going to do there? Repent for her sins? Uncle Pete knew every time Makayla went to church. There was a new episode of disaster. As she considered herself so mystical. A lack of consideration for others came with it.

Makayla had moved on with her life. Clarissa would never be able to travel. In the same circle as Makayla. It was hard for her to stand or walk unaccompanied. Clarissa's body had taken a turn for the worst. Uncle Pete thought Makayla was just trifling. She definitely needed more than church. Uncle Pete knew Makayla was the master of manipulation. With a criticizing spirit. He was hoping that Makayla. Did not cause him to kill her too. For telling Clarissa no love lost. That is something you tell your enemy.

Makayla just didn't care. To help Clarissa mentally or physically. Due to her getting all the attention. Makayla also suffered by living a nightmare. Under Marshall's rules and the wrong type of people. No compassion was given for Makayla. She was filled with hurt. That she was not the center of attention. Her jealous spirit had consumed her thinking. About being held hostage as a prostitute. Uncle Pete knew he had to suppress. Makayla's malicious toxic ways. She had rattled Uncle Pete's chain. He started thinking; if I can kill once! I can kill again! He will take Makayla out. Over any selfishness or bull shit concern Clarissa.

Who was Makayla involved with? That was the question? Were there anymore pieces to this puzzle? That was left out. Makayla was glad Marshall was out of her life. He became her best teacher. She learned how to take care of herself. Makayla did not feel inexperienced as far as street life was concerned. Would the street become Makayla's worst adversary? Did Marshall's death mean; she wouldn't have to suffer anymore? She wanted to be the center of attention. With no consequence for her actions. Makayla's was only concerned about her integrity. She was in denial of her existence. In all the emotional, corrupt disasters of ratchetness. That occurred in her thug life of sex and drugs. Which turned out to be deadly. With dangerous suffering of self-destruction and betrayal.

Makayla was rich now from all the money. That she stole in Marshall's suit case. It was like Marshall left the money. In his life insurance policy for her. To change the rowdy life and sexual reputation. That caused intense life altering struggles. Makayla really appreciated it. After all she worked for the money; and now she was paid in full.

Makayla left the house and made it to the church. She had fellowshipped with everyone in the parking lot. She stayed for a while. Then she went to her car and drew out the suitcase. While no one was watching. Makayla hid the money in the church. Then she stood at the altar and prayed to Father God.

Forgive me God for I have sinned. She asked God for a blessing. I would like to put all my problems on the altar. For I know you understand me better than anyone. I have no one; that I can talk to. If you're listening. I would like you to be my decision maker. I recognize I am not good at making judgements. I have hidden a suit case. In your house God. I would like to claim full recovery in my life. To make things easier. I believe my mind need healing. I need someone to point me in the right direction. Starting my life over won't be easy. My mother told me a long time ago. Read your Bible then you would recognize. That with God all things are conceivable! Tell me Lord is what; I have in the suit case my blessings. I paid one-tenth of the money, for my tithes. This house of worship is falling apart inside. Also, it needs a new roof. The money I concealed for myself. Is this truly the favor of God? I pray you send me a sign. I will keep it in your house. Until I feel my advancements. Has been moved in the right direction. Lord I thank you for your gracious hand. Amen...

23

THE HOSPITAL

Roslyn OFlaherty

Clarissa pain became unbearable. Uncle Pete was giving her OxyContin two tablets every four hours. That was maximum daily dose. It made Clarissa feel high. The pills had worn off. She commenced to begging Uncle Pete for additional pills. Uncle Pete went to provide Clarissa with the tablet. Clarissa screamed I can't move my leg. Uncle Pete called an ambulance. They reached the hospital. Clarissa was seen right away.

Seven hours later a doctor strolled up to; Uncle Pete and introduced his self. Hi my name is Doctor Dermas. I am Clarissa's physician. I am sorry to say Clarissa had a miscarriage. She lost the baby upon her arrival. The child had stopped developing inside of her. It was a baby boy. Dr. Dermas continued to have a word with Uncle Pete. Silently Uncle Pete was trying to comprehend. What the doctor was saying. Clarissa has damaged her spinal cord. This caused Paralysis. She lost movement in her leg. On the right side of her body. She also needs surgery in her rectum.

Was the baby a tragedy? To her misfortune of being sexually abused? Clarissa lost Gods child which was now looked upon. As a rape baby; given to her by Marshall. A sexual aggressive person. Marshall was the father of the deceased baby; Clarissa always said she would never! Have a baby out of wedlock. She stated it was a sin. Not exactly perfect without matrimony. Her destiny with her baby's father must include being married. So, they can raise a family together.

Uncle Pete said, Lord the family secret about Clarissa baby is between me and you Lord. Lord I can't understand. How one man could tear apart a whole family? This situation is frightening. Uncle Pete started thinking to himself. Would the baby's DNA confirm Marshall? As a deceased rapist the father of Clarissa child? Clarissa uterus wall was damaged; she lost her three-month-old baby boy. Dr. Dermas said they would do her admission papers. Then Clarissa would be taken to her room. She is sedated and will be hospitalized for a while. He asked Uncle Pete what happened to Clarissa. (Uncle Pete and Clarissa did not want to tell the doctor the family secret.) He was still hanging on to the fact that Clarissa had a miscarriage. Marshall and his infant son were dead. Clarissa the infant's mother was crippled. Makayla was mentally living on the edge.

Uncle Pete told Dr. Dermas that Clarissa was badly beaten and raped. I have to call the police. The crisis intervention specialist. Will be visiting Clarissa. They are from the Rape Crisis Center, for the mentality of distress. This will be very beneficial for her emotional state of mind. My name is Mr. Pete I am Clarissa uncle. I raised her. I do not want anyone to inform Clarissa she was pregnant. This information would not be conducive to her recovery. My phone number is 1 632 555-****.

Doctor Dermas put the information in his notes. I understand your concern about Clarissa; being informed of her miscarriage. Clarissa had told the Doctor Dermas. She had been raped against her will. It was a malicious attack. She did not recognize the individual. Who had done this to her? He had a mask over his face. Marshall was a tyrant. Uncle Pete was glad he was lifeless!

Dr. Dermas kept Clarissa sedated. Her situation was heart gripping. Uncle Pete started wondering. If Clarissa knew she was pregnant. Had she kept it a secret? So, she did not want to answer about the crime? What could happen next? Did the pain killers cause the baby to die? The baby stayed on Uncle Pete's mind. Wow could the doctors take any DNA? The baby had Uncle Pete puzzled. Uncle Pete was calling Makayla's cell phone. He wanted to tell her Clarissa was in the hospital.

There was no answer. He started wondering why it was not possible. To get in touch with Makayla. He had come to the conclusion. That she did not want to be found. Uncle Pete's brain kept telling him. Just because someone is related to you. Doesn't make them a decent person. Makayla was a controlling person. Uncle Pete felt insecure. When it came to Makayla. He could not figure her out; but he knew she was shady.

Uncle Pete did not want to develop any kind of hatred for Makayla. He did not like being around a lot of nonsense. Makayla unrealistic perception about her significance in life bothered Uncle Pete. He felt she was treacherous to herself as well as others. He was not terrified of Makayla. Uncle Pete did not feel blameworthy about killing Marshall. No matter how much misery Uncle Pete and Clarissa tolerated Makayla always felt she was superior.

He was trying to comprehend her self-absorbed personality. Always thinking she could change humanity. Makayla was walking around destroying people's lives. Uncle Pete was not comfortable with the circumstances that were dominating his life. Uncle Pete wanted to believe. Makayla had a warm heart and was compassionate. Uncle Pete assumed since he took so much crap off her. Makayla was blocking his blessing. That God had for him. Makayla was only concerned about no one but her dam self. She was living with hatred; in her heart. And drama in her soul. She abused people for her own suitability.

Uncle Pete knew he had to keep up with Makayla. All the negative things Makayla gets into. Uncle Pete felt it was necessary. To believe it was not intentional. Uncle Pete did not know which direction his family's life was headed in. So, Uncle Pete prayed to the Lord for spiritual guidance. He wanted him to look after; Clarissa in her condition.

This was not the time to get side tracked. Uncle Pete needed order in his life. That would bring forth positive intentions. Being consumed with Makayla's nonsense was not healthy. Doctor Dermas had Approached Uncle Pete in the waiting room. You can go up and see Clarissa now. Take the elevator to the 4th floor. Clarissa was put in the ICU unit for observation. Uncle Pete went to see Clarissa. She seemed so comfortable. He did not want to disturb her. He was concerned on how. Clarissa was going to manage when she got out of the hospital.

As Uncle Pete stared at Clarissa. Thoughts ran through his head. He was now a killer. Marshall was the destroyer. Of many people's lives and for this reason. He was now lifeless. Clarissa was paralyzed in ICU. Her right leg was lifeless. She was not suffering from pain anymore. Uncle Pete watched the tubes in her body. Administering the medicine that she needed. Clarissa was even given a Morphine drip. The Nurse said they would not let her use it yet. They needed to watch her leg on the right side of her body.

Uncle Pete was worried if the Doctor Dermas identified. His niece's leg as being paralyzed. Clarissa was given a medication. That kept her a little confused. She was able to comprehend. What was being said? When the hospital staff had to speak to Clarissa. About how she felt. Uncle Pete was just glad to see. She was not suffering anymore.

24

DECEASED

By Roslyn OFlaherty

Makayla was ready to start her life over. Marshall was now irrelevant and she did not fear anything. Makayla was drug free. Torn between the worldly people and the church. Makayla did not want to be bothered by anyone. She had turned off her cell phone. Got in her car and just drove looking for somewhere. To escape for a while. Trying to make the dreadful experience. With Marshall and Alina, a closed chapter in her life.

Alina was in a top-security Jail. Trying to prove she was not connected. The homicide concerning Marshall. Makayla knew Alina would be tied up. In this case for years. She could try to play the insanity plea on this murder charge. Marshall was dead cremated. Ashes were all that remained of him. When Alina found out; there had been no autopsy. She tried to hang herself in her jail cell. Money can make anyone disappear. Marshall was residing in an Urn. Makayla had set Alina up. The same way Alina had set her up to be a prostitute for Marshall.

Makayla would never forget. How Alina gave her the cocaine that contributed. To Marshall becoming her pimp. Alina was living in hell and Makayla wanted her to die there. Makayla decided to only keep. In contact with Tyree. He was the only one that ever cared about her. After all Makayla had been through. Tyree still met up with her; from time to time. He was the only man that she dealt with. That did not want her for sex.

Makayla had taken enough money. Out of Marshall's suit case to start a new life. For some reason it made her think. Of the time she went to the Chet's house. She began to think was Chet living in a world of spells. This was where she wished to obtain a lot of money. Hell naw... He couldn't have had anything to do with. The turn of events that took over Makayla's life with Marshall and Alina. The thought of this scared Makayla. She did not believe in spells.

The rest of the money was left in the AGAPE CHURCH OF WISDOM AND FAITH. When Makayla was in the church she smelt. The same aroma from the man Chet's house. Where she asked to be rich. This was only the second time in her life. She smelt that smell. Makayla felt no one would find the money. In the house of the Lord. Taking the Money from Marshall was not unsurprising. Was Marshall's money the reason, she had taken a bath for? She poured the whole bottle of blue substance. Over her body for five hours. Makayla was now rich!

Marshall's life and money had been stolen from him. Makayla did not see this as a wrong doing. This justifiable sin was; fair game as far as Makayla was concerned. All this was carried out on a spontaneous impulse. Which did not make it right. Makayla should have been careful, for what she asked for.

Now she lives drained and confused with crazy thought. Makayla need a cleansing from this life of sin. She needed to confess what happened in prayer. It was time for her to stay prayed up. Makayla was clueless about the manic journey. That keeps emerging in her life. She was humiliated with the whole ordeal.

25

THE POLICE

By Roslyn OFlaherty

Uncle Pete started thinking maybe. He should turn his self in. Then he thought his time could be served. Better by taking care of Clarissa. The whole situation had drained him. He sat down in chair next to Clarissa bed. He started to pray. God please dispense your angels around Clarissa. Uncle Pete could not finish his prayer. To God because two officers walked towards him in ICU. Sir can you follow us?

My name is Officer Burns. We need to speak to you outside a minute. When Uncle Pete saw the police. His heart started beating so fast. It felt like his spirit had dropped on the floor. Had they caught up with Makayla? Did she implicate Uncle Pete in Marshall's murder? His common sense started racing with views of being deceived. As the police spoke Uncle Pete could hardly comprehend. What they were speaking about. All the questions at one time kept him saying. Whoever did this to Clarissa they need to be taking off the streets. No one else needs to get hurt.

Look at my niece she never bothers anyone. I'm glad they did not take her life. I pray for God to give her strength to heal properly. Clarissa will be seeking professional help. From the Rape Crisis Center. I'm worrying if she was penetrated. With Any kind of sexually transmitted disease? Could she be pregnant? She will need a therapist and rehabilitation. Whatever you think is needed the officer replied. Uncle Pete held his composure as the Police asked him questions. Then the Officer stated. We will find her rapist. If she remembers anything call this telephone number. Again, my name is Officer Burns. I will be working this case. Thanks officers, for stopping by the hospital. It means a lot to me. Uncle Pete dismissed the police. Informing them that he would; keep watch over his niece. Officer Burns said bye and then left. Uncle Pete knew now the police. Had not talked to Makayla. He went back in ICU and Clarissa's eyes were open. She stared at him. I still don't have any feeling in my leg. She cried out!

Clarissa was in shock. Uncle Pete please help me; she started screaming... This has to be a bad dream! Clarissa the doctors are doing everything they can do. The nurse came in asking Uncle Pete to leave. Uncle Pete looked Clarissa and, watched a tear fall from her eye. He was too choked up to say anything. He acknowledges her discomfort. It bothered him to see Clarissa in ICU. He was unprepared to explain the damage to her leg. Uncle Pete left the room and called Makayla's cell phone. Wow she turned it off. He was furious with her right about now. Clarissa needed Gods almighty power.

Clarissa was raped and beat, because of Makayla. Uncle Pete knew they were betrayed. With Makayla's utter sinfulness. He took her actions as a personal attack. Makayla was relentless. He understood now that; she was operating in crisis mode. Oh Lord please help Makayla. I can't be troubled about Makayla and Clarissa circumstances too. Makayla actions had unsafe burdens that were annoying. He now knew she needs a psychotherapist.

Uncle Pete truly loved Makayla. Her actions sometimes became mind draining. He knew if he did not get her any help. He would never see Makayla have a normal life. He could no longer coddle Makayla bull shit. Could Makayla take the required steps to get better? He knew she would be overpowered by the streets because of her. Unlucky survival skills. Makayla had to be found.

Makayla thought the church was her hospital. This was not truly the case. Even though prayer helps Makayla. It was not the time to turn her back. On the fact that Marshall assaulted Clarissa. Makayla's spirit just was not correct. Uncle Pete truly believed in his heart. Her behavior was inconsiderate. Makayla's plantation mentality would. One day have her enslaved within a mental institution. Uncle Pete didn't know what her diagnosis would be. For whatever triggers her personality disorder. Many of her associates thinks she is a psychopath.

The nurse came to the waiting room. To inform Uncle Pete it was ok to see Clarissa. It sickens him to see Clarissa in the bed helpless. She was lethargic. He knew he had to man up and take charge. He enters the room and could observe Clarissa wanted answers. Where is Makayla she asked? She is obnoxious to people. Always using everyone for her own personal benefit. Wondering around the streets like a vagabond. Uncle Pete knew. He did not have time track down Makayla. He would keep her out of Clarissa remembrance. In order for her to recover properly.

Clarissa knew what happened to her. Was not completely unintentional. On Makayla's part in this disastrous incident. Her actions with Marshall played a significant part in Clarissa's life. Makayla should understand that this horrible. Agonizing experience has destroyed her. Clarissa explained to Uncle Pete. That Makayla had no regrets or shame. There was not even concern. Why didn't she come see about her cousin's health?

Clarissa started yelling again. How she absolutely could not afford. To pay for this hospital stay. She did not have any extra cash saved up. For medical purposes or financial insurance. Medicare would never help Clarissa. With medical copayments; ambulance and emergency room. She wanted to see a social worker. Before leaving the hospital for rehabilitation costs. There would be no assistance from the county Health Department. Makayla felt she was not obligated for her cousin at all. Clarissa was worrying about paying. For critically struggling towards recover. Anxiety gave Clarissa concerns about her drug obsession. It had got increasingly worse. From all this pain medication. She was given morphine every 4 to 6 hours as needed. Makayla never discusses Clarissa at all! Her cousin hated her for that. As she prayed not to have a health condition. That was out of control. For a pre-existent drug addiction after being discharged. Would be devastating! Clarissa needed to lean on God.

Uncle Pete could tell she spoke dangerous words of disgust. He never heard the words of hate and killing. In Clarissa's jargon before. Makayla needs prayer. Her soul needs cleansing. From the inside out spiritually. Makayla really need to work on changing her character. Clarissa couldn't deal with her cousin right now. Makayla destiny waits at the hands of the devil. I will harm Makayla if I see her. It's not good to use words. With intense hostility, Uncle Pete said. God could deal with Makayla. Better than you can Clarissa.

Are these comments coming from Uncle Pete she thought? He was nothing but a murderer, in Clarissa's eyes. Uncle Pete had run frantically outside the house. In the pouring rain an intense thunder. Like he was gully. Filled with feeling of extreme exasperation; to kill Marshall. After finding out Clarissa. Was raped and assaulted by Marshall. Was this premeditated murder? Why did she pay attention to Uncle Pete? He shot Marshall in point blank range. And watch the rain wash Marshall's; blood run down the street. As the thunder echoed in Uncle Pete's head from the sky. As his slipped into thoughts. Of the blood bath he encounters. As he showered in the rain. When Uncle Pete finally returned from his heroic killing. Requesting Clarissa and Makayla to uphold the new family secrets? Would this implicate all of them? In Marshall's death in one way or another?

Clarissa hoped that the families dirty little secret. Would never cause her to be incarcerated. After the following events. That had taken place in their family life. In such a short period of time. All the lies and manipulation made the whole family damaged goods. Clarissa asked God; please help me Lord. My life is one big mess. Please grant me peacefulness. Help me walk again. So, I can walk away from this chaotic situation. Please Father God! Take my issues into consideration for a blessing. Make me strong enough. To think about my health care needs. Father God I will comply with you; and you alone. In Jesus name Amen!

26

THE WEAPON

By Roslyn OFlaherty

It was time for Uncle Pete to get rid of the handgun. The gun was not registered in his name. Since the gun was used to murder Marshall. This was not the time for the death of Marshall; to be tied to Uncle Pete. The weapon was not even used for self-defense. He could not believe. He was engaged in conflict. That was Makayla's disarray. Uncle Pete did not need tragedy in his life. That could be used to make him a convicted felon.

Uncle Pete decided to pawn the gun. There was no interest for the first month. Uncle Pete had a Glock 32: .357 SIG HAND GUN. He thought it would be better. To sell the gun to the pawn shop. Since his friend was willing to buy the gun. Remove the firearm serial number. With no papers and no questions asked. Uncle Pete peddled it to him for one thousand dollars. Even though he, could obtain more money for it. It would cause all sorts of legal issues. For the person who purchased the weapon. The pawn shop had weird paper work. That would be used to re-sell the gun. Your social security number was not required. The papers had nothing. To do with the gun control laws. The papers were just bogus.

The pawn shop had the handgun. That was used in the brutal assignation. Of Marshall and they did not know it. Uncle Pete was glad that the gun was out of his life. He had enough confusion with Makayla and the family secret. Uncle Pete needed some quite time in his life. This chaotic journey he was on. Did not allow him to relax. Feeling his whole life was now wasted up in devastation. On so many different levels. When

Marshall became deceased. Uncle Pete could not anticipate the conclusion of this horrific crime.

Uncle Pete was mentally divested. He wonders what happened. Destruction had set in. On the peace and stability in his life. He felt it was time for him to pray. Uncle Pete asked God to point. Him in the right direction to righteousness. Never in his life did he think. He would be asking God for forgiveness. The worlds system had affected him. Now he is searching for direction. And meaning in his life without corruption. Uncle Pete was not reluctant to admit. Some of his deviant behavior that caused sin. He was ready to bow down to the blood of Jesus! He trusted in the Lords atoning blood.

27

CENATOE ISLAND

By Roslyn OFlaherty

Makayla contacted Tyree on his job. He would be landing his plane on Friday. Makayla was ready to see Tyree. She needed some adult conversation. Makayla had an apartment. In a remote area off Cenatoe Island. She wanted Tyree to keep her company. He agreed to meet her. At seven thirty pm. Makayla was excited the island had a casino; with a restaurant. She ordered food to her private residence. So, they could eat. Makayla ordered lobster, shrimps, and king crab legs. She also ordered her favorite Salmon with a chef salad and soup. She was looking forward to enjoying Tyree's company.

Makayla got dressed. Without a care in the world. Her favorite perfume smelt wonderful. Makayla looked elegant. The doorbell rang she was nervous. Makayla answered the door, Tyree stood there looking handsome. Makayla could smell him instantly. When the door opened. She smiled as Tyree greeted her with flowers. Then he kissed her on the cheek. They sat down on the couch talking and laughing. While they enjoyed; each other's company. Like they always did.

Tyree said to Makayla. Can I ask you something personal? Makayla wondered where Tyree. Was going with this. I don't usually ask you. About your personal business Makayla! You can tell me to mind my business. I know where not married. I'll be fine; if you don't want me inquiring. Whatever you tell me. I will still love you Makayla. Tyree you can asks me anything! I'll even, tell you the truth. Ok! Makayla, I had a passenger on my plane last week. I won't tell you his name. Makayla stated he paid you. To have sexual intercourse with him. Makayla almost choked on her words. She was still able. To use her fast thinking ingenuity. Since you want to know Tyree! Makayla stated she would be honest. Tyree I was a prostitute obsessed with Cocaine! Beaten wore black eyes; while laying on my back! I had been threatened by my Pimp! Marshall ran what he called an escort service. I have been abducted by men in a van. They ran a train on me. I was living a battered lifestyle. Anything else you wish to know. I escaped that life. With all the negativity I encored. There is not enough room for me to be embarrassed. I was seeing you while all this was happening to me. You could not save me. I had to save myself. So, I could find a clear direction in my life. So, Tyree! Makayla said, I hope. I have provided you with. An adequate amount of information to your question?

Makayla I'm glad you allowed me to. Ask you your personal business. I'm sorry you had to endure pain and mental stress. Don't be sorry Tyree. I've been through worse. I've been penetrated in places. You could never image. So, Tyree are you ready for dinner. Or do you wish to cancel? Your choice because my life is what it is. Makayla went to the table. Tyree sat there wishing he had kept his mouth shut. He felt like Makayla's feelings were pressed against his brain.

Tyree believed Makayla heart was full of love and courage. He was shocked! Was this the way. Makayla made her money? In order to live this luxurious life style. When Tyree met Makayla, she was driving a Honda. While living in a neglected tenement building. Now she's pushing a Benz. Living in water front property. Tyree came back to reality. Makayla felt there was no need. To discuss her past over dinner. She put on some Jazz music. Tyree and Makayla enjoyed the delicious sea food. They were conversing like they were at. The beginning of their first date. Tyree really enjoyed Makayla. Every time he saw her. She was still the woman he wanted to marry. This night had taught him. They could be honest with each other. Tyree really respect Makayla for that. He was still her virgin. Tyree wanted sex after marriage. He was content with the circumstances. That he had learned about Makayla.

28

JAIL TIME

By Roslyn OFlaherty

Alina's time in jail was traumatizing. Moods of being trapped in a cage. Had set in even though. This was not her first incarceration. Alina was cocaine sick. And stayed in the infirmary. Detoxing made her very uncomfortable. Whenever the opportunity came about. She would lay on her bunk. Alina would be shaking under her covers. Feeling fatigue with superiority and nervous tension. As the wetness pored over this woman's body. Alina knew this bid would definitely. Be unlike former jail time. For prostitution and indecent exposure. Alina could never imagine. Catching a murder charge.

Alina's earned income in the outside world. Was from sexual exploitation assistance. From her personal escorts service in prostitution. That was started from scamming money. From Marshalls establishing a prostitution ring. Alina market of selling ass. Felt unsafe and vulnerable. Forced to trust a former john. During her incarceration. He protected all sexual activity and investments. Alina needed freedom. Lawyers had to be paid. During this Catch-22 charge with evidence. Alina's former acquaintance Makayla. Could not be found. Alina did not need anyone to kill. Her mental heaven of hope. She needed freedom.

Marshall was deceased. A dilemma bringing on a sudden. Turn of events that emerged; hard times of imprisonment. With a killing altercation. That should not have Alina's. Name all over it...

Alina was in love with Marshall. Even though he treated her bad. Conflicts made it easy. For her not to be loyal to Marshall. To a certain degree. Symptoms of depression had set in from time to time. Because she had a crush on him. Alina was considered faithful. In Marshall's prostitute ring. He bust her ass from time to time. The word murder was causing instability in her life. She needed to take care. Of her money affairs. Alina did not need to become penniless. It was time to move on with life. While she was incarcerated.

Alina started wondering. Who she would fuck. To get commissary money in her account. The realism of sexually preferring. Men and women. Would play a big part. In her sexual decision making. Alina desperately needed to pay for a lawyer. Alina new the cause of Marshall's Murder. Had Makayla's name engraved all over it? Makayla was living a journey of destruction.

Alina knew that obtaining ducket's. Was her top priority. It would be time to spread her legs. When she felt better. Getting in population was a must. Thoughts of manipulation. Was taken into consideration. Which helped Alina conquer. A plan to be moved. Out of the cell housing area she was in. A little money could rectify that situation. Alina wanted to live on a dorm. She knew from being incarcerated before. She needed to eat. Someone out for inmate protection. Her tongue action would be working. To claim that; I don't give a fuck rank.

The cocaine withdrawals had her feeling. A little defenseless. It was time for Alina to prostitute. Get on her grind and fuck for a hefty price. A survival trait she learned. From her ex-pimp Marshall. Alina's hyper hardy sexual behavior. Usually enables her to find good prostitutes. To start a prostitution ring. Without causing burden to her profit plans. Alina felt it would be easier to screw. The officers for petty cash. Women and men officers. That loved working the wheel. Alina would play them. For their overtime money. There were inmates with street clout. That had more money. Than Captains and the Warden.

Alina would seek out inmates. That were incarcerated. Hiding white collar crime money. Jail was taxing their ass. For the decisions they made. White-collar crimes, had made them rich. And Alina being accused of killing Marshall. Carried more jail time. Then the person that became rich. Off their white-collar crime case. Entering back into society; independent without a struggle. Their white-collar crime profession. Made them comfortable. Besides being laid back during their bid. Their manipulating well-thought-out plan. Retired them for the rest of their life.

The majority of Captains and Wardens had mortgagees. Paying college tuitions for their children's schooling. Their cash flow was broken by the American Dream. Without the picket fence. Alina probabilities of making millions. From coins in jail were slim. A quest of becoming released. Was the decision Alina was looking for? Concerning Marshall being murdered. Her short term goals. Was to make a little money. For this bid, she was facing. There would not be a commitment. To this bogus charge. It needed to be over turned. With no contempt!

Right about now the Wardens pockets. Plus, status was looking good. For Alina's long-term safety net. She would not mind using. Warden Duncan as a pawn in her game. Alina would insist in seeing. Warden Duncan and him only. Becoming a pest; every shift the warden worked. Requesting to see him. Alina was always acting up. Stripping in front of the officers. Mashing her naked body, against the gate. Every chance she got. While assisting to see the Warden Duncan.

Warden Duncan sent Alina a message. Informing her to write him a letter. So, Alina did as she was told. Writing him three letters. During his shifts for a whole month. The letters always said the same sentence.

Warden Duncan,
With all due respect HELP!!!
Alina #00020149XX

Warden Duncan was sick of the letters. Three times a day the word HELP!!! He was sick of it and decided. To take matters into his own hands. Warden Duncan requested to see Inmate #00020149XX. Alina's plan had worked. Warden Duncan had agreed to see Alina. She walked through his administrative center. Where she was searched. Alina was escorted across the hall. To Warden Duncan's office.

The officer knocked and, opened the door upon command. After seeing how beautiful Alina was. Warden Duncan stumbled over his words. While asking the officer to leave. The warden locked the door behind him. Duncan could not get over; her banging body. Alina new it as soon as their eyes met. Alina had thoughts of fondling and seduced Warden Duncan. As soon as he stood up.

But it was now time for Alina. To turn herself into the warden. When she entered into the office. The Warden Duncan was staring. Alina was a beautiful woman in his eyes. She stared at him back. As the bulge grew in his pants. Alina stood in front of him. Reached for his crotch and said ok. What you got for Mama... As she struggled a little. Exposing his great old donkey dick. Oh, Duncan she giggled. What a great chocolate hard on. Just like I like it, circumcised dick. The warden was ready to nut off on her. He knew Alina had a body to kill for.

Yeah Baby come to Mama. I got milk for you. Alina pulled out her double D's. Getting him ready to give her milk money. Warden Duncan turned Alina's ass around. Place her ass on his desk. Yeah Duncan I knew you were a manly man. Take Charge!!! Yes, baby you know what I came for. Duncan parked that donkey-dick. Way up in her pussy. Alina said slap my ass ride me Duncan. Why did she say that? Duncan pulled his donkey-dick out. Oooh shit Alina said. Duncan wipe his donkey all over her ass. Then spread her ass cheeks. Wiping his dick up and down her butt crack. He lifted Alina's booty up. And shoved that chocolate in fast. She was moaning; oh baby. That what I came here for. He penetrated her ass. Alina's clit was cut out. She would never let Duncan know that. But she imagined him tasting it. The warden's great-big-oh-donkey-dick. Was on of a kind. It felt like it had a pulse. Alina could feel it throbbing. As he nutted off in her...

The office it smelt like sex. Alina now knew she could fuck. Warden Duncan every chance she got. It was time to play. Mind chest with this idiot. To obtain all her needs. Alina fondled him. One lick of Duncan's donkey dick. And he was hard and moaning. Alina sucked that chocolate. While swallowing that cream. Duncan scream like an out of control little bitch. She almost gagged. As she pleasured him. Alina was a sex addict; just like Duncan.

The warden's great-big-oh- donkey dick. Was not shooting blanks. Alina was slobing the knob. While rubbing his balls. As everything just gushed out the head of his dick. Duncan was shaking his Johnson. Screaming swallow, the cum Alina! Wow Alina thought he remembers my name. Ching-Ching you can write me a check baby. I know I'm entitled to it.

The warden stated he would send. For her when necessary. Alina's sex execution would get her. In Warden Duncan's pockets. It was easy money. Alina was ready to control his work status. Warden Duncan's title would be controlled by Inmate #00020149XX aka Alina.

The institution would pay. For her lawyer's fees. While she was incarcerated. The warden would pay. A hefty price towards her freedom. Alina would make the best of her time. She was definitely a wrongly accused victim. Alina did not consider herself a murderer.

Alina was part of a sexual escort service. Her brain was functioning fast. She was thinking about sex trafficking. From one institution to another. Alina would be the Madam. And the prostitutes in jail would be called Harlots. They would be identified by the title Harlot. With the last three numbers of their inmate number. Yellow Harlot Identification cards. Would read as follows #harlot-369. You would have to use it with your inmate identification card.

Alina was ready to market her Harlots. Plus, Warden Duncan would assist her in getting her freedom. Everyone involved would get paid. They would be criminalizing pimping in jail. The inmates in the reformatory. Would take them to the good quality of life. Alina had to be released. Her goal was not to stay incarcerated. She had a score to reconcile with Makayla. Makayla was the only one. That could identify the murder weapon as a Glock 32 .357 SIG... The hand gun that tied the Murder of Marshall to Alina.

The information on the weapon as well as. Just how many gunshots. Was never revealed to the public. Alina was allegedly accused of murdering her pimp Marshall. Who she truly loved? The newspaper article was entitled —

A SUSPECTED PROSTITUTE
PLEADS NOT GUILTY
TO THE MURDER OF HER PIMP

29

THE DOCTORS

By Roslyn OFlaherty

Clarissa blocked out various parts. Of her brutal rape. She found herself struggling. With her suicidal thoughts. The Intensive Care Unit. Was killing her spirit. Clarissa was suffering. From a rape trauma syndrome. This did not need to play. A major part of her recuperating. She was definitely in shock. Besides needing to pull herself together. Clarissa certainly did not need symptoms of procrastination. Her mind and body had to work. Together in order to heal. Uncle Pete thought he could help. Comfort Clarissa in her recovery.

Clarissa knew that she just wanted. To be without any assistance. That came with a pity party. She was tired of Uncle Pete. Just sitting in the chair. Staring as she laid in the bed. Clarissa was glad Uncle Pete went home. To shower and change his clothing. She knew that positive thinking. Would be beneficial to her health.

Clarissa was trying; to get some rest. When two full-size men. Entered her hospital room. They were dressed as physicians. They spoke at the same time; saying good morning. Clarissa wondered why they were waking her up. At the crack of dawn. One of the doctors bent over Clarissa. Then pulled out a knife. The other man choked her. Clarissa's eyes began to bulge. Out of her dam head. She began to imagine dying. In her hospital bed. Clarissa started choking. Also grasping for air. He placed the knife on her breast.

Clarissa could feel her heart. As it beat rapidly. The man spoke in an unsympathetic voice. Where can we find. Your fuckin cousin Makayla?

She went to say. I don't know. The man ripped out her intravenous device from her vein. Clarissa could feel the blood. Discharge from her hand. The other man had his hand. Over her mouth as she tried to scream. The conflict began to get out of control. Clarissa thought what Makayla could have done. She was horrified. Just from the size of these men. We need you to give. Makayla a message. Tell Makayla if she doesn't bring. Back our cocaine and money. We are going to viciously kill your Uncle Pete. Clarissa you will continue to suffer. Every time we see you.

You're lucky Clarissa your bastard. Rape baby from Marshall died. If he was alive. We would go to the nursery. Then crush his mother fuckin skull in! Clarissa was startled, what the hell. Was this man talking about? His words raced through her mind. Baby! What Baby! What fuckin baby! Clarissa was thinking back. To when she was admitted. Was that the cramping she felt? Before she passed out in the emergency room? What did this man mean my rape baby? She knew not to ask. About the baby while the man. Spoke to her in a condescending way. The thought of having Marshall. As her baby Daddy. Was hard for Clarissa to comprehend.

While imagining the fact. That Marshall's baby was growing. Inside of her body. Clarissa got an instant head ache. She thought to herself. I had a miscarriage? Tears rolled from her eyes. Then Clarissa found a focal point on the ceiling. Too just stared at it. God please help me! To rap my brain around this situation. Don't let me lose my mind Lord. Clarissa started praying Lord. I know my baby is lying. In a cradle, in your house in heaven. Is this considered giving birth in sin? This child did not know morally. What is right or wrong? Please check on my first child. My baby is in heaven! Thank you so much Lord. For keeping me from bugging out.

The Doctors or Uncle Pete have not mentioned. The deceased baby to Clarissa. Makayla's criminal life style; would have her killed. Clarissa snapped back to reality. She was able to hear. The phony doctor speaking to her. We need you to assist us. In retrieving our money. Plus, the cocaine Makayla; stole from Marshall. The man took a knife. Pointed it in the direction of her heart. Clarissa imagined the blade puncturing it. The trifling doctor used the knife. To cut the hospital gown. Her breast was uncovered. Clarissa was terrified! The man pinched both her nipples. Wiping the knife across her tits, ever so softly.

Clarissa closed her eyes. While praying in silence. Oh God, please don't let this phony doctor. Cut off my nipples. She could feel the man bend over; as he bit her nipple hard. Clarissa thought it was going to fall. Off in his mouth. While being assaulted. In her hospital bed paralyzed. The Doctor whispered. There will be a hit out on Uncle Pete's life. Right about now! Uncle Pete was unimportant to Clarissa.

Clarissa was breathing heavy. Praying to Father God. Please encircle her with your favor. Freedom from humility and negative spirits. That has attached its self to Clarissa's spiritual energy. Unable to hold a thought. As her minds focus point diminished. There was a force of evilness; standing over her bed. She repeated for the need of assistance. Over and over again in her mind. Clarissa feared for her life. This woman continuously prayed. To rebuke the chaos of hurt, lies and truth.

Imagining faith from betrayal. Her body was soak and wet. Looking for comfort from agony. Just resting there with her eyes closed. Imaging a brutal vendetta against Uncle Pete. Who had treated Clarissa improper? With a life that is consumed in lies. With fear of retaliation in this toxic situation. Clarissa was having flash backs. Of her attacker Marshall. Who may be her baby's daddy? According to the phony doctors. If she was truly pregnant. Lord I know you hear me. I want to thank you for watching over me. Please help me stay prayed up. Clarissa could feel the knife. Being removed from her chest. She laid in silence. With the devil hanging on her shoulder. All walks of this confusion. Must now be categorized. As a thing of the past for clarity. In order for her to heal. Uncle Pete would be addressed about. His contribution to all this bullshit.

Nurse Beverly came in the room. Ok honey! I'm just going to change your IV. I need you to take this medication for me. The nurse looked at Clarissa. Why did you remove the IV? Clarissa was full of anxiety. Unable to express her thoughts… Clarissa stayed silent. She could not confide in the nurse. Although the nurses voice. Sound like heaven to her ears. She pulls the blanket over her breast. Clarissa revealed her arm so the IV could be replaced. The men had left. She was ready to open wide. She welcomes the medicine. More dismay was not what Clarissa needed in her life. For Clarissa and Uncle Pete's life; to be threatened was pretty serious. What the fuck could happen next? Clarissa realized mistakes teaches us about our self. Petty, ignorance of full-grown ass thugs; deplorable street life.

Which was converted into a night mare. Clarissa had to put on. Her grown woman panties. She was dumb tight. It was time to drop them panties. Show these notorious; characters their actions are inhumane. The next person who showed brutality towards Clarissa. Would have to kill her. She no longer worried about the probability. Of death and fight back. Marshall fucked Clarissa head up. It was time to let people know they could kiss her ass. And she was dead ass serious. The obstacles of conflict. Needed transformation! This woman was caught in the middle of a bad situation. She could not keep that hospital bed on her back. Rehabilitation would help her identify with her past, present and future. Clarissa was fuck up in the head. And could not envision. Makayla having their cocaine and money. They wanted their suit case back. What could Makayla know about the cocaine, money and drug dealers? Makayla spoke of Marshall as being her pimp. Was he a dealer consistently? Makayla never mention any kind of money to her or Uncle Pete.

Clarissa had to see Doctor Dermas. It was time for her to leave the hospital. To have phony doctors. Coming to Clarissa's hospital room. Giving her uncalled-for threats. Was definitely inappropriate for her illness. She needs Uncle Pete to come and help her. Address the matter at hand. Lord Clarissa spoke out loud. I really don't know what to do. My lack of knowledge does not allow. Me to deal with such wicked spirits. I'm going to purchase a gun. No fury like a scorned woman A bible verse quoted to them. At this point may. Only come amendable at their funeral. Or in a prison sentenced to. Being a lifer for punishment. Without an option a being released.

It's unthinkable to think. Of what these men will do to her. Even though Clarissa said. She would not let the phony doctors take her pearl. While living in doubt of emotional cruelty. Clarissa would like to find comfort in the presence of the Lord.

30

HOSPITAL STAY

By Roslyn OFlaherty

Uncle Pete came back to the hospital. As he walked into Clarissa room. He noticed she was shaking. Clarissa was having a panic attack. Uncle Pete could not contemplate what happened. Clarissa opened her mouth. The words poured; out of her mouth real fast. Slow down Clarissa. I can't make out what you're talking about. Her communication was so distorted. That she had to write a short summary. On paper for Uncle Pete. To understand the events that had taken place. In her room that morning.

Clarissa what did the men look like. After giving Uncle Pete a description of the men. She could tell he knew exactly. Who she was talking about? Clarissa watched him panicking. As she stated the men had threatened their lives. Uncle Pete knew exactly what he would be dealing with.

Clarissa began to speak. Uncle Pete why didn't you tell me? I was carrying Marshall's baby! Then Clarissa started screaming out of control! She lost her child? My three-month-old son! My innocent baby! I did not even have time to name him. You knew Uncle Pete and you did not say anything! Clarissa said you left my child in the hospital? To be disposed of just like his father was. My baby tossed to the trash; like garbage. What the fuck! Were you thinking Uncle Pete?

This was a loss that was. Unmanageable to the brain. Imagine not being able to hear. Your baby's heart beat or first cry Clarissa said? God why did this happen? Uncle Pete I don't think. I can forgive you! For not telling me Clarissa said. The way she found out about her baby. Was a heart crusher, just horrifying! You don't even know if they. Took my babies organs; without permission.

Uncle Pete I don't ever want you to. Utter words of my son's existence. What a fine uncle you turned out to be! Clarissa said, by the way Uncle Pete. My sons name is Malachi. The word of the Lord. Was sent through Malachi. Unlike you Uncle Pete. You just kept your mouth shut. About my baby boy Malachi. Clarissa said; Father God I return your child. Malachi back to you in which you lent me.

1 Samuel Chapter 1: Verse 27 thru 28 says –
Verse 27-For this child I prayed; and the
   Lord hath given me my petition
      Which I asked of him:
Verse 28-Therefore also I have lent him to
      the Lord; as long as he liveth he shall
      be lent to the lord. And he wor-
      shipped the Lord there.

Mommy loves you Malachi. Lord Clarissa said; I want to thank you. For allowing me to hold on to my sanity. She stated; I'll never make reference of my son. Malachi again to anyone. Clarissa said you Father God! Are the true Father of my child Malachi.

Uncle Pete had to have Clarissa moved out of the hospital for her own safety. Clarissa was looking for a bereavement period. She had to be given a tranquilizer. That had reduced her anxiety. Uncle Pete thought of where he could hide out with Clarissa. She was moved from the hospital with a factious name. It was a wise decision. To change their appearance, and names until they reached. Their destination of safety.

Uncle Pete called in some favors. So, Clarissa was moved to a convalescent home for skilled care. She was placed in a body bag. Put on a gurney, and taken to the hospital roof. Where she was air lifted to the destination. Where they would hide out. The room was big with a full bathroom. It was like a five-star hotel. It had two beds which enabled them to share a room. Clarissa would continue to receive medical attention. Clarissa, and Uncle Pete would be able to have food. Brought up to their room. Instead of going to; the dining area to eat.

The accommodations were perfect. Clarissa did not know it but they were being accommodated. In a federal witness protection program. As a favor to Uncle Pete. Uncle Pete had promised. To bring forth evidence on street crimes. Uncle Pete made sure their well-being was now protected. It reminded Uncle Pete when he was in solitary confinement in prison. He worried about Makayla's safety. Uncle Pete believed Makayla was a narcissist; who needed to remove. All the Voo-Doo curses. With spells against her. She was not to be trusted.

The discrepancy's Makayla started. Caused Uncle Pete, and Clarissa to have a hit out on their life. Uncle Pete knew who was behind. All of the intimidation, and who ordered the hit on them. Clarissa and Uncle Pete's life was ruined. He wasn't sure if Makayla knew. Her life was in jeopardy. Makayla actions made Uncle Pete; go against the codes of the street. He now had to obey. The laws of the land for protection.

31

OUT TO EAT

By Roslyn OFlaherty

It was a beautiful Sunday morning. The sun was shining bright. Tyree decide to go see his mother. At church, and ask her out to eat. He had a few things that he felt. He needed to talk about with her. He saw his mother fellowshipping. In the parking lot like always. Hi Ma! Mrs. Jenkins turned around. She was surprised to see her son. What happened, now Tyree she asked? Nothing Ma! Can't I pick my mother up from church? Without anything being an issue. We'll let me finish my conversation? With Pastor Rachana, and I will be ready.

Ok Ma, I'm parked over here. Tyree decided to tell his mother. He wanted to get married. He was not sure how Mrs. Jenkins was going to act. In response to the news. Especially if Tyree told his mother it was Makayla. He wanted to be married with. Mrs. Jenkins approached the car. Tyree was worried, and his mother. Did not even get in the car yet. When Ms. Jenkins approached the vehicle. Tyree jumped out of his seat and, opened the car door. For his mother. Ms. Jenkins sat down. Taking in mouthful of air. Wondering what happened now.

Tyree entered the car quickly, and said Ma. Can I take you to lunch? Oh, where doing lunch! Is there a motive behind us eating out? No Mother, I just wanted to have a conversation. With you about something. He took Ms. Jenkins. To one of the finest restaurants in town. Tyree had made reservations and, their table was ready. As they entered the eating place. They order an entrée before the main dish. They began eating the food.

They talked for a while. Then his mother said Tyree. What did you wish to discuss?

When Tyree stated; he wanted to get married to Makayla. Mrs. Jenkins started choking, and the food fell out of her mouth. Ma you alright! Why in the world! Would you want to get married to Makayla? Tyree are you kidding! You don't know this woman! Ma if it was up to you. I would never get married. You always have something negative. To say about the women, I'm interested in. First it was don't get serious. About a woman until you are successful. Then it was I need to establish my finances. Well I've done what you said Ma!

I really feel a fondness for Makayla. Tyree told his mother; he was in love! Admitting Makayla never told him. She loved him. Tyree said, I can tell. She is ready to be committed. She has a soft spot in my heart. I am going to ask Makayla to marry me. I just wanted to tell you first Mother! Mrs. Jenkins yelled get a prenuptial agreement before you marry her. You want me get a prenup. Makayla source of revenue is better than mine Ma! I would go bankrupt for Makayla. I would depart this life for Makayla, Ma. Tyree don't say that! I love her Ma. She makes my heart beat. Every time I'm around her. I'm not getting a prenuptial agreement.

I'm really in love with Makayla. I don't doubt that; you love her Tyree. I just don't want you to make a big mistake. If Makayla loved you. She would have made it known to you by now. Don't you think you should get to know her more? Ma, I know more, than you think about Makayla. We are truthful to each other about everything. I genuinely love her. I want her to be the mother of my children. Mrs. Jenkins said Tyree! I just don't want this end up. In a separation or a divorce. What she really wanted to say was. I don't want any grand children from Makayla. Ms. Jenkins thought she knew. Way more about Makayla than her son knew. The way that church folk had spoken. Of Makayla would never. Come from Tyree's mother's mouth. Ms. Jenkins would never come. To her son with Church gossip. She knew Makayla was a drug addict at one time. Her life as a prostitute had been discussed. After church on many accusations. At the parking lot fellowships. Mrs. Jenkins did not want to discuss. This with Tyree because Makayla was his first love. He was a man and she respected that. So, they continued to eat their meal in silence.

Then Tyree said Ma, you did not even say! I have your blessings. You do Tyree, you do! That's good me and Makayla. Will set a date and make all the arrangements. The conversation ended, and Mrs. Jenkins just wanted to leave. She was so frustrated, angry and upset. About Tyree wanting to propose to Makayla.

Mrs. Jenkins felt Makayla was, an unpleasant person. For her son to marry. She could not even think straight. After speaking with Tyree. Makayla prostitution life style. Kept making her think of aids, and other sexual transmitted deceases. She just wanted Tyree to find out more about Makayla's temperament. Ms. Jenkins knew Makayla was truly a handful. Ms. Jenkins felt it from her guts. That Tyree's marriage to Makayla would be a life. Changing mistake for her son.

32

MADAM

By Roslyn OFlaherty

Alina was now a Madam. She represented the facilitation. Of sexual experiences that made money. For locked up individuals. The staff was prepared to escort inmates. The extra money, they received kept them silent. The jail had become a brothel. Human prostitution trafficking was now. Being run from institutions; from county to county. Alina also had a prostitution ring. Being run on the outside. It gave her powerful ties on the streets. She had a phony organization participate. With transporting women on the inside of the jail.

Women gay and, straight were being scheduled. To come on certain visiting days. They were screwing in dorms. That were emptied out. Cubicles and air mattresses were supplied. Through catalog orders which were received through the mail room. Certain areas were used for congenital trailer visits. The inmates would pay for sexual experience. From civilian's sexual partner. They were dealing with on the outside. Courtesy of Warden Duncan. Oral and anal sex cost the most. Split fee was given. To those individuals who; participated in orgies. Orgies were only given to the Wardens and Deputy Wardens. They were allowed to bring a person. To intermingle as an outside civilian participant. The Captains and Correction Officers got straight up sex. Inmates that participated in sexual favors. Were given early release. From the parole board. Some women left the facility. Into jobs and motivational programs. Only because they got pregnant while incarcerated. Inmates were suffering. With sexually transmitted diseases that were spreading through the establishment. The administrative authority did not recommend inmates. That were not in population. Like killers and rapist to be eligible for early release. Psychiatric rehabilitation centers and drug programs were also used for early release.

Alina knew she could not get caught. Being a Madam. She needed her case dismissed. If she was to get sentenced. On Marshall's murder. Her time would be running concurrently. With the charge of running a brothel from jail. She knew soon her jail house empire. Would become a problem. People were talking shit about things. They knew nothing about! Everyone who was getting paid! The inmates were getting coins and passing them. On the outside to support their family, commissary and lawyer fee's.

They had to pay the officers. In the mail room; to transport money. Alina new this could. Not go on much longer. Jail was no longer a jail. It became a recreation center for sex. Alina would appoint someone. To be the new Madam. When the time came to buy her freedom. Alina was just trying to figure out. How her case could be handled. Through the court system. She felt she could snitch. On the confinement sex operations... Being run from all Jails.

Alina was ready for her; freedom to the streets. An investigation would be held. Before they would come up with. A condition of release. The Judge continued to postpone. Alina's court date. She would give up everyone. Because her freedom was worth it. Heads would roll. Information would be given. On the notorious jails, and its inmate sex participants. Alina had everyone under investigation. It was time for her to dead this operation. Alina was ready to return to society. Heads had to roll on behalf of corruption. To inmates in a prostitution ring. While incarcerated and falsifying documents. Arrest were being made; Wardens, Deputy Wardens and Captains on down. Alina had implicated. Everyone but herself. This sort of freedom had not been given. To anyone else before. She gave everyone up. And was given her freedom with protection. Alina knew if she ever came through the jail system again. Her life would be ended. Coming through the receiving room. Alina knew she would not make it to a cell area. Some of the money Alina made. Was filtered to the streets. Alina was paid and her money. Was waiting on the outside. Makayla here I come...

33

THE RINGS

By Roslyn OFlaherty

Tyree could image; spending his whole life with Makayla. He was ready to serve her. Like the queen she was. He was worried that Makayla might say no. He loved her and wanted. To be with her the rest of his life. Tyree had already purchased Makayla's engagement ring. Makayla ring had gemstones. It was a beautiful pink diamond ring. With precious chocolate diamond stones. Tyree had a diamond wedding band. With square edges, and four chocolate stones. His ring was made to match Makayla's wedding ring.

Tyree met Makayla at her house; on Cenatoe Island. They were going to have dinner in the casino. He had planned a little. Out of the ordinary event. Tyree took Makayla in front; of her house at seven o'clock. He asked her to look up in the heavens. His pilot friend Dan. Took an air craft, and wrote in the sky. Would you marry me Makayla? The Message was sky written 12 miles high. The Smoke trail was written at a low altitude. The sky was a nice clear blue. Not a cloud insight. Makayla said yes! As the tears came from her eyes. Tyree smiled and reached over. And started to hug and kiss her. They were both happy.

Makayla wondered why. He did not purpose a long time ago. She felt love for Tyree. The first time she met him in the library. She had given him lots of nonverbal hints. Of wanting to be his future bride. Makayla thought to herself. She would now have to make. An effort to get along. With his mother Mrs. Jenkins. She worried how her; soon to be mother in law. Would take the news. Makayla new she could not be concerned.

With what Mrs. Jenkins or anyone else felt. She was ready to enter. Into the grand institution of marriage. Makayla started thinking love, honor and obey. Until death do us part! Huh… Tyree reached in his pocket, and put the ring on Makayla's finger. From that day on. He was going to keep. Makayla close to him. He prepared a home that would suit them both. They would both make a decision. On all the wedding plans. Love was in Tyree and Makayla's hearts…

Makayla and Tyree did not make it to dinner. They went in Makayla house and talked. They enjoyed some wine. Tyree wanted to make obsessive love to Makayla. Tyree was determined to stay a virgin. He would establish their sex life after marriage. Makayla decided to try, but Tyree refused. Now Makayla had sex on her mind and lust in her heart. Being a prostitute for Marshal all those years. Made Makayla believe she was not worthy of being with Tyree. She now knew. That after marrying Tyree they would be as one.

34

SKILLED NURSE FACILITY

By Roslyn O'Flaherty

Uncle Pete and Clarissa were still staying. In the Skilled Nurse Facility. A case manager assisted Clarissa. In navigating her health care. Clarissa was given all the care she required. She was given therapy on her legs. Clarissa was also given acetaminophen for pain. Naproxen to bring down swelling. Exercise was the key. To good physical life style. Clarissa did not mind. When they massage her body. As long as it was a woman. Due to her life of abuse. She had learned how to sit up. For long periods of time.

Clarissa was being trained on how. To get around in a wheel chair. She welcomed the challenge. Wheel chair classes were given by. The "Body and Fleshly Needs Program". The motorized wheel chair would ease the progress of Clarissa. Becoming independent enough; to oversee her own life.

Uncle Pete was exhausted from being locked down. With the aging and the disable. The nurses thought he was living there; for senior assistance. Clarissa was feeling a little better. So, Uncle Pete was moved across the hallway. In his own room. They were still getting protective custody. From the Federal Bureau of Investigation. They never used their factious names. Or changed their appearance. Prior to leaving the hospital.

That night Uncle Pete was assigned a new nurse. Her name was Nurse Estelle. Although Uncle Pete was handsome. With a strong back.

She would try to stay away. From him because she knew. If she got close to Uncle Pete. It would be fraternizing on the job. Uncle Pete and Nurse Estelle had been flirting. With each other here, and there. Through sexual eye contact. She started to turn Mr. Pete down as a patient. That's what her mind. Told her to do. Her heart was full of lust for the man. So, she kept Mr. Pete on her schedule. Nurse Estelle knocked and entered his room. She introduced herself. Hello my name is Nurse Estelle. I'm going to be, your nurse for tonight. Is there anything I can do for you? Yes, you can Nurse Estelle if you don't mind. That is what; I'm here for Mr. Pete.

Your help will be well appreciated. I have pain in the top part of my thigh. Can you take a look at it for me? Nurse Estelle said sure, that won't be a problem. When she pulled back the blanket. Up by his upper thigh. There stood an erection. A big beautiful healthy hard long fat penis. His dick looked like; he could pleasure any women. Uncle Pete's dick had got harder and out oozed. A little wetness from the head of his dick.

Well what seems to be the problem Mr. Pete? He held his dick. To move it out the way and ask her. Nurse Estelle can you hold this a minute. So, I can show you. She held his dick and giggled a little bit. As the inside of her pussy got moist. Uncle Pete rubbed his thigh moaning. Its right here! Thinking don't let my hard on go. Uncle Pete has something for you baby. When she bent over to look at his thigh, Uncle Pete pushed his penis in her face. Nurse Estelle's hand stroked his big long dick. With a firm stroke. She was ready to pleasure Uncle Pete.

After the first stroke her mouth flew open. Nurse Estelle thought it would be ashamed. For Uncle Pete's sperm to reach his balls. So, she started licking the cum. That dripped from the head of his dick. Nurse

Estelle began to jerk him off. Uncle Pete was circumcised. Encouraging her with certain instruction. On how to please him, and that was what she enjoyed. A man that knew what he wanted.

He could tell Nurse Estelle. Wanted to be eaten out first. He moved her out the way. Got up and put her in the bed. He locked the door. Was it a miracle? Uncle Pete could walk, his thigh did not hurt.

Uncle Pete went back to the bed. Pulled his nurses thong off. Exposing her big round juicy ass. He was surprised. When he looked between Nurse Estelle's legs. Her pussy had been shaven bald. It was a beautiful sight. As far as he was concerned. Shaved pussy yesss! I'm coming to lick that clit. He had not run into that in a while. Uncle Pete ran his tongue up her pussy lips. He spread the lip and played with her clit. Oh, she moaned a little. Trying to close her legs.

No open wide for Daddy, let me get that. Uncle Pete's head was now between her legs. Licking and sucking her twat. With a commitment to her clit. It was pink. Nurse Estelle said softly, Dam suck it baby. Suck it… 'Suck my big pussy Pete. You like a big twat don't you. Yeah this is what you wanted. Uncle Pete sucked her clit. And stuck two fingers. In her pussy at the same time. Yes, baby this is what I wanted. She moaned like, she liked it. Let me show you what I really wanted. Uncle Pete tried to put all five. Of his fingers inside her cunt. Her pussy got wet. Wetting the sheet like she urinated on herself.

Uncle Pete jumped up and placed Nurse Estelle on her Knee's. Sticking his head between her legs. And started tongue kissing that pussy. As he looked for that clit again and sucked it in his mouth. Nurse Estelle came all over his face. Oh yes that's right baby cum. That's what I like!!! He continued to taste it. As it dripped out the side of his mouth.

He licked the juice from; the crack of her ass. Then he tried to push his tongue. In her ass hole. Uncle Pete got up and pleasured himself. With that big tight bootie. While trying to put his dick. In her butt hole. Nurse Estelle screamed, a little with displeasure. Uncle Pete had a nice fat- long- circumcised- dick. He was hung! Uncle Pete said ok baby. I see you're not ready. For that yet and slapped her across the ass.

Uncle Pete started thinking about. How he would train Nurse Estelle. To take it in the butt. He stuck his pointer finger in his mouth. Drenched it with saliva. And penetrated her asshole. Slowly with his finger. When he finished. She got up, and sucked Uncle Pete's dick. She sucked it and enjoyed it. Now his hard on. Made his dick bigger than ever.

He turned Nurse Estelle over. Pulling her to the end of the bed. Uncle Pete I got something for you. Shoving his man hood. All the way up in her pussy. It filled every inch. She felt like it was. All over her uterus. With every stroke. Uncle Pete humped all over Nurse Estelle's pussy. With his long wet hard on. It feels good doesn't it baby. Oh yes it feels good, Nurse Estelle yelled! Her legs were shaking. She knew Uncle Pete was a good fuck. His dick was perfect for her pussy.

Uncle Pete pulled out, and cum dripped. All over her shaven pussy. Then he held his dick straight. Wiping all the cum off her pussy. Rubbing it all over his dick. Uncle Pete was ready. To give it to his new nurse. Baby eat and swallow the rest. Off my dick; I saved it for you!!!!!!! Wow your good. Nurse Estelle climbed off the bed. Uncle Pete eyed Nurse Estelle's tits.

As they dangled, her nipples were ready to be sucked. Nurse Estelle said forgive me Father. For I have sinned. Nurse Estelle was married with two kids...

Uncle Pete got up with no remorse. He dismissed her from his room. Giving Nurse Estelle the impression. That he was tired and it was late. Nurse Estelle left his room. With a wet ass smelling like sex. You would have thought Uncle Pete. Had to go to work in the morning. He was content with his action. For some reason Nurse Estelle. Had to taste his juices.

Nurse Estelle loved the bad boys. Sex was taught to Uncle Pete on the street. He did not know how to show. A woman affection, Love-in and respect. Pleasuring her never entered his mind. He began Squeezing and wiping the sperm from his dick. It felt awesome to him. He had no regards to Nurse Estelle's feelings. Uncle Pete got out the bed. Grinning from ear to ear.

Like he was a real macho man. With the same individuality he had. When Nurse Estelle pulled the cover back. Excited about his big fat long erection. Uncle Pete had a hard on as his balls. Were laid out on the sheet. Waiting for fore-play. She held on to his man hood. Like she was ready to fuck Nurse Estelle had wanted to get up out of bed. With the same respect she felt. Before she laid down. Feeling like a woman.

Not full of emotions, of being disgusted. Nurse Estelle started thinking. She should have just let Uncle Pete. Eat her pussy, and stepped the fuck off. Shaking her ass in his face... In her eyes; right about now. Uncle Pete was a dog. Nurse Estelle fucked this mutt. She did not make him use a condom. They had unexpected sex. Uncle Pete was walking around. The Skilled Nurse Facility. With his chest poked out, he had done. What every man in the facility. Wanted to do, with Nurse Estelle.

She had excited all the men. By walking around the Facility. With a tight ass see through. Nursing uniform dress with a thong. The men now looked at Nurse Estelle. Like a thirsty freak. Uncle Pete was the Man! You would have thought that the climax. Was Uncle Pete's biggest sexual aspiration of his life? Nurse Estella new that was hellah shady.

Uncle Pete's face was glowing; like a pregnant woman's... He told the fellas it was from the pussy juice. When Nurse Estelle left work, and returned home. She felt dirty. She smelt like sex, and had to clean herself up. Before her family returned home. Uncle Pete could put it down, in the bed. Better than her kids' father, and her husband. She had not had sex. Like that with any man. Was this sexual encounter. Worth ruining her marriage? It was the best sex. She ever had in her life. Nurse Estelle could not lie. She did enjoy sucking and fucking Uncle Pete.

He had the biggest erection. Her pussy felt good and warm. When he pleasures her. His dick was even bigger than her B.O.B. Nurse Estelle really could not figure out. If this sexual contentment she felt. Had been a blessing or a curse to her marriage. Nurse Estelle knew it brought her closer to her husband. Had another man's hard on saved her marriage?

Thinking about Uncle Pete's dick made her wet. And Nurse Estelle would climb on her husband to get him off. It was like she was enjoying the fuck from her husband. With thoughts of Uncle Pete's big dick. Pleasuring her in many sexual positions. Which bought on flowing orgasms of pleasure. To share with her husband.

She knew going before God. To marry her husband. Had nothing to do with sex with another man. Nurse Estelle sexual involvement. Was not the act of kindness. Needed for her marriage vows to work. The wedding vows. That where stated by Estelle and her husband. Was to be as one forever. Nurse Estelle knew. She was sexually and morally wrong? Nurse Estelle's husband really loved her unconditionally. In his marriage vow he quoted; KJV

Proverbs chapter 18: verse 22-
Whoso findeth a wife findeth
A good thing, and obtain
favor of the lord.

Uncle Pete had Nurse Estelle; emotionally drained spiritually. Uncle Pete was glad Nurse Estelle was his skilled nurse. Nurse Estelle started to feel. Like she was Uncle Pete's jump off. Was she??? Hmm...

35 PART 1

THE DRUG GAME

By Roslyn OFlaherty

The Drug Lords had stepped to the neighborhood dealers. They had threatened to murder. The street dealers. If Marshall drug money and cocaine. Was not returned. Makayla had put everyone's life in jeopardy. Marshall's well-kept organization. In the drug game. Left the streets dry with no narcotics. The man-made drugs Marshall obtained from the Drug Lords. We're not available to dealers on the streets.

Dead men can't talk; neither could dead presidents. The law of logic told everyone in the streets. That Marshalls missing drugs money. Would be focused around death and violence. The drug Lords money had to be accounted for. Or drug connects, and their families would pay. Until all the product and money. Was accounted for. Pharmacy medication over the counter pills. In capsules with white powder was used. For coke heads to sniff. Dealers had to go back to working the streets. Selling unlawful pills Black Beauties and Sunshine out of desperation. In order to make their money to re-up. The dealers were feeling stupid. Because they did not nowhere Marshalls stash was. The money and drugs just vanished. Along with Marshalls prostitute Makayla. She was the only suspect and was wanted for dead. Word on the streets was to keep Makayla alive. The drug lords would deal with her.

The addicts were disappointed about the drug prices. Sometimes it would take two or three days. For the connects to re-up. The junkies still spent their dollars. Even when they knew; they were being sold garbage. They know longer lived in junkie's paradise. Thirsty dope fiends on the nod. One hit away from death. Willing to sell their drug paraphernalia and their ass for a hit. They were desperate and the dealers knew it. Pharmaceutical drugs and dope. we're not being sold on a regular basis.

The Drug Lords were ready; to sell anything to bring street profits it back up. It was hard to tell what drug addict was on. Drug were mixed up with other drugs. Making addicts feel like they were speed balling. You could have sold them dope or coke. With cleanser in it and they would be content. The sad thing was that when addicts. Died from a dealer's product. That's what a junkie considered good shit. So, everybody wanted drugs from that connect.

A drug is a drug at this point of time. In an addict's life. Street drugs was a tragic death sentence. This made the streets dangerous. Addicts would wait and watch. Junkies buy their drugs and kill them for it. The crime rate had gone up. A Junkie would take or do anything. Not to be dope sick; have withdrawal symptoms. From pain medication or street drugs abuse. Junkies were thirsty for street corner drugs. They were getting locked up left and right. The police officers were sick of them.

With their vicious cycle of crazy beat downs. Altercation in the households sometimes brought on death. Parents were physically abused for their pay checks. Social security checks or rent money. Battling beatdowns to the point. They would have to be hospitalized. Family members were scared of the uncontrollable violence. They brought upon the household. So, they let them back into their residence. The vicious cycles continued. Along with chronic addiction relapses. Gang members were running rapid. Prostitutes were happy. when they were incarcerated. The streets were hell on earth. Even drug programs were saving the women and men prostitutes. Their Johns would not bail them out. For fear of catching a beat down. Being locked down in jail

Allowed them to have safety in numbers. Prostitute were sticking together...

The junkies did not bring the drugs to the neighborhood. Yet they were being accused of bring; sex crimes to the street. Junkies in the community were now ready to sell you anything ass, jewelry and appliances. Food from a pantry, welfare cheese along with food stamps. Some drug addicts were so thirsty. They would sell you bacon powder as nose candy. While trying to convince you it was cocaine. Junkies would stand in your face and lie out of desperation.

People were being killed for dope and methadone. Methadone was used to keep drug addicts chasing the dope. As far as the dealers were concerned. Their soul was so thirsty for the drugs. They did not care about deceiving the next person. This was not the steps; God ordered for them. Yet they were stuck. Not knowing what to believe in.

Youth sex and labor trafficking are increasing. Juveniles' were stand on the corner selling ganja. They needed to be in school. Respect for adults was not acknowledged. The village that could have help raise them. Know long held a foundation for the youth. Grown adults feared them and were constantly verbally abused. Adolescents were recruited to the drug game. Straight from the playground. Youngsters sent straight to the Juvenile Detention Centers.

Wow olden times is repeating itself. While the Dope Fein's nods on the corner. It was time to let God be the glory. Through the ratchetness controlling them. To challenge their forgetfulness. That had them lost from the leadership. They once found in their true emotions. To themselves that had been lost in shady endeavors. That was nondiscrimination to one's life.

The drug lords connects were living on the streets. Under a bridge under path. Selling drugs when it became available. Was this politically correct? Or morally wrong? They were also able to sleep on the floor in the shelters. Where they continued sell product. Junkie's personal identification and property were stolen in the shelters.

Even Adults, children and veterans were treated unfairly. The price of drugs had doubled and people. Were get getting evicted from their homes. They felt safer under the bridge with card board boxes. That was used for furniture. They stored their possessions in bags, boxes; and super market shopping carts. Spreading blankets over the card board to get a good night sleep.

When you walked under a bridge or under-path. The homeless made you say good morning. The under-path was fixed up like an apartment. All their possession was in order. Cars drove through their turf quietly. They knew this was their norm. They worked all their lives. And, received their Social Security Checks in a Post Office box. The under path it was clean, not messy at all. They paid the drug lords for Security Safety Services...

Their retirement check was not enough. For them to have an apartment. Drugged out military men with honorable discharges. Dope sick living homeless under the under-path also. Some of them came home from the military with an itch. Now they had a junkie slur to go with it.

The homeless folks, were not allowed to drink or drug. nodding off or be dope sick in the under-path. They protected one another sleeping in shift. The cement ground was sectioned off. Like little bed rooms. Clean hygiene of their skin. Was a must to control bacteria. This took place in public facilities. Which the homeless paid to use. Disrespecting one another was not tolerated. They would greet you as you pass through. The under- path saying good morning.

The drug lords would toss their place. Every now and then. The cops would tell them to evacuate the area. Like they were in their back yard. Besides the fact they knew. They would always come back. The homeless became disrespected individuals. So, police could make their quota. Of arrest for the month.

Prays went out for God. To take narcotic cravings from their soles. Some dope sick addicts prayed to kick their drug addictions. Others did not want to relapse; they prayed often. They needed God's blessing. Even when they were acting scandalous from time to time. They were Gods children.

Cocaine was scarce and dope was on demand. People became obsessed with ambulance rides to get methadone. Now becoming the reality of their struggle. They shot dope so much. All their veins clasped. It seems like we lost a creation of people to drugs, the streets and jail. People had the nerve to judge them. Stating they had a plantation mentality. The drug lords and paid officer could not be concerned. With the lost souls' children and infants born with a habit.

God had another plan for them along with their parents. Who really needed opportunities mentally, physically or spiritually. Religious leaders fought the Drug lords; and their churches were destroyed. People went to the place of worship in need of love and food. The church was the hospital for individuals. Hurting and sick in desperate need of that feeling of affection. Their congregation was under duress.

People may as well believe. Marshall had shut down the drug game. They were expecting law enforcement to put a stop to violent behavior in the streets. They were not being paid from drug sellers any more. So, they did not care. The Drug Lords are going to bring the drug game back. This was just the beginning of the vicious cycle.

35 AS PART 2

SPARKY

By Roslyn Oflaherty

CONTINUES THE DRUG GAME

Drug Lords came to a surrounding area of woods. On Ramona Road and told the head dealers. To get in the car. They pulled off and they were taken; to an out-of-the-way area. There was a large beautiful motor home on wheels. Wow this was the traveling; drug store everyone spoke of. Sparky the head of the transporting drug business. Came outside from this beautiful home. Sparky was well dressed from head to toe.

Who the hell is this Makayla, I keep hearing about? Who is Makayla? Sparky screamed! Marty said I don't know. Sparky took a knife and proceeded to dig. Marty's right eye from the socket. The more the blood ran down his face. The more he hollered from the pain. Marty took a beat down. From Sparky's body guards. As he dropped in the dirt. Marty was stomped to death. Sparky still did not have any indication who Makayla was.

Now does anyone know who Makayla is? Well I don't wish to waste my time discussing her. Heads will roll, until someone figures out who Makayla is. Now take that body, and do away with it! Marty's wife and children will be dead next. If the drugs and the suit case. Full of money are not returned. Sparky knew he was looking. For more than one suit case. Sparky would not let it be known. The true value of money or drugs. That were missing after Marshall's death.

Everyone was silent they knew. Makayla was a prostitute. They did not talk about it. Fearing that a fatal mishap would pop off. After the first sentence. Especially if Sparky did not get the reply. He wanted to hear. The Drug Lords were not use to the street game. They dealt in the inside operation. Of transporting drugs and Makayla had their re-up money. They knew they had to find Makayla.

No one had idea where to look. They search everywhere for Makayla in jails, hospitals and the morgues. Favors were called in for any information. That could be given about Makayla. It was like she vanished off the face of the earth. Sparky killed one drug lord a day. If they did not have their product sold and his money. Makayla did not have a clue, that she had ruined people's lives. Maybe Makayla just did not care to recognize. What was going on in the streets. People's emotional health and personal worth was at stake.

36

MRS. HENDERSON

Roslyn OFlaherty

Tyree wanted to take Makayla to his moms' residents. To tell his mother Mrs. Jenkins. That he had officially proposed to Makayla. Makayla wanted to have her mother. Ms. Henderson go along with her tactics to get married. This way they could have. Their parents get together before the marriage ceremony. Makayla went to her mother's house with Tyree. She had not seen her mother in years. Because of her mother's trifling ways. Makayla and her Moms were both head strong. With opposite views about everything. This did not allow them to get along. Even though they tried to be cordial to each other.

Mrs. Henderson was not a petty individual. She was content with her life. Makayla was just overbearing at times. She was just tired and fed up with Makayla's crap. Makayla held in breath as she entered her mother's residence. When Mrs. Henderson saw her daughter Makayla she was surprised. You could have called before visiting. She was wondering who the young man was. That was with Makayla.

Hello Mother, this is Tyree. Mrs. Henderson did not like the looks. Of this guy Makayla was with. Tyree said hello and Ms. Henderson gave him the impression. Of being discussed about the visit. So, what do you need Makayla? Nothing Ma! I just came over to introduce you to Tyree. We are getting married. I am engaged! Oh, Makayla please! Why would someone want to marry you? Give me a break! I can't believe you brought this young man here. To tell me this nonsense.

I'm going to marry your daughter Mrs. Henderson. I want to take our love to the alter. Before God on our wedding day. I love Makayla! I came to ask for your blessings. I won't have cold feet; Tyree explained! This wedding will go on! Your marriage to Makayla! Does not require my blessing! This marriage idea has, insanity written all over it! You need a blessing from God... If you're going to put up with; Makayla and her temperament. Mister... I don't mean any harm. You could never. Handle Makayla's passive-aggressive, vindictive ways.

Sir, let me tell you something. You are a brave soul. To even consider doing anything with Makayla. I'm opposed to this marriage. Makayla is going to harm you; in one way or another. Believe me a mother knows her child. I birthed that! So, don't come up all in my space. With this nonsense Tyree! First of all! Makayla could never be obedient. To the vows of matrimony. Let alone an affiliation with you.

Makayla is a pathological liar. The only Men that could control Makayla are the bad boys. I feel its best you stay away from Makayla. Now, is that a sufficient enough blessing for you Tyree! Come on Makayla; Tyree shouted! Where leaving... I'm not going to let you get disrespect by anyone. Not even your mother! You have a good day Ms. Henderson. By the way I am a man. It's time to say goodbye. I am not going to tolerate this nonsense.

You don't even know me Ms. Henderson. I find you to be totally disrespectful. I would never disrespect your household. So, I'm going to depart from this situation. My Mother raised me better. Tyree grabbed Makayla's hand and started toward the door. Ms. Henderson started shouting back. Makayla some men came by. They kicked my door in... I don't know what you're into Makayla. You better watch your back. Or, you will wind up in the morgue. With your toe tagged. One man had a weapon drawn at my head. They left you a message. He said to tell you! Sparky is going to murder you Makayla.

Makayla heard that name Sparky before. She did not know who, he was. Saying something about you; returning the money and drugs! They stated you stole it from. A man name Marshall. The money and drugs that Marshall had in his business location. Had been authorized for Sparky's people to flip. Marshall just took charge. Of his prostitution ring from that specified place. They told Ms. Henderson she would be sorry. If they had to kill her daughter Makayla.

Makayla you must comply with their request soon. I told the man mister my daughter Makayla. Has been dead to me; a long time ago. So, you do what, you have to do. The man replied he hoped. He would not have to honor my request. Well Makayla if they come back; I'll let them know. Makayla came by with her fiancé Tyree. Makayla was informed that she was going to die! Tyree slammed the door. He thought Makayla's mother was discourteous.

Ms. Henderson was being straightforward. She was really concerned. About the circumstances that had been brought. To her attention by street thugs. Ms. Henderson knew Tyree was not ready for the truth. Makayla was ready to live a lie. She felt Tyree should know. What he was getting himself into. When they got in the car. Tyree started yelling! His voice and diction sound scary to Makayla. What in the hell! Is your mother talking about! Makayla stated that she did not know anything. About drugs that belong to a man name Sparky. Tyree, I don't know anybody name Sparky!

Then she changed the conversation. Makayla was not lying to Tyree. She had no knowledge about any drugs. Maybe Alina had them stashed somewhere. Why were these men. Specifically asking for drugs? That belong to Sparky? The money was in Makayla's possession. Truly fully her feeling allowed her to believe. She worked for that money. Tyree was emotionally drained. From the trip to Makayla's mother's home. He felt disrespected! With worthless uncontrolled moods. Towards Ms. Henderson behavior.

Makayla, I think we should go back to your house. We can meet with my mom's another day. Tyree knew he could not take another mother episode! Makayla knew Tyree was right. One mother was enough for one day. She knew Tyree's mother would be truthful. When Tyree said they were getting married. Makayla knew Mrs. Jenkins was not fond of her. She just went along; with everything for Tyree's sake.

Makayla could not wait to get married. Tyree being a virgin was causing sexual issues. She had to stop sleeping around. This was not the time to become pregnant. With a one-night stand. That could destroy Tyree spirit. So, she would make love to herself. That would be the only solution to her sexual addiction.

Makayla's love and affection were. Supposed to be for Tyree Jenkins. For some reason Mrs. Jenkins. Could see right through her crap. Makayla's life was one big mess. Being married to Tyree was Makayla's dream. She would not let anybody get in her way. Makayla would be faithful to her vows Till Death Do Us Part. Amen!

37

ENGAGED

Roslyn OFlaherty

Tyree was not secure in his relationship. After the visit with Mrs. Henderson. He was already engaged. It was not the time. For Tyree to crumble under pressure. Makayla was wearing her engagement ring proudly. Tyree found himself wondering. Was Makayla lying about loving him. Would a prostitute make a good wife?

Would he ever label his bride to be? The whore she was coerced to become. Was Makayla truly a slut? Would this relationship push him? To the arms of another woman. Would life care for him better. If the marriage was called off? Makayla was truly preparing him. For her love. He was ready for Makayla now! Was she ready to marry Tyree? He might not be ready to marry Makayla later. Regrets of not having a romantic wedding would be horrifying for Tyree. We make our own matrimony choices relentless or not!

Was Makayla camouflaging her love? Was their room for deception! Through her sexual exportations with other men? Tyree started to believe that the truth. Would be manifested by God. Would this marriage tear down the relationship? With him and his mother. Makayla was controlling Tyree's emotions. His head was now full. Of a lot of thoughts and concerns. Tyree knew deceit wouldn't bring triumph to their marriage vows.

Mrs. Henderson also had Tyree doubting. The association between him and Makayla. Mrs. Henderson had made Tyree feel. Her words and threatening actions were wicked. That Makayla's nonstandard behavior was nothing to get attached to. Tyree loved her and was not ready. To abandon his engagement to Makayla. Tyree loved Makayla since the first day. He laid eyes on her. He had trusted in love at first sight.

Tyree could feel Makayla's presence. All through his body. When he was around her. He enjoyed Makayla's spirit. He would make love to her soul in time. Makayla's mind was full of sexual over the top. Things she could teach her virgin man. Tyree knew now that Mrs. Henderson and his moms. Would never understand his unconditional. Confused love for Makayla. It would forever be in his heart. That is where he wanted to keep her. Tyree decided to step up and be the man. He was raised to be. While claiming Makayla as his wife. Till deaths do us part was that the question or would it be love, honor and obey?

Tyree was ready to raise his level of commitment. Makayla start to feel, telling Tyree. She was prostitute and a coke head. Brought on a lack of admiration. She brushed it off in her mind. To entertain the thought of Tyree not loving her. Should she have kept her past. Dirty baggage to herself. Tyree had to hold respect for her. Till sex do us part; was not going to be love making in their spirits.

God please let Tyree continue to respect me. Until we make it to the altar. I need your blessings. I'm always the first one to say; God don't bless mess. Makayla knew she was just messy and a thief! She said thank you to God. For knowing she needed a savior for her convictions.

38

TIMED SERVED FOR ~
ALINA AKA DARIEONO

By Roslyn OFlaherty

Alina verdict in jail. Was over and done with. She would no longer be incarcerated. Lawyer L. Barnett had her case thrown out. The lawyers opening statement. Killed that noise. Alina could not be linked! To the shooting of "Her Pimp Marshall". Alina did not plead. Guilty to the fatal shooting. There was not enough substantiation. That Alina pulled the trigger. The witness turned out to be. An anonymous phone caller implicating Alina. No one ever identified her at court. The prosecutor closing statement. Allowed the charges to be thrown out. She was being held discriminatorily for said case.

At first Alina thought that she was locked up. For being a prostitute. Truthfully speaking the law wanted Alina to catch a bid. With Marshall's murder written all over it. Alina was going to be released. On the attack charges. That caused Marshall to die. Case dismissed was like music to Alina ears. Assault with a fire arm. Could have sent Alina to prison for life. Justice had gone in her favor. Alina's days of being a madam. Over the brothel ran in the correctional institutions. Was now shut down.

She became a criminal informant in jail. Alina had snitched on everyone. In the whole prostitution ring. She was released and did not have to finish her bid. Jail earned money gave her independence. Quite as it was kept! The existence of the prostitution ring. Had shut down! Alina had made a hefty profit.

Alina had to keep a low profile on the streets. She had camouflaged herself as a man. Alina's new name was Darieono. Everyone thought she was a dude. Alina's sexual preference. Were women all along. Now that Alina came out the closet. Darieono identified her as a man. Life as a male would go onward. Darieono was now known. As the new pimp in his old vicinity. He had established his clientele. From a penitentiary he found out about. While net working. Darieono would only inducing rage. On his women if necessary. Money was not a problem. The prostitutes kept him paid.

Darieono had set up an apartment. Right outside Cenatoe Island. Where Makayla resided at. He was kept private investigators. Watching. Makayla and Tyree. Alina had been released. Being identified as a man name Darieono. Who had a score to settle with Makayla? She would pay for all the tragedies. That she caused him. Darieono could have easily put a hit. Out on Makayla's life. Makayla needed to know. Darieono would be her worse nightmare.

Makayla had treated him so inadequate. They were fuck buddies when he was Alina. He turned that pussy out. Wet ass Makayla was strung out on coke. Like Marshall wanted. then turn over to her Johns. Makayla despised Darieono because he set her up to be a hooker. When Darieono did suffer in jail. He often wondered if there was a God. He would pray for forgiveness. Of all his wrong doings.

Darieono was not brought up in the church. He was waiting for God to interpret the bible into his heart. Darieono, felt the evil forces taken over him at times. Spirits he could not explain. He was confused why. He played both sides of the fence. Thankful he never forgot how to pray. Darieono was a lost soul. To debts, rough sex and being shady. So, he prayed for glory from his Father in heaven.

> Our
> FATHER
> which art
> in heaven.
> Hallowed be thy name.
> Thy kingdom come.
> Thy will be done in earth,

as it is in heaven.
Give us this day
our daily bread.
And forgive us our debts,
as we forgive our debtors.
Lead us not into temptation,
but deliver us from evil:
For thine is the kingdom,
and the power,
and the glory,
forever. Amen...

Darieono had asked for forgiveness. On so many occasions. Alina was Bisexual would God forgive; her sexual preference to be a man? Now that she was Darieono. Some religious people would say. Alina you will burn in Hell. Whether you called her Alina or Darieono. She trusted God and his understanding. God's mercy and forgiveness let him know. He was cherished regardless of his sexuality. The Lord was in his heart. Darieono was a spiritual person. Truly believing we are all God's children. Even though he felt. He was born bisexual. The good part of his life was balanced. With positive productivity in the LGBT community. They kept Alina AKA Darieono from. killing himself on many occasions. They were his mental sponsors. Everyone interpreted Gods love differently.

When Darieono hit the streets, he did not complain. His business was started while he was incarcerated. The identity politics in the house of correction would continue. He had not been; what society called reformed in prison. Darieono was no longer considered. A paid pimp-convict incarcerated. He welcomed his early release. Without any potential danger. He was not looking for any difficulties. He was living courage with faith.

Darieono had approached his living situation. As if he was still incarcerated. Despite the fact he had more advantages. The quality of life was better. Nervousness would set in. Makayla had given Darieono. The stimulation to stay alive. While he was incarcerated. He was living for revenge. With no forgiveness in his heart. Makayla was one of his main concerns.

Makayla had caused unsteadiness in Darieono. Her actions had him. Living on the edge. Makayla had taken him. There with her personality disorder. There was defiantly a lack of insight. That existed in Makayla's life. Once Makayla hurt you. Her symptoms would make matters worse. Then you could understand. Her true mental capacity. For what it was worth. Darieono wished to deal. With her as a coke head. Then he would be able. To shut her down quick. He was curious to know. Where Marshalls cocaine was! Darieono was hoping. To obtain it before Sparky. In jail you knew more. That was going on outside, in the streets. Than people living in the public society.

39

THE ENSLAVEMENT

By Roslyn OFlaherty

Uncle Pete was still doing the nasty. He was strung out. In the Skilled Nurse Facility. His dick was enslaved concurring. A different nurse almost every night. His old behind had the nerve to brag. About the facts of his sexual; arousals to the others. Walking around the facility. Like a walking Ding-A-Ling. Uncle Pete needed a hotel room, Hmmm. Clarissa had spoken to her Uncle Pete. Telling Uncle Pete, he should feel discomfited. Walking around with a hard on all day. Clarissa knew he was bored. She was also bored to death.

Uncle Pete we have to get out of here. I can't take it! I can get around in this wheel chair. I won't continue to be enslaved. To this living situation. Clarissa could not believe. That the altercation with Marshall. Had taken place in her life. This living condition needed change. Its time! Uncle Pete that we find a way. To start a life for ourselves. We must locate Makayla to find out. What can be done to clean up this confusion? She has gotten us into.

Uncle Pete how long do you think. We can continue living like this. In our hidden safe place of protection. Full recovery; will come into my life. This disability is what I have to work. With at the present time. The obstacle that we have occurred. To be in this society may be. Better face in the general public.

Uncle Pete looked a Clarissa. Like she was crazy. Obviously, she did not know. What they were dealing with. Clarissa this is our life, believe it or not. Death will be brought. Into our lives if we leave. Haven't you been through enough. A beat down, raped with a weapon? If we depart from here Clarissa. We are as good as dead.

This was as good as it gets. Uncle Pete would rather stay hidden. While he played. With the nurses sexually. A bed along with some food and shelter. He thanked God for that. Marshalls ex- drug dealers. Had spoken death over his destiny. I won't face this predicament until. Makayla returned their possessions.

Marshall is dead and so many. Lives are being sacrificed? Truth be told this is the beginning. Of the rest of our life. This is the enslavement. We have been dealt. Chaos has been thrust upon our lives. We must not waste this chance. To be happy; forever how long. This experience continues to last. Clarissa consider yourself blessed. Uncle Pete no disrespect. Speak that nonsense. Into your future not mine! I did not come this far. In this trauma just to be enslaved. To this ongoing situation.

40

EVIL SPIRIT MINDED PEOPLE ARE BUSY BABY

Roslyn OFlaherty

Makayla went to the church on Cenatoe Island. She was baptized at AGAPE CHURCH WISDOM AND FAITH #2. The Cenatoe Island Church. Enabled her to pray to the lord. Fellowshipping was something Makayla couldn't do. She decided just pray. Makayla never worried about death and damnation. Her ways were not socially accepted. Ms. Henderson said her daughter. Was born with bad genes. Her rude behavior was toxic. Especially towards the family. That really hurt Makayla.

Makayla was strong minded with a weak ego. Church was Makayla's hospital. Mrs. Henderson was shocked to be threatened by Sparky. The money Makayla had stolen from Marshall. Was still hidden in a suit case. At the AGAPE CHURCH OF WISDOM AND FAITH #2.

Marshall had drugs and hookers in his life. The dispute over stolen drugs had to be settled. After Sparky had threatened Mrs. Henderson Makayla knew her moms. Would never attend the wedding. Ms. Henderson, was really pissed off. Makayla doubted if Tyree. Would take her to discuss. The wedding with Ms. Jenkins. Makayla's life was progressively getting worse. While Makayla was in church. It made her think about Clarissa. She prayed lord; let her be safe. Makayla did not know if she left the hospital. Alive with her critical condition.

Makayla knew Uncle Pete; had enough street smarts. To keep him and Clarissa safe. Trying to contact them would. Only bring forth deadly danger. Makayla had no feelings of repentance. It was only predicted agony from the drama. Considered as an unfortunate consequence. There was no real desired affection. For anyone but Tyree. Makayla was truly devoted with admiration.

Makayla clearly wanting her mother blessings. On the major choices in her life. The marriage and coming together as family. With her fiancé Tyree would mean so much to Makayla... Mrs. Henderson had shocked Makayla back to reality. They never agreed on much. Neither one of their arrogant dispositions had a chance. Towards a better positive relationship. A real quality of love. No matter how hard life's regrets gets.

Mrs. Henderson knew her daughter. Was shady, a real intolerable human being. She knew if Makayla wanted her dead. She would continue to attack. Taking her mind captive; emotionally and spiritually. Draining it with thoughts of nonsense. Mrs. Henderson was not going to stress. Over the situation that had. Trickle down to her relatives. She slept with the door open. With the windows unlocked. She was not going to hide. Showing weakness would only. Make Makayla manipulate the situation. Through her creepy ratchetness.

Mrs. Henderson believed that God knew. When her time would come to be dead. She disregarded the untruths of her enemies. That was implied chaos. On what was considered nonsense. She would not intervene in solving. The enemy's problems and illegal acts. Evil spirits are busy

41

CONNIE

Roslyn OFlaherty

Connie was a Tyree's old girl friends. They reunited at a hardware appliance store. Connie was considered despicable. Messy when she was thirsty for dick to soothe her. She was tall and slender. With a shapely big bust and a nice firm butt. A Unique physical beauty. Wrapped in a chocolate complexion. Natural short jet-black afro. She was charming and always made. Sure, everyone feels good.

Connie was beauty and brains. She loved Tyree and could not fasten her brain around. The thought of his number one rule. No sex! Until marriage was thrust upon their relationship. Everyone called Tyree, Baby Virgin. Tyree loved being called him Baby Virgin. You would have thought. He was being called Baby Jesus.

Tyree truly respected the name Baby Virgin. Connie just slept with women to get over it. Connie and Tyree's past relationship had been ruined. Due to Connie's admission to a good University. Her parents were well-off. Tyree believed the University earned a hefty profit. Which presented an open-door policy. Entrance into the University of high prestige. They were strict when it came to her schooling. So, Connie inconceivably enter the University! She graduated with high honors.

Connie's education took her on a journey. She was not moved by circumstances. Just the knowledge, wisdom and understanding. That she should not compared her life to others. This enabled her to understand her worth.

Connie always walked around telling people to:

"LIVE TO STAY ALIVE; IN THE BUSINESS WORLD". She started many business ventures. That have had positive outcomes. Connie was able to sponsor students. To the Universities of their dreams. With contributions for their cost of the books. University students would in return. Intern by sharing business knowledge. In several community colleges. Whether you were an attorney, working in billing and coding or just grant writers, etc.

Everyone in Connie's circle took care of each other. They were a loyal, honest. Dedicate business minded family. A support team of individuals. That were hungry for success. Serious when it came to accomplishments and taking it. To a whole different level. Business associates able to persist. Finding out who they were in the corporate world.

Connie's University life was her best teacher. With lots of street survival skills. She became sneaky always partying. Hennessey was her preferred drink. This was the private life. The family did not know about. Living off campus in an apartment. Where pay parties and orgies took place.

Most of the bisexual student came to her parties. Sexual males looking for head. Dykes hungry for intercourse. With promiscuous lesbians and whores. Craving for orgasms with desires and motives. They did not fit in a lot. Of events given on campus. One thing you could say about them. Is they spent money to party. They did not allow. Conflict in their environment. Connie sold wine, beer, weed and fish. Dinners at her parties. She also lived in campus living quarters. That her parents paid for. Two bedrooms in RAPHEAL RESIDENTIAL DORMITORIES. She rented them out like hotel rooms.

Connie always kept a brand-new car. After she finished school. While shopping in the hardware store. Connie and Tyree's eyes locked. They said hello to each other. Tyree kissed her on the cheek. It was like time was unmoving. Their feeling for each other. Were stronger than ever. Connie perfume smelled beautiful as always. Connie was not seeing a man. And welcomed the possibility. To get back with Tyree. If he asked her. Tyree was fine; well dressed. With proper voice and diction. She still considered him. The love of her life. Sex was never an option with Tyree.

Connie would welcome the opportunity. To have sex with Tyree. if it was presented to her. Feeling fortunate to have run into Tyree. She was not sure if he felt the same way. Tyree was formally invited. To her house for dinner. Tyree had accepted and did not tell. Connie he was engaged. He decided to discuss his relationship. With Makayla over dinner. Connie gave Tyree the address. They also exchanged telephone numbers.

Tyree could still smell the scent. Of Connie after she left. He could not believe. How hard his penis was? Connie still kept her figure up. She looked gorgeous like. He always remembered her. Tyree continued to run his errands. Then went home showered. Changed his clothes put some cologne and left.

He arrived at Connie's house at eight o'clock. The domain in which she lived was beautiful. Tyree was impressed; he could see. Connie was well established. He rang the doorbell. When she opened the door. The place looked like a mini palace. The table setting was beautiful. Connie said dinner will be ready soon. Can I offer you something to drink? I have wine in the fridge. Will that be ok. Tyree said sure honey and paused. He did not know where. The word honey came from. He stared at her body. It was as if she; no longer had a face.

Tyree and Connie sat on the couch. While drinking wine they discussed. A lot of old stories from. When they were in a relationship. It reminded him of how much. He really cared for Connie. She was a passionate person. Its scared Tyree to feel this way. He did not want. To act on his feelings. Tyree had not felt like this. In a long time not even with Makayla. It worried him a little. Because when he got up from the coach. To be seated for dinner. He had a hard on.

Tyree felt a little embarrassed. Connie peeped out the situation. She thought it looked inviting. Tyree was seated close to the refrigerator. Connie wanted to ask him. To get her some ice. Anxious to see if Tyree's dick. Was still standing at attention. She felt like Tyree could salute her anytime with his bulge.

Connie could not wait. To get Tyree back on the sofa. Her heart was pounding fast. Her mind accepted his. Spirit of love quickly. Tyree had made her horny. Connie was feeling the; eagerness for this virgin. She did not see Tyree in years. Connie knew he had to be dating someone. Given up the sex-not... Tyree had to be dry humping her. She could clearly hear. Tyree's voice in her head. I'm waiting to get married. Then I will be ready to have intercourse.

From the welcomed bulge in his pants! Connie knew Tyree did not need to wait. To penetrate a good woman. Baby virgins' pants. Looked like they were going to bust. He needed to release himself soon. Mama wanted to play. Connie wanted his stiff; action toy tonight. Tyree would feel incredible. With his first sexual session in eating. Connie's panties were damp.

As Connie and Tyree ended dinner; the doorbell rang. Who could that be Connie thought? Connie opens the door. It was her women Marlene. Marlene knew she... Wanted Tyree to penetrate her. When they were introduced. Marlene walked over to Connie. And started to tongue kissing her. While revealing her breast. Marlene was looking at Tyree. With one eye open as she moaned.

She knew Tyree wanted some. Of the sexual encounter. That could go on with his consent. Tyree was breathing heavy. From across the room. Marlene tried to figure out. Why Tyree was speechless. Most men would have reacted. The women expected him to act. Like a kid in a candy store. Knowing there was definitely room. For his participation in a small orgy with bedroom candy.

Marlene spoke freely about sex. Letting Tyree know she was. Interest in men and women. Connie poured her some wine. Connie went to refresh Tyree's drink. He acknowledged it was time. To carry his dick out the door.

Some men would love to engage. Sexually with two women. The females started acting like. They were anxious to have. Unprotected sex with him if necessary. The next thing Tyree knew. They were both butt naked. He stood there holding down his Johnson. The women were beautiful in his eyes.

Marlene invited Tyree to join them. Connie knew he wouldn't. So, she indulged in sex with her woman. Connie enjoyed the thought of Tyree. Watching her make passionate love. While having a climax. She knew that was the opportunity. To have her legs cocked opened. Showing, Tyree her hedges were trimmed. He finally saw her twat. Her legs were wide opened up in the air.

Tyree exploring her vagina with his eyes. This was the closes thing. To having sex with Tyree. Connie was fine with that. It was the best time. She had spent with her woman.

Tyree did not want to compromise. His pride for sex and being a virgin. He was saving his body. For the day he would marry Makayla. For that was truly. Where his heart was. The women were tempting. Tyree's body oozed with pleasure. Had Baby Virgin had a form. Of foreplay that could have. Been considered having sex? The whole room smelt like sex...

Ladies I enjoyed your company. I have and engagement. That I must attend. I will have to come back. Another time and take you ladies out. Connie give me a call; an let me know. When it will be convenient for you. Connie knew Tyree was lying. She was tired of tip toeing around his meat. So, she just opened. The door and let him out. He left the premises. Got in his car and drove off. He never got a chance. To discuss Makayla with Connie.

42

TYREE TIME TO PRAY

By Roslyn OFlaherty

Tyree had not prayed in a while. So, he decided to pray. My heavenly Father I am grateful. For understanding the need to pray. For people all over the world. Please send a blessing to underprivileged individuals. Especially the children Lord. To those who are fighting addictions and critical illness. Those suffering with family, death and dying. That are in need of a blessing; from you Lord. Let blessings go out to the homeless. Along with the people. Who are poverty stricken and unaided?

Individuals who have been locked up. Due to false convictions. Causing overbearing negative dysfunctions. God please be the vindicator. For those who have just lost their way. Father God please watch over them. Until they get it right. Place a shield of faith over them. That can be activated through prayer. I ask that you provide them with food, water. Clothing with a safe haven. World peace is truly needed. In our uneasy times. That could cause nations against nations. As we fight amongst ourselves. On our own government soil.

People should have been born color blind. Racisms - superiority is a no brainer. A movement of unnecessary hatreds. Truly a sign of ratchetness. In our disaster of economic times. I thought we were all spiritual beings. God's global people. Father I pray that my prayers travel. All around the world and touches many lives. Father God we all need favor of church. In hope over our life's changes. Along with this doom's day existence of a world.

I would like to pray for myself also. For some reason God. I feel the need to ask you to keep me safe. Lord thank you for waking me up. At the crack of dawn. I will always honor you Lord. Give you the credit for the church giving me a voice of reason. I am not perfect! With my walk; with you Lord. I want you to know. I truly respect you. Lord please take me and show me the way. I would like to comfort. People through prayer. I will always talk to you lord. While paying attention to the word. My mind is always open to you.

Please keep me safe in these complicated times. I am proud to be a child of God. Please bring me closer to your beliefs. Father I would like to comprehend. What you put me in this world to do. I will continue to praise you. Lift them up in prayer. In hopes that you sow a seed into your children's life. Hallelujah... Lord I believe the importance of prayer is to activate faith and worship. I will put you first and worship you everyday Father God. I feel your people are enslaved by man. I am ready to walk with peace in my life. I give you the glory and will always praise you. I love you God.

Through my struggles and blessings. I tend to run in my life's. Continuous struggle of brokenness. Is Death really enslavement or living? I am your anointed child. Amen... Then Tyree studied the following scriptures from the Bible.

The Holy Bible KJV
Authorized King James Version
Holman Bible Publishers
Nashville Tennessee

1st Corinthians - Chapter 8 Verse 5 and 6: Verse 5 says- For though there be that are called Gods, whether in heaven or in earth, (as there be Gods many, and lords Many,) Verse 6 says- But to us there is but one God, The father, of whom are all things, and we in him; and one Je'-sus Christ, by whom are all things, and we by him.

Psalm Chapter 83 verse 18: Verse18 says-That men may know that thou, Whose name alone is JE-HO-VAH, art the most highest over all the earth.1st Peter Chapter 2 – verse 21: Verse 21 says- For even hereunto were ye called: Because Christ also suffered for us, leaving us an ensample, that we should follow his steps.

Mathews Chapter 16 verse 24: Verse 24 says- Then said Jesus unto the disciples, if any man will come after me, let him deny himself, and take up his cross, and follow me.

Revelation- Chapter 1 verse 5: Verse 5 says- And from Jesus who is the faithful witness, and the first begotten of the dead, and the prince of the king of the earth. Unto him that loved us, and washed us from our sins in his own blood,

John Chapter 17 verse 3: Verse 3 says- And this is life eternal, that might know thee the only true God, and Je'sus Christ, whom thou hast sent.

John Chapter 5 verse 20: Verse 20 says- For the Father loveth the son, and shewth him all things that himself doeth: and he will shew him greater works than these that he may marvel.

Acts Chapter 1 verse 8: Verse 8 says- But ye shall receive power, after The Ho'-ly Ghost is come upon, you: and ye shall be witnesses unto me both in Je-ru-sa-lem, and in all Ju-dae'-a and in Sa-ma'-ri-a, and unto the uttermost part of the earth.

Luke Chapter 8 verse 1: Verse 1 says- And it came to pass afterward, that he went through out every city and village, preaching and shewing the glad tidings of the kingdom of God: And the twelve were with him.

Acts Chapter 5 verse 42: Verse 42 says- And daily in the temple, and in every house, they ceased not to teach and preach Je'sus Christ.

Mathew Chapter 28 verse 19 and 20: Verse 19 says- Go ye therefore, and teach all nations, baptizing them in the name of the Father, and the Son and of the Hol'-ly Ghost:

Verse 20 says- Teaching them to observe all things whatsoever I have commanded you: and, lo, I am with you always, even unto the end of the world. A'-men

Mathew Chapter 24 verse 14: Verse 14 says-And this gospel of the kingdom shall be preached in all the world for a witness unto all nations; and then shall the end come.

John Chapter 17 verse 3: Verse 3 says- And this is life eternal, that they might know thee the only true God, and Je'-sus Christ, whom thou hast sent.

43

MAKAYLA

Roslyn OFlaherty

Makayla's mother had an awful repetitive behavior. Mrs. Henderson felt she was cursed. The disrespect and the control. Makayla had provided to her. Mentally with no compassion. Mrs. Henderson became a horrified. Shocked victim from her; daughter's dangerous behavior. She kept herself prayed up. Against Makayla's egotistical. Toxic manipulating moods swings. That played a part in her mental health disorder. Makayla still lived in a distressed soul. Her mental state was living actions.

Off Tyree's saintly ways. She started idolizing Tyree. Like he was her personal Ordain Minister. Tyree kept her confidence level up. Giving her thoughts of having. Hope of Another chance. To take charge of her disturbed and crazy life. Makayla believed Tyree was truthfully. The only one who understood. Her drugged, pimped out the life. Her past involvedness with Marshall. Would not be the end of her happiness. Due to the fact Marshall was dead. Makayla was preparing. To get married to Tyree.

Marshalls money was for Island hopping. Tyree did not know the money existed. The experience of traveling. All the time would be her wedding present. To her husband to be; Mr. Tyree Jenkins. Makayla thought of having. Marriage counseling with Minister Gharries. She knew he would be the only. Minister that would go along with. All her wedding ceremony wishes. Minister Gharries was one of her sex customers. That she had met through Marshall.

That's the reason Makayla. Chose Mr. Gharries to be her minister. Makayla thought of having marriage counseling. Makayla knew her and Tyree needed counseling. In order for their wedding vows to work. She was to trifling and petty. To make it happen. So, the idea was dismissed from her brain. She feared the counseling would. Prolong their wedding day. Her mind was stable about. An agreement she made with God. When it came to vows concerning Mrs. Makayla Jenkins.

The presence of God. Was needed in Makayla's life. To keep her grounded. Not many people had love for Makayla. Everything in Tyree's life was about her. Did Makayla truly love herself? Marriage is a union before God. Makayla also needed salvation. The tongue that speaks against Makayla. Should know God forgives people. The manipulation and mistreatment that goes. With it because of her pass. Seems to make people heartless.

Makayla believed that; she has been forgiven. Of her past mistakes. God's love remains with her. Some folks have not figured out the fact. That no one has the right. To pass judgement. They need to kick rocks... It would be easier. If they all just honored Father God. God could deal with Makayla's pass. Better than anyone. Amen.

44

MALACHI

ROSLYN O'FLAHERTY

Uncle Pete and Clarissa left the nursing facility. And moved into a private house. Uncle Pete is still dating. Nurse Estelle on the outside. Uncle Pete welcomed the Nurse Estelle. Every time she came around. Estelle had become; Pete's sex toy. Pete just felt her husband. Was not putting it down right. So, he would have sex. With her no love or money. Attached to the situation.

Estelle's flesh was still weak. She was stripped of her dignity and self-esteem. Estelle's husband found out about. The secret sexual affair. She fights with her husband. To acquire a little self-respect in their marriage. Estelle does not believe in divorce. Her intentions are. To keep her husband and Pete.

Clarissa had plans for Uncle Pete. They were living together. Once again in her domain. She despised Uncle Pete. Just as much; as she hated Makayla. Uncle Pete was the kind of enemy. You keep close to you. Until their luck runs out. Forgiveness had not entered Clarissa's heart. When it came to Uncle Pete's concerns. Uncle Pete kept the existence. Of Clarissa three-month-old son Malachi from her. She was done with him. It angered her how a stranger had. To inform her she was pregnant. She had an infant by her rape attacker. Marshall was her. baby daddy!

Uncle Pete was family, and Clarissa felt. She should not have endured the pain. Of being told about the loss. Of her son from a complete stranger. Who called her son Malachi a rape baby? Yes, Uncle Pete was trying to make Clarissa's miscarriage. Another one of their family's dirty little secrets.

My heavenly Father I pray. To get close to your precious holy spirit! What happened to our family's contentment? Our family genes are contaminated. I feel like a lost soul. I am reaching out to you. So, I can remain in your worship God. Help me at the same time. As I lean for your willpower. The tears are flowing from my eyes. Allow me to pray away. The kingdom of darkness. That keeps following me. With Makayla and Uncle Pete. For me not to forgive the negative drama. Plus, mishaps I know it is not your way. I feel that Makayla and Uncle Pete will carry our family curse. Thank you for listening about my DNA Father God. I Promise you one thing. I will not let family, friends or associates control my destiny anymore. Amen...

45

WEDDING PREPARATIONS

Roslyn Oflaherty

Makayla and Tyree enjoyed each other. Preparing themselves for the wedding. They went to the doctor together. For their blood tests. Makayla irrational thinking made her claim negative results. For not contacting HIV or any diseases from her John's. Tyree knew he was physically healthy. Mr. Virgin never slept with anyone. In Tyree's mind Makayla was the reason. Why he asked her for an aids test. Tyree kept asking her when they were going to get it done. You would have thought. Tyree was asking her for a prenuptial agreement. He was relieved to find out. They were both healthy and in good physical shape.

They shopped for their clothes. Money was not a problem. They picked out what was appropriate. To wear on their wedding day. The clothes were delivered to Makayla's house. When the alterations were completed. They were happy and spoke to Minister Gharries. On decision on preparing their wedding day. Their mothers could not be bothered. They were still trying to digest. The fact they were invited to the wedding ceremony. Mrs. Jenkins and Mrs. Henderson could feel and see. The real dichotomy of the Bride and Grooms marriage potential.

Tyree and Makayla could not have been happier. They were ready to become as one. In their minds and spirit as far as being married. Makayla and Tyree were both convinced their wedding. Would be the best wedding ever performed by Minister Gharries. It would be the best day ever. Makayla and Tyree would take a stand. In glory to the Lord and their wedding vows. They truly loved each other. They wanted God to bless them every day as Mr. and Mrs. Jenkins.

They talked of traveling for a while. Then they would settle down and becoming parents. Tyree and Makayla asked the Lord to be blessed and prosper in their marriage. Amen...

46

THE WEDDING DAY

By Roslyn OFlaherty

GAPE CHURCH OF WISDOM AND FAITH #2

The house of worship was full. With all the general public. Who were part of Makayla and Tyree's existence? At one time or another. Everyone was dressed in their finest garments. Michael Kors pants suits, Givenchy Gowns, and Tuxedos in all flavors. The men and women had on red bottom shoes. Everyone smelled so good. Ange ou estrange perfume and hand bags by Givenchy. Louis Vuitton clothing and men accessories. Made a fashion statement at the wedding.

Everyone looked ready to share; in this joyous occasion. This was the day that Tyree and Makayla would be as one. They were both looking for the marriage design by God. Their coming together as one man and one woman. Held in respect at all times. As they become as one. The wedding had become public knowledge.

Alina AKA Darieono had put the word out. That Makayla was having a wedding traditional style. Alina had sent out invitations to all Makayla's ex-Johns. Who she knew had seen Makayla fuck face before. She invited Marshall's personal friends. Alina invited ex-inmates from the brothel she ran in jail. Alina gave them personnel invitations signed from Makayla.

Alina truly despised Makayla… This intense dislike had become a sickness to Alina. Alina was stalking Makayla. She was ready to fuck with Makayla. Every time she saw her. Alina hated the bitch so much. She knew a feeling of joy. Would come from pestering. Makayla's husband to be after the wedding. She had no intentions of letting Tyree or Makayla be happy. Life after marriage would be an extremely. Awful experience of destruction. Alina did not care that Tyree and Makayla were ready. To put forward their commitment. Of love for each other with a marriage license. Alina felt it was about a bunch of bullshit. Because, Makayla was a shady ratchet bitch… Who glorified her personnel, unacceptable harmful behavior.

Clarissa and Uncle Pete had come to the wedding ceremony. When Makayla saw them, she hunched over. To ask Father God for forgiveness. Makayla had literally shit on the Clarissa and Uncle Pete. She was shocked they were at the wedding. Especially when she noticed Clarissa. Sitting up in a wheel chair. Makayla had no idea Clarissa was crippled and wheel chair bound.

Makayla really did not care. All her selfish ass was concerned about. Was her fiancé Tyree AKA Baby Virgin. Makayla could tell Clarissa had a nasty vindictive attitude. If looks could kill, Makayla would be lifeless. Right there on the spot; where she was standing. Makayla knew not to greet them. Until after the wedding. Clarissa did not think about the fact. Makayla did not speak to her. Clarissa knew she had invited Sparky to Makayla wedding. The invitation kept Sparky and his people. From killing Clarissa and Uncle Pete. Clarissa knew Sparky from Deluxe Lounge. That was the lounge where Makayla met Marshall.

Clarissa told Sparky everything. That she could think of about Makayla. Clarissa wanted Sparky to demolish Makayla Spiritually. Clarissa even told Sparky. About Makayla's fiancé Mr. Tyree Jenkins.

Clarissa knew Sparky would know. What to do with the information. He had received from her.

Makayla had too much baggage. That she needed to be the owner of. Sparky would stop in Deluxe Lounge. From time to time. To pick up the drug money; along with his money. From being part title-holder of Deluxe Lounge. Sparky would always buy rounds of drinks plus food. For everyone in the VIP Room. When he entered Deluxe Lounge. That is where Clarissa met Sparky at. She was Sparky's eye candy. It never went any further, than a few drinks. Sparky never knew Makayla was Clarissa cousin.

Makayla did not feel. She needed love from her family and associates. Who thought she inherited her cruel evil ways from her family. They did not define her. She was classified as a good person. By the church officials especially the elders. Today's church parishioners, was like a blast from her past. Makayla had erased most of these folks from her brain. Was this going to be the wedding from hell? Being forced upon Makayla. Due to all the dirt she dished out. Karma had a striking resemblance. Of Makayla's; I don't give a fuck attitude.

Who gives these two people, Makayla and Tyree away in holy matrimony? A candle was lit by Makayla's mother; Ms. Henderson and she answered saying I do. She would not have missed. This day for the world! Makayla was shocked and almost shit on herself. When she heard her mother's voice. Makayla thought her mother was going to sabotage the wedding.

As Makayla looked around the room. There was standing room only. She identified individuals in the crowd. That bought back bad memories. There were faces of men. Makayla never saw before in her life. There

were twenty men; surrounding the wedding party. They were wearing three thousand-dollar Gucci Tuxedoes. That matched her husband to be Tyree's. Makayla was wearing a white Vera Wang wedding dress. With diamonds around the cleavage area and around her waist. Diamond went all the way down the beautiful train.

Everyone was silent as Tyree and Makayla exchanged vows –Tyree's vow - I loved you Makayla from the first day I met you. I pursued you at the library to get to this day. I wanted you to be Mrs. Makayla Jenkins. My love for you has always been in my heart. He handed her a piece of paper it was owner ship papers to a mansion in Cleaver Hills. It was in both their names. This is where we are going to live. I have saved for this place. Ever since the day I met you. I will love you always. I will never deceive you Makayla. I want you to be my wife till the day I die!

Makayla's Vow – I love you Tyree Jenkins. I except you as my husband. You have been the only man in my life. That did not want something from me except honesty. I disclosed part of my past, that you inquired about. Whatever the bad life incidences. I had in my life before our wedding day. I leave at this alter. Tyree when you and I depart. From this church my pass. It will no longer exist in our lives. God will watch over us as one. I love you Tyree Jenkins. I will be your wife Mrs. Makayla Jenkins...

Sparky had got up and stood with the groom's men. Like he was part of the wedding party. Shit was about to get ugly! Minister Gharries spoke does anyone have anything to say. Why, Makayla and Tyree should not be joined; together as one in matrimony. No one said a word. Tyree and Makayla exchanged wedding rings. Makayla was shaking. Tyree and Makayla's wedding rings were beautiful.

Alina knew Makayla did not deserve baby virgin. Tyree did not need a slut for a wife. Alina was concerned he would be sleeping with the devil.

Baby Virgin would be sleeping. With Alina's ex-sex partner Makayla. After the wedding she planned on telling Virgin Tyree. About all their Sexual Exploitations. Alina felt it would be the right time to tell Tyree. He could have milked the cow for free. Tyree would know that she. Played all up in his wife's twat. She was going to offer to teach. The Virgin Tyree how to hit that spot.

Alina planned on inviting herself to the honey moon. For a three some with them. That would be an awesome wedding gift. As far as Alina was concerned. Alina was shocked that no one replied to Minister Gharries to discontinue the wedding.

Everyone knew this was the wedding from hell. An Ordain Minister should have never let this marriage go on. Makayla and Tyree needed marriage counseling...When Minister Gharries said I now pronounce you man and wife. You may kiss your bride. Makayla and Tyree kissed a long passionate kiss. Tyree finally touched Makayla's ass. He was breathing heavy... Sex Addict Makayla wanted to go. Straight on her honey moon. People started throwing rice. As Mr. And Mrs. Jenkins hopped over the broom.

The mob snatched and held Tyree. As he completed his jump. Over the broom with his bride Makayla. Mr. and Mrs. Jenkins were in shock. Sparky had a gun point at Tyree. Does this gun look familiar Makayla? This is the same handgun. That was used to kill Marshall. Uncle Pete Just looked. He was in shock. Uncle Pete knew his ass. Was going to prison. Sparky told Makayla he had brought it from the pawn shop.

Sparky shouted! I want my money and drugs now Makayla! Makayla yelled hysterically. I have your money right here! Clarissa knew she invited

Sparky. To Makayla's wedding; it kept Sparky from killing her and Uncle Pete. Clarissa wanted Tyree Makayla's husband dead. Clarissa baby boy Malachi had died. Makayla needed a love loss. As far as Clarissa was concerned.

Makayla ran to the back of the church. Screaming please wait don't kill my husband. I love Tyree... I have your money... When Makayla gave Sparky's men the suit case. Full of money, that was hidden in the church. She slipped over the train of her wedding dress. Falling on the floor head first. Laying in front of Connie and her girlfriend. Connie was Tyree's Ex women friend.

I knew you had my shit Makayla. Sparky yelled! Makayla you better come up with the rest; of the money and drugs. That existed in Marshall's establishment. All Makayla kept thinking what money and drugs. When Sparky shot Tyree in his chest. At that moment hostility and screams. From the people in the church began. As Tyree's chest burst open. A flow of blood poured out. From Tyree's open chest exposing meat and flesh. Some bloody money was on the floor. There were folks practically. Stepping over one another. Trying to leave the church.

Tyree crumbled in his Mama's arms. Like a new born baby. In agony as his life was slipping away. Mrs. Jenkins held his frail body close. She heard Tyree whisper. I did it Mama? I married her. I married Makayla. His mother said yes you did son...Yes you did... Tyree then laid in his mother arms. Mrs. Jenkins, just held her son rocking his lifeless body and, kept saying yes you did; yes, you did. Tyree's mother was in shock. Crying like she was ready to lose her mind. Tyree had gone home to the Lord. As soon as he died. Tyree's spirit went up to heaven. His mother held on tight to the shell of his body. Rocking Tyree's body was keeping Mrs. Jenkins mentally stable.

Makayla was married to a deceased man. Clarissa had tipped Sparky off. About the weapon that was used to kill Marshall. She found the pawn ticket for the gun. In Uncle Pete's room. She wanted Tyree killed with it. For the simple fact. That Makayla cherished him. Clarissa loved her three-month-old baby boy. She had come to grips that; Malachi had died. Clarissa had birthed a baby boy. She still felt the hospital. Had disposed of her son Malachi. Inside of a garbage can. She never got to see her son.

Clarissa's relationship with her son. Was between her and the Lord. The people who found out about Clarissa pregnancy. Called Malachi, Marshall's son a rape baby. Clarissa felt in her heart. Tyree had to die. In order for Makayla to ponder. About all the lives she destroyed. Clarissa wanting to pay Makayla back. For the entire trauma she initiated. It had become a distraction in Clarissa's life.

Makayla should not have been Clarissa scuffle. It was conveying too much negative energy and conflicts. Destroying Makayla's life should have not been Clarissa destiny in life.

Did Makayla sacrifice Tyree's lifespan? With the bath and the blue foam slime substance. In order to attain money. From Marshall without knowing it? The man Chet's friend that gave. Makayla the blue slime substance. Was at the wedding. Screaming in the middle of the floor. With a Satanic Bible under his arm. The dead chicken in his hand was dripping blood. Makayla could smell the scent. That was in the man's house. When she visited with Chet and obtained. The blue substance of slime.

Makayla started to think the man. With the bloody dead chicken. Was some kind of Witch Doctor. She never got to know his man's name. Makayla got to know him by an odor. Makayla felt like her heart had left her soul. She started speaking in tongues. Sweating, squawking and chanting with her hand in the air. Did Chet and the man with the smell. Cause wicked demonic events in Makayla's life? Could there have been a holistic solution? To the emotional circumstance's that occurred. After Tyree and Makayla wedding matrimony.

Mrs. Henderson looked at her daughter Makayla. I knew you were not my child!!! Who are you? Who the hell are you!!! I'm not scared of you!!! What have you done with my child Makayla? I love my child Makayla. Release her true mortality back to me. I birthed her. You have played with my family long enough.

Lord please cast all these evil spirits away. Please close the door that follows this prophecy. Demonic ways be departed. I rebuke the evilness of lies!!! I rebuke it to have; heavenly spiritual advice and direction. What kind of wedding is this? Where people come to die. Minister Gharries I question if you're; really following your calling. Even though it is not my place. Because you are a shepherd that preaches the gospel. Pray Minister

Gharries. "Forgive us our trespasses. As we forgive those who trust past against us"… Praayyy… Mrs. Henderson screamed!

Poor Tyree's mother will have; to forgive you Makayla. She will never forget your sinful ways. You are lost in this world of darkness. You must be saved by grace and mercy. You should not be existing in this sinful nature. You must be freed from this bondage. Let God Get The Glory!!!

Mrs. Henderson pulled some oil from her bag. Went to the back door of the church. She put a cross sign over. The doors and windows with it. She anointed and prayed with the people in church, The Reverend and other church administrators. Made sure the elderly and children were safe. Police – detectives and ambulance attendants. Carried out their moral obligations.

The Reverend called law reps from the precinct. Two elderly church members and, visitors had lost consciousness from shock. They were put in ambulances. The church was surrounded. With cops and the barrier tape. Crime scene evidence was gathered for the forensic science technique. Detective investigated the criminal altercation. The News Cast spoke. Of the horrific crime on television. Minister Gharries wondered if Tyree. Was going to leave the church in a body bag. The Cornier was on the scene.

Was this a demon evil doing or did this have? Makayla's name written all over it? Had Makayla's sins separated her from God. Due to this violent crime? She caused so much horror. All this time Makayla thought she had. Sewed a seed of favor. When she obtained Marshalls money. Makayla thought she became a better person. The money, bath of the foam like liquid; soft blue slime. Along with visiting the man's house. She went to with Chet. It had immoral incrimination all over It. Was this some kind of Spiritual damnation (witchcraft)? Even Makayla could not understand her distorted reality.

Makayla began to think. That a powerful fallen angel. Had heard her fall from God's Grace. It was easier for her to blame. Anything than to blame her wrong choices. Makayla thought she was a good person. Everyone was always taking advantage of her. Makayla grabbed the Bible and started screaming in tongues. Oh Lord, are you letting these vindictive people. Drive me crazy; because I stepped out of faith?

Did I not do. What you asked me to do Lord? Bring you the souls. Look around the house of worship God. Here are the souls that stand before you. Most of them are dirty and stinking with shady arrogance. Father God here they are. Here at my wedding. I pray that you bless them. And, they are able to walk in faith. For they are truly messy and wretched. They truly need Gods Glory.

After praying Makayla began screaming. Please someone help me. I want to kill myself! Makayla lost her mind and soul. From what she called a victim mode... It was time for her to cleanse her soul spiritually. Makayla and Tyree both loved Jesus Christ's. Along with his ministry. Makayla did not mean to go up against God. While questioning him in prayer. Why things were going wrong. She was confused and hurt with a disgustful approval. Of negative anger with God. In Makayla mind she truly believed. She wanted to walk in a God's image. Makayla's mentality was not there yet. She was no longer ready to surrender. To his love or reasons for commitment. Anger towards God was now. Consumed in her heart over Tyree's death.

Practically everyone left in the church was emotionally unspiritual. Towards each other they needed reconciliation. Makayla's husband Tyree never reached his fleshly desires. It was a thought in his mind. As, he slipped into death... Makayla's husband Tyree died Baby Virgin. In his mother's arms.

Mrs. Jenkins held her son rocking him. Crying, telling Tyree you're going to a better place. The house of gold. Ms. Jenkins was sure her son Tyree. Was going to the house of the Lord in heaven. Her son Tyree did not deserve. To travel in the same circle. As, Makayla and her associates. They all had a frightening; unexplainable sin in their hearts. This is how Ms. Jenkins defined them.

Mrs. Jenkins is starting to believe. That a demonic force can appear. In more than just a form of a serpent. Mrs. Jenkins held her sons' bloody weak body. In her arms as the breath left his soul. Tyree was lying in his mom's arm dead. Wearing his chocolate diamond wedding band. That was a symbol of Tyree's love. For his wife Mrs. Makayla Jenkins. He was a married man to Makayla; till death do us part. Tyree's Moms heart was crushed. She knew Tyree's spiritual existence was lent to her by God. He returned to his Heavenly Father. Tyree was deceased his mother. Was holding the shell of Tyree's body. Tyree was now; Mrs. Jenkins Guardian

Angel in heaven. She held her sons body close to her heart. And, began rocking him singing "Amazing Grace".

Amazing Grace! How sweet the sound. That saved a wretch like me. I once was lost but now am found. Was blind but now I see. T'was grace that taught my heart to fear and grace, my fears relieved. How precious did that grace appear? The hour I first believed. Through many dangers toils and snares I have already come. T'was grace that brought me safe thus far and grace will lead me home. When we've been here 10 thousand years bright shining as the sun, we've no less days to sing, God praise then we've first begun. I once was lost but now am found was blind, but now I see. (I see)

This was supposed to be Tyree's wedding day. His Moms, Ms. Jenkins felt like she was at a memorial service. There was no love, honor and obey... Had the evil angel and witch craft taken over Makayla. Was Tyree's death, an Exabition dominated by the homicidal fate of rage. The destabilized power only to show. A dangerous conclusion of chaos. Along with relevant facts. Through dramatic forces of events. To the real vows meaning? Of till death do us part at the wedding.

Uncle Pete went to jail for the murder of Marshall. He now awaits trial in protective custody. Uncle Pete started feeling that his mind was institutionalized. He did not understand why. Uncle Pete would soon be on lock down. In a prison cell as a lifer. The reality of this became over whelming. He welcomed being expedite to the penitentiary. The truth of Marshalls deaths main issues. Was the brutal rape of Clarissa and the loss of her child Malichi?

This was not life, just mental abuse. The destruction that caused a Haynes Crime. Tyree's death was caused by Makayla's relentless ass. Fucking the coke dealer Alina from Deluxe Lounge. Made Makayla hostage to confusion. That caused corruption with no accountability for malicious criminal offences. Uncle Pete would be looking for a solution. To the judge, jury and execution. Confinement and persecution would not kill his spirit.

Uncle Pete's comfort zone would be used. So, no one or anything could take his mind. During his journey to a life of imprisonment. He had three strikes against him and he was out. Prison had reclaimed him through the revolving door. To Uncle Pete's soul. Makayla was the obsessive force. To his heinous crime.

Now he was about to face the judge. On a murder charge. The judge and the criminal defense attorney. We're trying to make him a lifer in prison, without parole. Uncle Pete new Marshalls Associates in jail would have a hit. Out on his life when he arrived. Uncle Pete could not comprehend. What was the lesser of the two evils, the street or the penitentiary?

Makayla now resides in a mental institution. Where she rocks the same way her husband Tyree Jenkins. Did as, he slip into his death. Makayla is straight up cray-cray. She sings the song – JESUS LOVES ME all day long.

"Jesus loves me" This I know, for the bible tells me so; little ones do he belong, they are weak but he is strong. Yes, Jesus loves me,

> Yes, Jesus loves me,
> Yes, Jesus loves me,
> The Bible tells me so...

Jesus loves me he who died. Heavens gates to open wide. He will wash away my sins; let his little child come in.

> Yes, Jesus loves me,
> Yes, Jesus loves me,
> Yes, Jesus loves me.
> The Bible tells me so.

Jesus loves me! He who died, Heaven's gate to open wide; He will wash away my sin, Let His little child come in.

> Yes, Jesus loves me!
> Yes, Jesus, loves me!
> Yes, Jesus, loves me!
> The Bible tells me so.

Jesus loves me loves me still. When I'm very weak and ill; From his shining throne on high, come to watch me where I lie.

> Yes, Jesus, loves me!
> Yes, Jesus, loves me!
> Yes, Jesus, loves me!
> The Bible tells me so!

Jesus loves me! He will stay, Close beside all the way. He prepared a home for me. And some day His face I'll see.

> Yes, Jesus loves me!
> Yes, Jesus loves me!
> Yes, Jesus loves me!
> The Bible tells me so!

MAKAYLA KNEW TYREE WENT WITH JESUS. WHO TRULY LOVED HIM. MAKAYLA WAS TRULY LOST. IN THE LIFE SHE MADE FOR HERSELF. GOD JUST WANTED HER HEART...

Makayla depends on God's blessings. With, no resentment or guilt in her heart. Makayla spirit doesn't not comprehend. Having anything to with Tyree's murder or Clarissa rape baby's death. God was Makayla's Judge so. She lived with not condemnation; for she was in Christ. Her maker God will judge Makayla on judgement day. That was her conviction to being a damage soul. Makayla lives with a mental delusional mind; her conscious is not clear about her husband's death. She did not consider being held accountable for any repercussions. "That's right!" In her mind she has been forgiven for her sins. Makayla fought for the minster to sign her marriage certificate. That would be all she would have left; to bind her to Tyree. Makayla found a witness to sign with her. Will Tyree and Makayla meet one day in the house of God; to live in paradise? That plantation mentality and social dominance, had destroyed many people. Believe it or not some folks. Were released from the manipulating spirit of Makayla. There were other people who wondered. If Satin had told Makayla's truths. Tyree never signed a prenuptial agreement. He left Makayla well taken care of. His Mother was living on an insurance policy her son took out. She was the beneficiary. Tyree made Mrs. Jenkin feel loved and rich from the death benefits. Yet it could never take the place of her son. Mrs. Henderson turned her back on her daughter. Due to the fact she knew. Makayla manipulating spirit would never leave her soul. She kept Makayla in her prays. Clarissa still struggles with the death of her son Malachi. She still despised his father Marshall. Clarissa never her son a rape baby. He was a child of God to her. Mrs. Henderson and Clarissa and Mrs. Jenkins became a close net family. After the marriage of Tyree and Makayla. They understood the toxicity of their family composition. Their Lord and Savior stays knocking at their door.

1. Clarissa lost her son Malichi - Death
2. Mrs. Jenkins lost a son Tyree - Murdered
3. Mrs. Henderson lost her daughter - to a Mental Institution.

MAKAYLA KNEW; WE MUST ALL PRAY TO- THE LORD FOR OUR RIGHTIOUSNESS!!! Bible KJV - John chapter 15 verse 12 and 13

Verse 12 says – This is my commandment, that ye love one another, as I have loved you.

Verse 13 says – Greater love hath no man than this that a man lay down his life for his friends.

Your hostess Roslyn O'Flaherty invites you to read her short stories. You will read circumstances that society accept as inappropriate self-esteem, with hypercritical opinions. Should the truth of deceptions become someone's norm? Triggering pain with no significances. It is used to push one's concentration over the top. To have you feel like a scatter brain. This is the reason that over confident, trouble minded people try to comprehend why it affect them mentality.

Innocent minded individuals are looking to safeguard a cautious life. Recognized crises unfold with no consideration for anyone's well-being. Traumatized feelings in the silent majority's lives. Guiding standards of controversy and collateral obligations that have been exploited on the low. While demanding freedom for themselves and worrying who will save humanity.

Will those who are positive and motivated decline as they call a spaded, a spade. Misplaced in the system of lost wages, Student loans and credit card debt that is unable to be restored. The dangers of political problems bring anxieties into their daily day. Never imagining anxiety existing while trying to restore their respect and safety throughout all the drama.

Feeling fortunate when they can get money. Imaging why their culture has troubled out-of-the-way proceeding in set laws:

1. Bad Credit
2. Student Loans,
3. Being bankrupted into poverty…
4. Welfare, Social Security Medicaid and Medicare ~ people are concerned if these agencies are at risk of depletion
5. Climate controls – Category storms 1-2-3-4-5 that have names; causing natural disaster – tropical cyclones, tornadoes, mud slides, volcanos and hurricanes are causes of: bankruptcy, lost property and delinquent mortgage payments. Imaging wanting to get rid of your property with a lean against it. (Home insurance) I question is it worth the paper it is written on. – Remaining climate catastrophes victims are in need of relief.
6. Jail institutionalizing our youth who exist on probation with no future - Juvenile delinquent work programs needed. Allowing them a real future without judgement. Second chances were given

from the courts. For those with low classification. Sometimes society does not acknowledge their need for a second chance at all.
7. Mental health 8. Identity fraud – theft, national security risks. # Concerns if we have a draft will people be able to dodge the bullet as well as law enforcement issues etc. We watch families become poverty stricken in need of charity! Denied charity exist without direction due to lack of identification. Unable to obtain birth certificate, social security card. Due to the fact they are indigent or just not knowledgeable (mental disorders) enough to obtain ID…

Government Security breaches upsetting people's lives. (Global Terrorism) Self-confidence completely lost and can't acknowledge. Ever seeing grace or glory in this world. They find it hard to identify with their lifecycle of excuses. For not having positive growth as they live. Stuck under justified governance. Only to be deprived with denoting, crippling power.

Men are staying home taking care of the household. The women have become the bread winner. At the top of the tote-tum-pole. In many family structures. Some call this woman's (lib). Some women were liberated all along… To me this is just an opinion. To break up the family unit. Many parents lost respect for each other after a while. They became greatly in need of monetary growth.

With people there is power in numbers. Why is their always division in one's own mankind. (Financial gain, political unity- deliberated to us like we are empty headed). Society is sensible for wanting the government to talk their language. Not the laws terminology, as they back pedal on jargon. It's time to cut the world-perception; which is not beneficial. In making a difference in real life matters. Mortal rights are abused by the philosophy. Of so call superior minded people. It's time to free ~ We the People Of their Constitution of America's - Induction with Injustice…

Roslyn O'Flaherty

~ Gives thanks to her readers with 14 short stories: from past accomplishments! ~

1. Brutal Death
2. How we survived
3. Dear Mr. President
4. Daddy
5. This Isn't The Time To Jail
6. I Ain't Got know Crack
7. Mister Cheeba Man
8. Ice Ice Crazy
9. Beautified
10. Grown Adults
11. Beat Down
12. I live in Vietnam
13. God's child
14. Convert to the Lord and his kingdom

WE MUST INFORM OUR CHILDREN ABOUT THE RATCHETNESS THAT GOES ON IN THIS EARTH. EXPOSE THEIR ATTENTIONS TO THE TRUTH OF THE DIFFERENT SPIRIT THAT THEY CAN BE EXPOSED TO, AS THEY TRAVEL THROUGH THIS WORLD... IT IS TIME FOR OUR YOUNGSTERS TO THINK SMART WITH PURPOSE,STAY SAFE, WHILE AVIODING NEGATIVE DISTURBANCES AROUND THEIR SURROUNDINGS, WALK AWAY FROM TROUBLE, DON'T LET MISFORTUNES FOLLOW THEM, PUT SOME KNOWLEDGE WITH THEIR SURVIAL SKILLS, HUMBLE THEMSELVES, SHUSH WHEN NECESSARY, UNDERSTAND THAT THEY ARE DESTINE TO BE SET APART FROM STUPIDITY/ SHADE,TRY TO WALK IN LOVE WITH BRILLIANCE AND COMPASSION, GOD IS PURSUING THEIR HURT, SHAME AND WRONG DOINGS,

NOT TO HURT THEM, BUT TO MAKE THEM EXCELL IN LIFE, WITH SELF CONFIDENCE, TO STAY PRAYED UP AND BLESSED WITH GOD'S WORD. IN THE NAME OF THY SON A-MEN...

"GIVE GOD THE GLORY"

Psalms 127 verse 4
As arrows are in the
hand of a mighty man,
so are children of the
youth. KJV.

The LORD is my rock, and my fortress, and my deliverer; my God, my strength, in whom I will trust, my buckler, and the horn of my salvation, and my higher tower. - Psalms 18:2 KJV

RETAIN HOPE; BY MEANS OF FAITH...

47

BRUTAL DEATH

By Roslyn OFlaherty

Brutal Death; they killed my baby ran up in my shit. Just shot him dead. Gave him a severe harsh beaten. They were malicious gang bangers. Living in their world of organized crime. Acting like our neighbor savages; real cruel individuals. With the transgression that were just heartless. Without regards to God or Jesus. My son was murdered disrespected, assaulted by uncivilized thugs. These various ethnic wannabe gangsters. We're living with territorial boundaries. They just kicked in the front doorway and violated my residence.

My son died a brutal assignation of deception. He had home boys with so call gang intelligence. Where were they, when it came time to be of assistance to my child? The gang members claimed my child; was in a racial war of immortal violence. Is it possible they set him up? His home boys, loved the fantasy of armed conflict. The street gangs had the lack of consideration. For the life of each other's in my neighborhood. Their wickedness is why I found my child dead. He was pistol whipped beyond recognition. Stomped into unconsciousness. Shot three times in the face. As well as a bullet to the back of the head. My sons' heart was cut out and placed in his hand. The blood drained from his lifeless body.

Now my son lays six feet under covered with earth. I'm still paying my acquaintances; back for burying him. Monetary gifts were greatly appreciated. My baby boy's life was not even acknowledged. In our world problem with horrific crime, violent behavior. Gang members and big-time drug dealers. Did not give their condolences or support to me. They just recruited my child's life to the streets Which did not benefit him or his loyalty.

The leaders of the gangs. Had my son accepting their so call wisdom. Which made him think; they were his Daddy. He was looking for some place. That would give him the mental stability to fit in. He was happy because they addressed him as Son. Making him feel like he was a part. Of their street family unit.

Gang member thought they were qualified. To save this lost age group; of children they had recruited. I guess my son should not have trusted his peers. He really needed to be a leader. The king he was born to be, with good intentions. Instead of entertaining the idea. To be a follower of manipulation and lies. My foundation of strength came from. An organization called; Untimely Death Family Support Group - For Assassinated Children. My son's death stayed on my mind. It was definitely a senseless killing. To murder my son was not a revelation from God.

I recognize the fact that my son. Was not doing the right thing. He lived in a one parent household. Were all the nurturing skills from me enough? He told me Ma! You can't teach me how to be a man. You raised me well. You have done your job. To make matters worse. He made me feel like he was telling me. To step the fuck off. He decided gangs and violence made him a man. The violence armed and unarmed in the street. He was a wild dude. Truthfully violence; he really didn't want it. He couldn't even bring it. He was acting out of fear. Fright can be a deadly killer. I don't wish senseless death on anyone. I have found it in my heart to forgive his killers. Through the almighty Father in heaven and the interpretation of the word. I just wanted Gods Child to be picked up off the streets. To avoid any more beat downs and killings. In which our children; had become creatures of habit.

There were times I was going Cray-Cray. Now, I have learned how forgive; but not forget. So, from time to time I'm not going to lie. I would look for government officials, to sanction punishment for disobedience. My son lived above the law not giving a dam. He's now living beyond the grave. Maybe he should have gone to jail. For any criminal acts he may have committed. While under the street's authority. I wonder if being incarcerated would have kept him alive. I could have accepted that verdict for his dysfunctional behavior. Then him being brutally deceased.

My mind was destroyed by the reality to crime. His undeniable lifestyle and principles. Were made with his conscious decision. I just wonder if he was terrified. At the time of his assassination. He really tried to act like there was no fear. In his heart about everything related to dying. I thanked God every day for watching over me, while praying for my son spirit. To dwell in heaven peacefully.

Me and my child went for family counseling sessions. Using his manipulating spirit. He would talk vulgar slang towards the therapist. The direction he was given by this licensed woman to empower people. Had no real self-admission to his temperament. She confirmed to me again... That this year we will work with him Giving my son long and short-term goals for behavior adjustment. Which included coping with his actions in life events. Correcting and managing his emotions. While finding the triggers that needed to be balanced out. Giving positive productivity for his life style. Through managing his emotions psychologically.

My son stressed me out him and his gang family. The therapist modification goals were too hypothetically incorrect. To enable my son to get along; with others without aggression. Feelings of empowerment to claim his life. Through a mental facility. This was supposed to enable us to cope as a family unit. There was nothing wrong; with me and my son's relationship. The corruption from the streets had taken over our life. The Therapist stated that my son would be able to comprehend. That he should not have confidence in gang members.

He would learn how to control. His inappropriate behavior towards humanities cultures. I thought the therapist would be able to save my son. From harm and the welfare of her client's intensification to violent emotions. My son was true to the streets. The streets sucked the life out of him. And he lost faith in himself. (along with his hopes and dream).

He was initiated into a gang. Which he called his FAM. They used him as a sacrifice to no return. BANG-BANG your dead! Killed in the New Wild-Wild West. His FAMILY has moved on without him. He's Ghost! I wish my son understood that. God was a greater power than his so call buddies. Who convinced my son; a child of God. That God's Word was a spiritual lie of deception. He loved it when they would say. Come here Son; let me talk to you! He was just looking for his Daddy in the streets. I wish he would have Gave Father God a chance.

ISAIAH 54:17 says

"No weapon that is formed against thee shall prosper; and every tongue that shall rise against thee in judgement though shalt condemn. This is the heritage of the servants of the Lord, and their righteousness is of me, saith the Lord." KJV Bible.

The licensed therapist of so call empowerment stated. My child! Would be given the tools to articulate; his wants from his needs. So that he would be able to maintain a confidence level that would help him in life's situations. While understand that he had better choices in life other than the streets.

The therapist book smarts were not helping my son. My son needed to be able to think, rationalize and reason. In order to execute a plan to better his life. The therapist truly did not have any street smart. She was too damn cocky; to see past her title and degrees. I believe everything the therapist told me. Only because that what I needed. To have faith in her at the time. I should not have doubted myself. And, the expectant concern coming in my heart.

I sign a paper to agree to her long- and short-term goals. The thought of the outcome of my resolution never entered my mind. My son's life was in her hands. I stayed in court trying to get them to mandate my son to a group home. Until I could find a place to properly evaluate him. Nothing was being done about it. I worked every day and paid taxes. I feel the system was unsuccessful to my son's needs.

A brutal death along with betrayal. A real ruthless situation occurred. My only son is dead. Life was shattered by obstruction of justice. By the courts and a therapist in which I looked for help. His psychiatrist should have been dedicated to his life. He was a man; that could have help balance out his lifestyle. Along with managing; his emotional psychotic state. Yes, my son was off the chain with his bull shit. He did not care about learning humanities culture. Of code of behavior in the street. Or me being his custodial parent. Who's questioning justice the American way.

The murder was completed by my child's brilliant. Choice of gang affiliation. He took his existence; of being a gang member to his grave. The incident remains under investigation. No one was ever convicted of murder. As a court ordered mother. Everyone knew I didn't condone violence.

Adult leadership in our communities. That can help our young ethnic minorities. The absent parent in the house hold. Needs to carry more responsibility and pour love into the children's hearts. Religion might need to be placed; back in schools again. It's time to take our streets back. While we transform our communities to a peaceful place of residency.

We must stop letting violence go on in our own back yard. My sons' street level of loyalty and sacrifices. As being a low life gangster worried me. Stressing my mentality to the point. It showed on me physically. As a mother I had to repent for my sin of hatred. Towards everyone involved in the BRUTAL DEATH situation with forgiveness.

Who will stand up and advocate for our youth? The future; lies in young people's hands. Yet their future is in trouble; some youths don't have no true understanding of why! My son truly didn't! He lost his human rights to the streets. Hmmm, want to talk about; dead to rights? My son was my best friend. That's some kinda real $hit. That is deeper than water; and at some point, longer than blood. If there was such a thing. My child is someone. I can never replace.

*****God shows you stuff through life for a reason. It's like a mission for insight. Of the real truth and untruths that are never verbalized. To aid in the understanding of his Word. ***** Not one youth came forward. To tell about the cause of death or killer. They only gave off an unbearable demeanor. Of wanting to be warrior. They bounced back from adversity really well.

It was like my son was unfriended at his death. I always believed; that true friends. Could be your Angel. Through all negativity and discouragement, especially death. When I would see his friends in the streets. They had attitudes with no blessings. Me as a mother of a lost soul. I would like to leave this bible verses.

Too our youth and their parents; for closure. To the bereavement period of a child's death. And life's unpredictable lessons. That are caused from negative thinking. Wisdom is avoiding all thoughts and things. Which weaken you with negative consequences. That becomes attached to you. Mentally or physically causing deadly repercussions.

1ˢᵗ JOHN 1 Verse 9 - KJV

Verse 9 says – If we confess our sins, he is faith-ful and just to forgive us our sins, and to cleanse us from all unrighteous-ness.

1 Thessalonians 4: 13 – 18 - KJV

13-But I would not have you to be ignorant, brethren concerning them which are sleep, that ye sorrow not, even as others which have no hope.

14- For of we believe that Jesus died and rose again, even so them also which sleep in Jesus will God bring with him.

15- For this we say unto you by the word of the Lord, that we which are alive and remain unto the coming of the Lord shall not prevent them which are asleep.

16- For the Lord himself shall descend from heaven with a shout, with the voice of the archangel, and with the trump of God: and the dead in Christ shall rise first:

17- Then we which are alive and remain shall be caught up together with them in the clouds, to meet the Lord in the air: and so, shall we ever be with the lord.

18- Wherefore comfort one another with these words.

I would like to thank Senior Pastor. Who was truly my Shephard! I would like to send a prayer to the parents of God's children. Who have left us to soon! A-MEN!

48

HOW WE SERVIVED

By Roslyn OFlaherty

Poverty – Stricken! You invited me to lunch; spice ham sliced so thin you could see through it. Kool-Aid in a jelly jar. I remember this lunch; my Mama use to make. Now she reminds me to turn the light on in the kitchen. Or the roaches will come out. Exterminator came yesterday to give them a bath. The poisonous chemical did not work. Had me take everything out of the cabinets, for what? Now I must run down to the bodega to get the Black Flag. The condition has gotten worse.

I wasn't born with a silver spoon in my mouth. My birth place is America. I feel I'm a first-class citizen. I'm not an unfamiliar person to poverty and struggle. This is how we survived. I'm abandoned in life's games. I sleep with the pee-the-bed boy. Piss all over me; that's it! New strategy needed for sleeping arrangements. It seems meaningless to even let the asshole in the same bed. The requirements for his bed time should be to sleep on the toilet. Perhaps that will put some emphasis on the situation. The ironing cord just isn't effective. I can't keep going to school smelling like piss.

My dad's an Uncle Tom at his place of employment. So, he can get a pay check to provide for his family. Daddy never obtained a formal education to get a good job. Always Uncle Tomming for half the typical wages on a full-time job, which only perpetuates enslavement. His culture is disconnected from his soul. Yet he looks for leadership and a connection; to justice on this earth of opportunity. My Godfather comes to our accommodation a lot. He's my father's best friend and a womanizer, always acting like our daddy.

My Godfather walks around like he's ghetto fabulous. He stays bringing my family welfare pork in the can. "NASTY", if I regurgitate on the pork. I'm going to get the taste slapped out my mouth. I'd rather eat a ketchup or mayonnaise sandwich. My Mama loved for him to come by; when he brought her some welfare cheese in the box. She would make the best Macaroni and cheese with it. There would be enough left over for grill cheese sandwiches. Castor Oil and Cod Liver Oil were nasty but; we never had a cold.

The ironing cord, strap, or a switch off the tree. I wonder today which one it will be. This is not even considered child abuse. I stay getting my ass whipped; because of tattling neighbors. Pay parties held in the basement as, they gambled to pay rent. Blue lights, grinding on the wall. Old Mister, can in the hand sucking down his beer. One beer over a six pack and he's straight for the night. I lived in the drug era of the fifties. Drugs canceled out the leadership. Of some of the most intelligent individuals.

Let's not forget Swiss Up, Thunder Bird and Boones Farm Wine. The Cotton Club, Boston Road Ballroom, and Savoy Manor. Is where my Dad use to sneak off to and get his party on. My father always reads the Mahammad Speaks newspaper. The Muslim men would come to the house. Wearing a white shirt and a bow tie. Selling my dad fish and bean pies.

Mr. Boroughs is our neighborhood cop. He is a married man. Mr. Boroughs walks the beat on my block. You will have to pay a fine. If your caught walking on the grass; or hanging in the hall corridor in the building. Mr. Borough's lover is a heroin addict. Her name is Ms. Margaret. Ms. Margaret is a prostitute and a lesbian. She supports her family as a GO-GO dancer and a number runner, entertaining on stage butt naked wearing Go-Go Boots in the local tavern. She collects the almighty dollar, from time to time. I have witnessed Mr. Boroughs act in an unusual manner. Towards Ms. Margaret as if he was her pimp.

People do not show any compassion. To what some call war junkies; they are our heroes. Due to the fact they are constantly; looking for their pusher. Dope-coke-marijuana-pills-alcohol etc. We must be conscious to the fact. That Uncle Sam sent them home from the war like this. Some of them have mental or physical issues. Respect should be given; with considerations of their feelings. Honor and support should be given to the military units. They stood at the front line for us. And negative thoughts can stay on the back burner for them. Don't forget Uncle Sam Wants You...

Pot heads looking for a joint. Liquor mouths are murdering each other; over chicken bones. Bell-bottoms, afro puffs and peace power picks. "Right On" to the brothers and the sisters. They constantly listening to R&B, Rock and Roll with a little soul. Mama swears by hand-me-downs. She thinks spray starch and hand -me-downs; make you look on point. All you have to do is wipe down your patent leather shoes with a little Vaseline.

Mama would take us to 3rd avenue and 149th street in the Bronx to purchase clothes. She would stroll her children; up and down the streets looking for sales. Just when you believed Mama was finished shopping... Mama would say hold hands. Next thing you knew you were on the 3rd Avenue EL train. On your way to Fordham Road. You were familiar with Mama shopping. From Fordham Road and Webster Avenue; all the way up the hill. To Fordham and Jerome Avenue. Back down to Webster Avenue.

We would hold hands and walk with her. As Mama; bargained shopped. For deals from the Jewish merchants; to get what she wished to purchase. At the cost she could manage to pay. Mama was forever buying us Skips and Decks sneakers. Stylish shoes and sneakers that she would discover; on sale at Tom McCann's shoe store. I wanted Pro Ked's or Chuck Taylors. My brother loved his PF Flyers. They looked better than his buster browns. I could not stand the thrift shop.

When Mama finished shopping, we would go to Carvel for ice cream. Then we go home and eat Mama's delicious fried chicken, seasoned in a brown paper bag with flour. Then she would fry the chicken in a hot cast iron frying pan filled with Lard. It was mmm- mmm, good!

Mama's sitting in the corner sewing up the holes. In her drawers and pinning the elastic back on. Knowing dam well, it's time for them to go in the garbage. The holes in the soles of her shoes have card board over it. So that Mama's feet don't hit the ground. My mother loved to go grocery shopping. She would get (green) plaid stamps back with her receipt and change. You would have thought plaid stamps were gold. She would paste her stamps; neatly in her plaid stamp book. When she collected enough books, she would send them to the redemption center. They would give her gift that she picked out. Mama would give them away; as a birthday and Christmas gifts. Daddy would tease Mama when she, wrapped the gifts up. He called her the plaid stamp lady and, she would just smile.

Shooting crap, red light - green light, one - two - three! Kick the can, Hop Scotch and Johnny on the pony. I even know how to do the funky chicken! Don't forget run, catch and kiss. I'm going to my residence; so, I can take my brother outside. When he finishes watching Captain Kangaroo and Mr. MA-goo. His favorite television character is Lamb Chop. It's time to take the weight off my feet and sit on the bench and listen to 107.5 R&B Classis Soul. As children we would always say; cross my heart and hope to die. Mama said, say it again and I'm going to slap you in the mouth. That was a forbidden sentence.

Why do we fight amongst ourselves (gang's blacks, against blacks)? My Grammy walks around with Lye in a Soda Pop Bottle. She will eat your ass alive. Grammy doesn't play; she reacts first and ask questions later. Domestic violence, I don't get it. Is this all part of surviving or existing? In a casualty zone with, neighborhood assassinations? Folks say we live in the ghetto. Mama says ghetto is a state of mind. So, is this what some folks call a plantation mentality?

Mama's friends came over our house. They are trying to comprehend racism. Being used in a derogatory way of unfriendliness. I wonder if this has anything to do with derogation. I wanted to ask what racism stood for. What was its importance? Was racism part of what they spoke about; while they mentioned The Political Black Panther Party? I learnt Black Panthers were soldiers; who marched in the streets armed? I never understood why! I thought it was for social justice. What I did know was, they fought for race equality and underprivileged children.

I could not wrap my head around what white supremacy meant. Did this have to do with a race or the 13th amendment? Did it make one race of people superior to all races? To me the word supremacy meant supreme being. What I didn't understand what it had to do with the word white. I knew not to ask my mother. What she was speaking about. For Mama would start yelling. What have I told you about; being in grown folks' business? Respect your elders! Children should be seen and not heard. Go sit down some where! Get a book and don't be disrespectful! (Get a book meant read a national geographic - encyclopedia or the dictionary.)

Mama taught us about - "Rosa Parks activist in the Civil Rights (1913-2005) Movement. Born February 4ᵗʰ 1913 – Died Oct 24ᵗʰ 2005~ Rosa Park- "Stand for something or you will fall for anything. Today's mighty oak is yesterday's nut that held its ground" Rosa Parks- civil right activist refused to surrender her seat on the bus to a white passenger, spurring the Montgomery boycott and other efforts to end segregation."

"Nat Turner- Slave rebellion leader (freeing slaves). Lived from Oct 2ⁿᵈ 1800 thru Nov 11ᵗʰ 1831. Died at the age of 31. Cause of death hanging. In August 1831, one of America's largest slaves' uprisings strikes fear in the South and prompts some to call for an end to the institution of slavery."

"Doctor Martin Luther King Jr. American clergyman - activist and leader in the American Civil Rights Movement. His date of birth was January 15ᵗʰ 1929. Date of death April 4ᵗʰ 1968. Place of birth was Memphis. Cause of death Ballistic Trauma. Manner of death homicide, MLK JR. known for his speech – I HAVE A DREAM –AUGUST 28ᵗʰ, 1963… Speech- I have a dream that one day this nation will arise up live out the true meaning of its creed: We hold this true to be self-evidence that all men are created equal. (A dream for everyone to dream big…) MLK graduated High School at 15 – Got his Bachelors at 19 – His Masters at 22 and his Doctrine at 26) – MLK - WE HAVE BEFORE US THE GLORIOUS OPPORTUNITY. TO INJECT A NEW DEMENTION OF LOVE INTO THE VEINS OF OUR CIVILIZATION".

Happy Birthday!!! DOCTOR MARTIN LUTHER KING JR. "Doctor Kings last speech April 3ʳᵈ 1968 - I've Been To The Mountain Top… Doctor Martin Luther King was assassinated the next day April 4ᵗʰ 1968"

"John F. Kennedy at age 43 in 1961 was elected the 35th president of the United States. Born May 29th 1917 – Died November 22th 1963. Cause of death – Assassination. Believed in human rights at home and around the world." –JFK "IF FREE SOCIETY CANNOT HELP THE POOR. THEY CANNOT HELP THOSE THAT ARE RICH." "After JFK graduated from Harvard, he joined the US Navy. Near the end of 1963, in the wake of the march on Washington and Martin Luther King Jr's "I Had A Dream Speech", Kennedy finally sent a civil rights bill to congress. One of the last acts of his presidency and his life. Kennedy's bill eventually passed as the landmark Civil Rights Act in 1964."

You could not talk back to my Mama. Mama was always saying. I'm not your friends… My Moms is real old school. My mama was active in the Civil Rights Movement. Discussing whether some people thought civil rights dividing our nation. When it came to the business cycle. Of the recession declining in economic activeness. Her church family is always protesting and marching for different causes. They have spoken on our local television station, giving news bulletins about our transportation situation for elementary school children. Demonstrations were given to fight for school buses. The bus company would administer transportation. For project kids to get a better education. In what some called a middle-class neighborhoods. Yes, education is forever. They marched one time for financial freedom. Along with under minded citizens votes.

My Dads mindset was stuck back in time. Always speaking with a nasty temperament. He was bad tempered to the point that he seemed emotional dysfunctional at times. When it came to his immediate family members. Picking cotton until their fingers lose blood. The skin on their body. Had painful nasty bites from insects; which carried germs and funguses. Some owners of slaves. Branded his family members as slaves. Without even acknowledging this country was built on black backs.

Daddy swore us youngsters; didn't know nothing about hard work. He was stuck in a slave mentality of hatred. When concerning how his father's, fathers, father lived. Which many of them were grief-stricken with posttraumatic stressed from being born into slavery. A field slave made to market crops. His memorable words, were- don't never forget were we came from as a people. Never know if we have to go back; to where our descendants came from. You young folks could not handle this type of pressure. As a Youngster I knew a form of modern-day slavery will come to past. With the loss of societal freedoms of the Great American Dream. Where cotton mills and cotton fields still exist. As a people we would be straight up violated with our destiny controlled. This is going to come to the past even thou. The liberty bell was thought of as a sign of liberation. And, The Statue Of Liberty meant braking the chains for slavery.

My mother said that the statue of liberty. Was taught to her as a black female in chains. I think one day we will be in need of an antislavery movement. My father says we should give a salute to; our civil right discoverers from the past. Slavery in the other parts of the world needs to end. Freedom needs to be given to the slaves. We need to salute our Civil Declaration. That liberated slaves and understand our self-accomplishment.

My father said the military once again will fight. For democracy in a war know one truly understands. A combat that isn't even ours, with – segregation, oppression and discrimination. More acknowledgement needed for the veteran and their families. Who lived through the misery? Of our wars killing field! The impact on war. Has sent many of our war heroes' home in the body bags. Some of our military defense force went missing or injured. Fatalities that are often created by man's political ego. From our government and their heavy artillery. As the military men and women get to call on religion. For a moment of peacefulness and tranquility. Daddy believes there is an underground army. Committed for mass destruction. He says that a man can kill his self and others alone over some BS. Many folks think this is an impossibility of being brave. While rejecting his enemy.

My dad stays yelling at me and my siblings. Don't stay slept on the silent majority! As he spoke of the days of triple K's and burning crosses. Telling us the pure whites can appear once again. Everyone's not your comrade. Destiny can bring human predators; that are always ready. To let people of many nationalities, know the fire is still foreseeable. The pure man's animosity can travel massed with pointed hoodies.

I tried to understand my Dad. He brought his children up not to be prejudice. Was he hiding something from this problem? He spoke of with repulsion? Was there a double standard for those he calls the Triple K's? I was trying to understand why. He would not go in depth with this discussion. I still don't know what a Triple K is. I guess that's another secret. But he way Daddy spoke. They sound like uneducated fools. Daddy will take The Triple K mistery to his grave. He only would say don't hate people. You have the right to question their beliefs. For like us they are a different kind of folk... Well everyone can't wear their type of hood. I guess; daddy is saying hoodies are made for all nationalities. Hoodies should be worn with respect and dignity. We all bleed the same. With the same color blood. A sight that was seen as we fought in wars. Together with honor and pride.

We must all value life and well-deserved opportunities. Sounds to me like. Dad was flipping and flopping. When it came to this conversation. Was this just an inappropriate prophecy? Of expressive dislike amongst the silent majority and other folks? Well maybe; something's are better not known. I think we should walk around color blind. So, we can walk in love with forgiveness. Everyone is not the oppressor.

Modern day Masa has rapped his brain around money, new tax laws/ student loans/ jails and hospitalization/ abortions. Social Security has it become the new form of welfare/ Social Security with a retirement plan with health benefits. As many deprived people struggle with credit cards. Will Social Security become ghost in the future for generations to come after us?

Daddy wanted us to be truthful to ourselves. When we did dumb things. He taught us how to rationalize our opinions on life's situation. He stressed you must always think, and sometimes think out of the box. Your intelligence, will be challenged on many levels. My father also drilled in our heads. Know the reason why you do thing and have no regrets about it. He stated it was time. For us to know the glory of God. For he is our great creator. The author of many people resourcefulness.

You don't want to have a Masa in modern days' slavery. Own your own home and land. Work for, yourself. Many folks are taught to go to school; and come out and get employment. An occupation which is only good for daily living. Daddy said be an entrepreneur and control your own mind. Have the willingness to achieve more than you think you can. With a chance for, growth. Property gentrification; renovations exist in almost every neighborhood around us. Grow your own food; with your own dirt. Place homes on your own land.

Daddy has thoughts in his mind that modern day society. Is trying to have a Masa. That will take over one's culture. Making people field hand harvesting his potatoes and, cotton as their skin burns from the heat. Inhalation problems occurred from the air quality. Which is unsafe to the lungs. Crops are developed to feed a settlement for people.

Daddy's always saying! Why can't we just be left alone or get it on? I'm not trying to get along. With someone that wants to take advantage of me. We should not want to get along. With a system that's trying to abuse us. Refusing us equal quality or a decent chance. To obtain what some call the Great American Dream.

To him the Draft was another form of slavery. Was there racism against African American. Drafted into the military when he was coming up. Mothers losing their sons. Forced into a war; they did not even understand. For those people who didn't want to go. Men and women coming home. With Mental Disorders- suicidal tendencies, alcoholics and dope fiends. Armed forced persons come home. With no place to live. Their families have moved on with their lives. Men, women of the LGBT communities. Have taken up arms in a racist military. Destruction, Disaster, Disorder… Man kills his self alone. Not knowing one's self is the Destruction, Disaster that leads to Disorder. My Father thought it is time to stop cruelty; and not be muted as we fight for fairness.

My dad tried to remember the stories. Of slaves that were free but the struggle still increased. Abolitionist concealed these slaves. (Gun stash houses exist during those times.) The underground rail road of slave unity to freedom. Forty acres and a mule were bogus for many. For other folks the land was given and taken away. "Let my people go," Should have been the national anthem. Females sold in Auction blocks. Slavery in which many; were raped and killed. No promise land; just authorization to work in a cotton field.

A revelation of modern-day truth has been thrust upon us. Sometimes I worry; where do I come from. For, I do not know. This place we call a world with manmade corruption. Is the only place that shows. People all acting the same. Waiting to use you in their own little game. Seems their lost in their; own little confusion or maybe this all an illusion.

I guess, I better grow up quick mentally. So, I can understand what is needed to have a good future in my adult years. I have learned. I don't have to keep up with the Joneses. I feel victimized through the direction of my compass: NORTH, EAST; SOUTH AND WEST societies crap just won't rest.

This is not my life's calling. I feel: the history of poverty won't repeat itself in my generation. Through God all things are possible. My Massa won't be welfare! I am not uninformed about the poor quality of life that can be forced upon me. The baby boomers; with inadequate evidences of who is their baby daddy is. Sometimes forced to live with insufficient funds. Credulity play's apart in this in many ways of hardship. To be victimized in a new form of modern-day slavery. This won't be genocide. Reality has set in; I will survive! My neighborhood has organized crime: hustlers, pimps and number runners.

Jail time offering drug programs and, mental institutions opposed to incarceration. Some inmates in jail did not understand the two-facedness behind mental health. Finding it undignified for people to be victims during their incarceration. A big part of the hypocrisy was built around. What they identified as racism. With a false pretense that it didn't exist. They were victimized as human.

Many inmates wanted all people; locked up to be treated equal. They have paid taxes all their lives. Yet mental health was not available. For many who lived the inequality of craziness. As they looked for the interpretation of principles. Of life's standard manners. For common life and respect. All they were given was a whole lot of rhetoric…

My brother is in jail for health benefits. Three meals a cot with an education. Some of his friends have become religious in jail. To keep from getting raped. Not only was they raped by inmates. They were also molested by staff. The streets still have loan sharks. The human interaction of prostitution has escalated. Recruiting run away girls and drug addicts. Narcotics and gambling can be visualized; on our street corners. Dope fiends are on the nod.

Gays are beaten and, terrorized because of people's stupidity. Gay prostitutes killed while turning tricks. LGBT are in the closet fighting in our military armed forces. As they fight on the front line for our country. Race and genders are often misunderstood in this country. Men on the corner are inebriated. I can't tolerate listening and living dumb-idiotic BS … THIS WAS HOW WE SURVIVED!!!

This was the norm when people grew up. In what is called my generation. The lost generation in a place of dysfunction. This norm of the real-world. Can be a reality to overcome my struggle. Daddy must know that I must! Believe in myself along with God. I may be bruised as the psycho path. Of the worlds given regulation. Bruised but not disjointed. This life was hard; I am commonsensical.

I don't think of my sins as my final destiny. My hard times have made me a better human being. I made it through my realism. Which gave me intelligence and strengths. I am able to understand the infinite possibility to use my faith. Yet I felt no legal guidance in adversity or political stability!

My ancestors of color-built Churches and the White House. Governmental and Dutiful Leaders. Have very little to do with the poor and, the homeless in my community. Some people don't understand how to get personal identification. This lack of knowledge and not understand. How the system works keeps them indigent. Government institutions won't be happy. Until they have us living out of tents and robots take over our jobs.

My comfort in life comes from my inner assets. I am an activist in my survival skills. The revelation of hard time is here. I will live past my revenue. My mentor besides my Mom and Dad. Is, The Black God Father-Of Black Music – Mr. Clarence Avant. A man that is able to bring on change with victory and a purpose. He has touched many people's lives! He is respected and appreciated for his amazing gift. Of transferring his words negative or positive. Into truth and love towards wonderful things. When it comes to someone's aspirations, dreams and ambitions. Each one, teach one and you are taught in all circumstances. Good/Bad or Just a butt ugly opinion. From a negative individual and their deviant behavior. A person's prediction over your life is something no one has to except. That's what "Mr. Clarence Avant -The Black God Father of Black Music" taught me. That you can be a winner. You must be content within yourself! The destruction of my generation can't be my fate. I'm just waiting for the day that I will be free! I still have my integrity. I don't have to change. Just adjust in my own particular beliefs. I am only human, discovering how to be a child of God. Regardless of HOW WE SURVIVED!

I pray that in my life. I don't have to look forward to Modern Day Slavery. That will come for all (people of color) -Nationalities. I don't want to see another occurrence of the Military Draft. Which will cause mass destruction; a fight with nuclear bombs!!! I grew up believing detonating nuclear bombs. In wars could end the world. A curse specification for nuclear doom.

My mother believed in Psalms 23 - in the Bible, KJV.

1. The Lord is my Shepard; I shall not want.
2. He maketh me to lie down in green pastures: he leadeth me beside the still waters.
3. He restoreth my soul: he leadeth me in the paths of righteousness for his name sake.
4. Yea, though I walk through the valley of the shadow of death, I will fear no evil: for thou art with me; thy rod and thy staff they comfort me.
5. Thou prepares a table before me in the presence of mine enemies: thou anointest my head with oil; my cup runneth over.
6. Surely goodness and mercy shall follow me all the days of my life: and I will dwell in the house of the Lord forever.

My Dad and Mom were the back bone to the family.

HOW WE SURVIVED – Proverbs 31 verse 28 says: Her children arise up, and call her blessed; her husband also, and he praiseth her.

49

DEAR MR. PRESIDENT

By Roslyn OFlaherty

Dear Mr. President, I am an ex-draftee. I have returned home from enemy soil. I feel like I have taken a bullet from our economic system. I'm suffering from a system; that is not for the poor. I am just another statistic, silenced and feeling like I don't belong. To draw a conclusion on ethics is a bit overwhelming. Has American power destroyed this great nation; and the American dream? Does the decisions made for our country? Come from you or the Supreme Court. Have we gone from justice to injustice? What should I believe?

I was not sure where to address this letter. I have arrived home from the war with the Purple Heart. Life has buried my heart. I served with my infantry. I wound up in a blood bath. With foot soldiers that died. On this search and destroy mission. Your American hero is indigent! World ethics has me bound to capitalism. I am living like; I'm in the great depression. One war was enough.

I question who motivated the banks. To take my home into foreclosure. I returned home from the war homeless. I have nothing to call my own! Except the memories of killing individuals. The smell of death, blood and burnt bodies. Troop's blood slippery under my feet. A psychological struggle in which I hold within myself. I can't get rid of these images. Shell shocked in my dreams; of the dead and the wounded.

Terror lies in my heart as, my mind scatters for growth. To overcome intense fear. Of the enemy's ammunition and booby traps. I must believe that when I took a life. It was the enemy that had to be killed; or they would murder your troops. I served my country. My mind is destroyed over the fact, that I am homeless.

Was Wall Street waiting for me? The path they put me on just leads to failure. The stock market – BOWS DOWN TO THE BLOOD OF JESUS! I live in the bowery in New York City under a bridge. Mr. President, feel free to look for me; When you get a chance. I thought my Purple Heart would show me the right to equality and justice.

I was unguided by authorized representatives. I was thinking that our government communication. Would exercise my rights. I didn't understand the politics. I am living a heritage of self-destruction! Well the empathy is gone. I have to get myself together, the best way I can. I was looking for a great humanitarian for relief. Hoping they would act in the interest. Of the people with righteousness.

Well I better have faith and trust in myself. I won't let myself down. God has empowered my self-determination. I have a new found confidence. That I found in praise. The Lord gave me discernment. It is making me stronger with; endless possibilities for change. I found something to call my own. I pray in church; with my church family. Yet I feel like a victim of in justice. As I put my money in the collection plate. I watch funds being misused. By people who say; they have the calling from God.

I love my church family. I don't speak of misappropriated funds. I don't sow to the people. I sow to God. I question why my Church has an ATM machine at the front entrance. Well I'm living new beginnings.

Even though I have an honorable discharge from the war. It only makes me feel like. I'm living on the front line on government soil. I was drafted into this war's confrontation. My Purple Heart has become a symbol. With no substance. Sometimes. I wonder if many troops became disillusioned with a vivid memory of what the draft was all about. Did they think the war would not affect them? Once they returned home. Were they still bound to the war's destruction?

I took my tears, fears and prayers to the Lord. While trying to understand the 6th Commandment. "THOU SHALL NOT KILL" Mr. President was this really our war? Well Mr. President thank you for allowing me. To use my first amendment rights. In addition to the freedom of understand. Life's precedents however manifested. I am looking for the New York Department of Justice. To monitor my civil rights. This will help me give respect; where respect is due. As I rectify my outstanding problems. That needs to be address; through military personnel. I end my letter but not my love. For our troops and this great nation. In this war of oppression! They called me a draftee; but I am a vessel of God. Amen...

***** Lord I found the dignity. To continue to live my life. Although I am up there in age. I still have my faculty's. I am honored to say. I have lived long enough to observe. A great leader of the free world. He has contributed to my philosophies. He empowered me to greatness. I have learned; I must admit. I gave consent to my troubles. The happiness I am entitled to have. Showed me how to have self-confidence. The optimism to challenge my principles. My mentors name is BARAK OBAMA. He is the 44th PRESIDENT. JANUARY 20th 2009 thru JANUARY 20th 2017. The first black male president. Of the United States of America. I was so proud of Barak Obama – OBAMA ON TRAYVON MARTIN: 'If I HAD A SON, HE'D LOOK LIKE TRAYVON, THE PRESIDENT SAID WHEN ASKED ABOUT THE CASE IN THE ROSE GARDEN

ON MARCH 23, 2012 Martin 17 years old shot in 2012 February 26. Info cited from KNOWLEDGE on line. And cited from CNN,

Michelle LaVaughn Obama is the First Lady. Of the United States of America. From two thousand and nine; until two thousand and seventeen. The wife of the 44th president Barak Obama.

(Proverbs 31 verse 26 KJV says- She openeth her mouth with wisdom; and her tongue is the law of kindness.) They resided in the White House. While raising their two children. God Bless This family; in their future endeavors! Amen...

50

DADDY

By Roslyn O'Flaherty

Daddy never hugged me. He was a nightmare with a stress level. I was embraced in human; contact and no affection. I was permitted to call him dad. When he wanted to be a dictator. After I turned fourteen years old. I never saw him again. I knew I could not continue to look for him. I was compromising my morals. Trying to please my mom's by. Doing what she thought was proper. For our father and son relationship.

My mom's is not a man. She'll never know how I feel. I don't even have my father's last name. I wondered if he wanted me in the first place. He was my biological dad; but I was forced. To be the man of the house. I didn't want a phony father figure. My dad won't man up and give me. The parental guidance that I need. I find it difficult to communicate. With my so-called part-time father.

I decided to continue my life without my dad. I will no longer look up to him. The respect I have for him is depleting. My Dad really messed my head up. I have to protect my mind. I was crushed by my; dope feign fathers' needles, foil. Also burnt spoons hidden in the house. He would visit before he became strung out. Always finding a new place to stash his works. So, my mother would not find them. My dad started off snorting dope and smoking bud... After riding the horse. The next thing I knew he was a heroin addict; and I still loved him. Despite the lies and manipulations. I had endured in my life.

My mom could not allow daddy to reside with us. I wished they could get along to co-parent me... Dad abused Mommy and made her sell her body. So, he could get the dope. Mother did not retaliate when being abused. Yet she was tired of getting a beat down. Until She was black and blue. My dad's uneasy experience in the drug world. Always dominate our family's life. His excuse for his drug life. Was that growing up as an unhappy child. He was always misunderstood by his parents. He was what some relatives. Called the black sheep of the family. My dad told me he did not like. The liable harmful reaction of heroin. Being strung out all the time. When he missed his veins; not having any more heroin. Made his body crave it. He hated being dope sick! Laying in the bed in a fetal position. Shaking and shivering; every bone in his body ached.

Imagine watching your dad scratching and nodding. With a new mentality of a dope fiend. I have my own opinion of him. He was just too damn selfish! With no morals; a very perverse person! I was condemned by the experience. Of the existing circumstances. It was hard being the son; of a strung-out junkie. I could no longer watch the man. I loved beg, lie and steal for money. My Dad turned into a thief and went to jail on several occasions. After being released from jail. He was still a dam junkie. Discharged to Junkies Paradise.

Drugs were available for inmates. While they were incarcerated. My father said dope in jail. Was better that dope on the streets. I believe my dad could shoot up. In the veins in his neck and nuts if he had too. Track marks were all; over his feet and arms. All the veins in his legs have collapsed. I wonder if his hands. Hurt from closing them. Due to the dope swelling.

Lost wages have caused Daddy. To sleep on benches; roof tops and in hallways. At this present time. He has lost his take-home pay from employment. The repo man has kept his car. And, the judge had control over his driver's license. The only thing in life he really loves. Between the heroin being administered to dad's body. And, him not being able to keep his word. Roughly everything important has brought suffering to our family. Yet he is the one that stays. Whining over his poor choices.

The Methadone Program was like the keep program. It would keep dope fiend on morphine. Daddy would be on line outside the methadone clinic. With all the rest of the people. Which many folks considered them to be dope sick junkies. That kept going back for the morphine. So, relapsing didn't occur; causing a hospital stay. That is where; I would find my father. When I use to want to talk to him.

If daddy was able to stay clean; he was a ladies' man. Sleeping in many woman's houses. From pillow to post. A life full of secrets, crazy drama, and deception. He was never ashamed of being a male whore. Or not having possession. Of his own residence. Daddy was a scam artist a liar and a woman beater... Knock the $hit out of them in a minute. Which I considered criminally insane. He would never fight a man. Just punk up to that and fatherhood.

Women would buy him cars. Keep him well-dressed. Until that monkey was on his back again. Daddy's life was one big withdrawal. With an obscure personality disorder. Constantly showing destructive behavior. He has a narcissist complex. I don't have to condone my father's behavior. He has so many children. That I call my daddy; The Sperminator... He would dry hump a dog. If it stood still long enough.

Yes, my Moms raised me. I am activated with faith. A spiritual seeker looking for a solution. To stay blessed to obtain a genuine testimony in my life. Now that I am a forgiving person. I understand my parents love. It had made us what some call a dysfunctional family. God has a plan. For my family a blessed future. With a new revelation on life; with a faith level. We all turned our life over to God and Jesus.

I just can't spend my life. Wait for my Dad to become a man... I am content within myself. I want my Dad to know: -The Bible says honor thy Mother and thy Father. I love you Daddy! You see I have my heavenly Father.

REFRENCED: modeled from Church Bible KJV
THE LORDS PRAYER
OUR FATHER WHO ART IN
HEAVEN,
HALLOW BE THY NAME,
THY KINGDOM COME,
THY WILL BE DONE,
ON EARTH AS IT IS IN HEAVEN.

GIVE US THIS DAY OUR DAILY BREAD.
AND FORGIVE US OUR TRESPASSES,
AS WE FORGIVE THOSE
WHO TRESPASS AGAINST US

AND LEAD US NOT INTO TEMPTATION,
BUT DELIVER US FROM EVIL.

FOR THINE IS THE KINGDOM,
AND THE POWER. AND THE GLORY,
FOR EVER AND EVER. AMEN.

51

THIS AIN'T THE TIME TO JAIL

By Roslyn O'Flaherty

This ain't the time to jail. The Judge says I was presumed innocent on a drug charge. An innocent man should not have to cop out to jail time. Especially when he knows his shit is proper. I've never been in trouble with the law before. This has become an invasion of my existence. I believe if someone shows you; who they are believe it.

The drugs were found on the ground. There was nothing that was presented in court. That shows that; I should have been. Handed this unfavorable decision. There was no real evidence. That showed the heroin and crystal meth belonged to me. Well at least my color; did not make me guilty. I never personify people by color. To be threatened with an unconstructive warning. That was spoken into my future. It was like putting a knife in my chest.

My life was negotiated for me. Right in front of my face. It was a conflict of interest to my freedom. I should have the positive destiny. With the positive attitude that others see in me. My freedom used to lie in my hands. I was released in my own recognizance. Is this a warning? Are they looking for a second occurrence of mishap? To add on this court case? The deferred prosecution proceeding in this criminal case. Will be put off for a moment in time. I knew the court officials were waiting. For charges to progressively get worse.

I can't believe that I'm living under the obligations. Of the court's conditions. I'm praying that I hold up to societies standards. Well if my ass gets in a dilemma again. I better be able to get out of it. I realize if the term and conditions are met. The case may be dismissed. I can't continue to live; this life of politics. I don't think the courts stipulations. will be hard to abide by. I will be living in damnation. I pray to God, that trouble doesn't follow me. I just turned 18 years old and I don't want to be incarcerated. Living in a dorm with grown men. Men who have nothing to lose. They may never see life's social order outside. They will just have to adapt being incarcerated. While waiting to go up state to do a life sentence.

DAMN!!! I was picked up riding around. With my man in a stolen Mercedes Benz. The cop yelled, get out of the vehicle now. I got out the car and right away. I threw up both my hands. The cop spoke to me in a derogatory way. As he informs me the car was stolen. My self-importance was destroyed. So, I took it out on the man in blue. I yelled at him mister. I'm going to need you to find. Another voice to talk to me in. Bring down your tone or I promise you! You will be hiding behind your badge. And, that blue wall of silence. You and your precinct got going on. If you can't speak to me better than that. Just arrest me!

I didn't realize the bitch was stolen. The cops went to hand cuff me; and, I was thrown up against the car. I was inhumanly beaten. While they yelled! For me to stop resisting arrest. The man in blue yelled. I was resisting arrest. That was what he needed to speak. For a reason to whip my ass. Well that's what I got for asking. The man in blue to bring; his mental attitude down a notch. I definitely needed favor.

The police gave me a reason to yell. It reminded me of the day my mom dragged my ass to the precinct. Took me in front of the sergeant desk yelling! You see all these men. In blue uniforms; they are not your friends. You talk about a flash back. The reality of my new circumstances had set in. To make matters worse. An officer in blue uniform pulled a hand gun. From under the front seat. Where I was seated in the Benz. This man had a smirk on his face. That said alright you punk ass, bitch. I got you now. My heart was pounding like; I was going to die.

The realization of the gun. Let me know my case. Was now more than just foolishness. At this point regrets were not an option. It was not time to even plea bargain. With the cops my mom taught me; wasn't my friend. I could hear my Mama; in my mind saying. They're not going to let you go son. I had to get ready to suffer the obligation. Of said matter humbly.

Over home boy's actions; a gun and a car. The ride I took from dude. Was about to drive me straight to hell…

I started to wonder if the gun. Was used to murder anyone. That's all I needed; was to catch a body. That would be a horrendous new case. That I don't need right about now. Now I'm guilty by association. I needed to see an attorney. My friend can't be my codefendant. Our cases have to be split up. I only asked home-boy to give me a lift. To the Ave. three blocks away. The cops lifted my ass off to the precinct. Where I was put in a cell of secluded uncomforting confinement.

When I went to court. The judge didn't even lift his head. To look at me when; he made his decision. I assumed; I would be granted the privilege to be seen and heard. A detainee center was a perilous incarceration. Was I considered to be a first-time offender? Will my charges be running (simultaneously?

I didn't understand anything. Running concurrent at this point. I was feeling miserable full of shame. Did the judge make a decision to run the cases consecutively? All I knew was that I would be considered guilty. When it came time for me to inform. The Judge that the mistakes and assumptions. Of these opinions in these cases. Negative possibilities were just a viscous circle. Of stupidity on behalf of the criminal justice system.

I felt maybe I needed mental health improvement. A displeasure about worrying was destroying me. Would I be presumed guilty or not guiltier with this new charge. I lost my respect in the penal system. God knows, I didn't know the car was stolen. I didn't do anything wrong. I kept telling the police that the gun. Found under the seat wasn't mines. I was let out on my own recognizances from my previous dilemma.

Now I was picked up with Dude. This was not supposed to happen. I'm still in shock! Dude had a rap sheet a mile long. I had to have a word with God. About this catastrophe situation. I prayed a meaningful prayer. For his blessings and a trusting; legal representative! I Just turned 18 two months ago. I am terrified with emotional issues. My Mama told me to sit still. So, trouble won't follow me. I'm living under attack of serious dislike and immorality. Not gaining nothing but animosity. From all this civil cynicism.

My mom's upset with me; right about now. How could I be such an ass hole? Mama can't take the fact that her son. Was being accused of being a dope dealer. My Moms states that it's bad. To have the status of being a failure. With complications of a heroin dealer. That can have you killed. I wasn't a junkie! Ma said it's just as bad; as becoming a dealer. Having to challenge negative street attitudes for a living. She said I had the nerve to have a lot of tattoos. Which made me a walking billboard; advertising here I am. A moving target for the police.

I told you don't put those damn tattoos all over your body. You think your grown and I'm stupid. I'm sick of you right about now. Sitting in a car laid back. With no knowledge if it was stolen or not. I wish you could have felt the frustration. I feel every time you leave the house. I felt worrying if you caught a case. With a dead body. Well I guess you were bought up. To sit in cars with guns under the seat.

Which may now be considered yours. This makes you Mommy's big fuck up. Tell me how the hell you felt. When one cop had his gun drawn in your face. While the other one cuffed you. Over some dumb shit. This ain't the time to be jailing son. They could have blown your fucking brains out. Your guilty before proven innocent; you jackass. But you see there is a bed waiting for you in jail. As fast as one inmate leaves; that same day. They have the bed ready. For the next. Inmate stay slept if you want. Mama considers me an asshole. Looking for a bullet with my name; written all over it. I never rode; the white horse. I could never inspire myself to use or sell drugs. Something with a negative purpose. To cause people to die from a dope sick habit. Ignoring speed balling with coke mixed together. As the junkie craves the first high, they ever encountered. Which will never return. A depressing experience which keeps their soul; drained and mentally humiliated. The chase is on with doom. Which gives you a hard time; returning to the reality. In what you were truly grateful for.

Mama shouldn't be blamed. For my unhealthy lifestyle chooses. All I wanted to do is show. My mom's love and affection. That I was the young man she raised me to be. I got my ass handed to me. In a vicious immoral cycle of the constitution. We the people in jail; guilty or not!

I was given a bull shit legal aid attorney Who only came to visit me one time. An expert at never being in his office. I would use my slot time on the phone. Calling my mom's constantly. Begging her if she would consider calling my attorney. Mama was never able to converse with my lawyer. His answering machine always conveys a message. That he is in court leave a message. The phone calls only bought on confusion. Along with a reaction of aggressive behavior. From not being able to talk. To anyone from this law firm. I am angry. I need my lawyer to see me. ASAP!

Living with no judgement to incarceration drama. Not even to take a shower, shitting or shaving. Begging for toilet paper. Careful not to drop the soap in the shower. Jail correction officials stay telling you; This is my house your living in. If you don't comply to the rules. You will be transferred; to another correctional facility! You did not want to be transferred. Officers at the other institution. Knew you were coming there. You would catch a beat down. Right in the receiving room. After they ask you your name. Your ass was tossed in the receiving room cell. Getting the shit kicked out of you. The experience made you feel incredibly stupid. Now you are in another county. Which made it hard for people to visit you. Even your lawyer! You learned to digress in conversation. With correction staff to a certain degree.

Presently in jail I came across this MF... Which I considered a double ass hole at times. Just plain old stupid and confused. Always talking out his ass. According to inmates' gossip in jail. "Yes, Inmates Gossip" Men gossip more than women. The gossip hardly ever; offers a solution or respect. Dude has nothing to lose but time. The word in the dorm. Is that dude's facing life without parole. People think he is an idiot. He stays talking loud, screaming and distracting others. While punching himself in the face and head. Dude feels it's time to get an appeal on a federal level. At this time, he is in a confused state of mind. Striping and masturbating while; calling out his girl's name. Now he has hard on. This big dick mother fucker. Came in his other hand. Licked it and said it taste like his girl's juicy pussy. Now how nasty is that? The feminine gender males; are enjoying the entertainment. While cheer him on. I feel it's time for this dude. To be placed in a psych housing area. What were the attributes for his life skills? (SPIRTUAL – MENTAL – PHYSICAL – SOCIAL FACTORS) Psychologically his mind was not there yet. He could not see things; in the spiritual or in the natural eye! This man's attributes for life skills were. (BITTER – NASTY- HATEFUL- SPITEFUL) You could tell dude never learned how to love himself! "It was time for deliverance" There was no growth from the word. Not even in crisis intervention care...

His foolishness gives him confidence. For his future to be able to return to the streets. Yet his ignorance is boundless. Dude tries to act unstressed. I feel he should get some respect. For staying in the law library. Collecting information on the law. Legislation which has been passed by congress. On a Federal crime level. The law library brings down. The anxiety from his life's consequences and legal rights.

I've learned to digress in my conversations. While presently in jail. I came across this man name Kash. I know it was not slang for money. He stayed broke. I consider Kash to be dense in the brain. The talk amongst inmates was if this man. Was found guilty on his case. Kash will be doing life, without parole. This inmate is supposed to be; going to prison. According to jail gossip. Kash has a slim chance. In wining his case. Jail house popular opinions says. Kash has nothing to lose.

I believed he has; but I'll keep that too myself. Kash has tear drop tattoos. Going down the side of his eye. He never uttered a word on what the Feds wanted. I would just listen to the nonsense. Kash did reveal to me. Some inmate stated that; he did not belong in a dorm area. He belongs in a cell area in protective custody. While confined in this detention center. Some people conversed about Kash. Killing a man on the street.

It was a hideous over kill. The man's face was smashed. Continually into a building wall. With a level of strength and energy. You probably couldn't imagine the appearance of his face. It was totally disfigured. His eyes were popped out of his head plastered. To the brick wall. Along with his blood, snot and tears. When the Police came, they had pry; Kash's hands loose from the corpse. Which looked extremely horrid in the newspaper. The district attorney and judges. Have hard core evidence. On the level of Kash's insanity.

Kash walks around with the intent. For people to believe his case is just messy one big collusion. Nothing was his fault. The word in our housing area is that. Kash strangled a man with his bare hands. Without a body being found. This accusation is just hear say. I know Kash could bench press me for wreck. Me jailing, is one big nightmare. For Kash it's just a conspiracy.

It's disgusting to see a male. Loving to be fucked by another man. Who is only confused of his sexual preference? I wake up with a hard on. Holding on to my dick; all the way to the shower. The crazy make-believe heterosexual men are only a woman. When they become incarcerated. I have nothing against LGBT people. They have the right to exist. In this world like everybody else. Grown men jailing; wanting to be real fish. They stay tucked to the max with swag. It's not a real safe look. They could be rapped. Fucked each way possible at one time. While waiting to be turned loose. A victim of an unwanted; uncontrolled rape orgy while incarcerated. Some of the men from the LGBT community. Are the most intelligent people. I've met while doing my time. They are sneaky; I treat them within their due rights.

It's not fun when you're in jail. And, have to hold on to your manhood. I'm tired of being stripped searched. Lined up with other naked inmates. With my dick and balls hanging in front of me. While the officer tells me to bend over. Spread my cheeks and cough. I think these mother fuckers get off on this shit! As soon as I'm asked to strip and bend. I just lose it. I just ask the officers; the same question. I don't know why? You want to see my dick all the time! What do you want? For me to rub my nuts for you?

I'm always removed from the line. The officers would take me in a corner. Away from the cameras. And, beat the shit out of me (punched, kicked and - stomped me). I would catch a beat down. Which gave me a fucked-up face. Soreness that made me vulnerable. To any other attacks. The officers would still write me up. I'm just not with that bending shit! It felt like they just asked. To screw me in my ass. And, I would have to suck their dick next! Jail makes it really easy to become rebellious. Right about now; I don't give a fuck. I feel that it is so degrading. For a man to look up another man's ass. I speculate who else is being, housed in my dorm. I will man up and protect myself if necessary. I made a weapon to defend myself. I'll jig a mother fucker! I thought; I made an ingenious weapon. I'm starting to think, was a weapon a good idea? I know that if I stab someone. I can catch a new charge. I'm trying to identify with my new struggle. Guilty until proven innocent. In the court of law...

Realizing I now had a reason. To be disturbed and live in fear. I'm not anyone's bitch but violence took place; On the dorms all the time. This doesn't justify taking someone's life. Just to let everyone know I'm the right one to be fucking with. I had something for their ass. I could bring it with no hesitation. In my eyes; I was innocent. I was not a criminal. Like all these other bitches. Now I realize; This Ain't The Time To Jail.

An old man told me to meet him. In the law library. He would show me how to study up, on my case file. So, I can get a better legal representative. He stated I needed to apply for an 18B attorney. I can't believe that my mom won't help me anymore. She won't put anything in my commissary. My Mama won't even assist me. In obtaining any clothes or sneakers. I had to get clothes and slippers from the facilities clothes box. Inmates would leave me clothing. When it was time for them to be released. From this horrible detention facility. Where I lived as a detainee

My mother had to be sick of me. And, the bull shit that came with my existence. I know my mother acknowledges; me as the son she raised. She kept telling me to get myself together. No women want a man that's not established in life. I now understand what she talking about. I need some slot time on the telephone.

I have to get in touch. With this Lady friend of mine. We are fuck buddies. I like her because she has a fat ass. Girlfriend is Hood-Rich! I guess if I step up. My game and tell her; I love her. Then all I have to do is convince her that. We will be getting married. Which in my standards of life that hood-money! Will make her my common law wife. Then she will visit me. To bring me a care packages on a reg. We will have something in common. Her keeping my commissary full. This Lady was

definitely living large on the streets. I am going to allow her; to do this bid with me. As my sex tourist. She will travel back and forth to see me, While I am incarcerated. She is trust worthy. I found a job in the detention center making. Twenty-five cents an hour. I only work three hours a day. Do the math! Is this slave wages or what? These mother fuckers will work you until your balls clap. The institution calls this an honest living. The job keeps me out of trouble. I need the money for stamps and envelopes. To write my lawyer. Until my Queen shows up! It's a dam shame that incarceration showed me.

THIS AIN'T THE TIME TO JAIL...

It's time for me to apologize to my Moms. I didn't mean to hurt the only lady that truly ever loved me. I need that bond of her unconditional; love which I am always grateful for. I need her forgiveness. God in your Son's Mighty Name. I ask that you please. Keep my mind stayed on you.

I believe my flesh will die on this earth. Which is my physical death. In my physical form. As I try to stay alive the devil. Will try to throw me off track. My spirit, heart and the brain; will be beholding to you.

> Heavenly Father my Lord and savior I come to you. To ask what is the judgement day? Will I be held behind the gate? I come boldly to your throne to ask that Jesus be my Lord and Savior. I have used my supernatural gift that God has given me. To be inspirational to others. I must be stable in my being; from negative thoughts. In this world who is worthy; who is unworthy. While I try to keep the faith. I remember the spiritual entrance of life is greater than me.

I need to pray to God; and ask him to keep me safe. God keep your mind strong. So, I can make it out of this system of agony. It's time for me to dead this abnormal spirit, I'm living with. I must stay prayed up and keep a sane connection. Between the supreme being, myself and praise the Lord. A-men

Bible KJV- 2 Corinthians verse 12 and 9

Verse 12 says – For our rejoicing is this, the testimony of our conscience, that in simplicity and godly sincerity, not with fleshly wisdom, but by the grace of God, we have had our conversation in the world, and more abundantly to you-ward.

Verse 9. says – But we had the sentence of death in ourselves, that we should not trust in ourselves, but in God which raiseth the dead.

52

I AIN'T GOT KNOW CRACK

By Roslyn OFlaherty

I ain't got know crack.
I cooked my coke
all in my pipe. I puffed
and puffed with all my
might. The sight I seen,
the rush was mean.
The chip of ice that burned;
I yearned, for another puff.
Can't get rid of this stuff
coke, smoke, tears I choked.
Have no money and I'm still
broke. I want some more I
know for sure, that will be my
only cure. My craven is here.
It's time for some more. I can't
afford to pass, the crack dens door.

MISTER CHEEBA MAN!
By Roslyn O'Flaherty

Mister Cheeba man,
nickel bag on the corner,
seeds burning my clothes.

E-Z Wider, Bamboo! Just one sheet for morning
spliff, joint made from roaches. Now I have a buzz.

I run into a pothead;
inviting me to smoke a blunt.
Umm, ganjas,
puff, puff, pass
tokes of grass
smell of fonta leaf
that I had stashed.
Phillie, White owl,
Chocolate smoke.
Smoked a whooler was no joke.
The herb and crack, it was great.
I'm mellow now. This Wasn't Fate.

ICE, ICE CRAZY
By Roslyn OFlaherty

Ice, Ice, Crazy
Meth,
Cooking in the basement
Factory! Determining my future.
Hitting that glass pipe.
Watching it burn.
    CRYSTAL METH…
You've been my head ache for years.
Annoying me!
Feeding on my human misery.
      To Escape Crystal…

          The chase is on while looking for
          my first encounter. I owe money
          and sexual favors. Revelation
          with no judgment. Three and four
          times a day I shoot up.
          My level of spirit,
          has gone to the devil.
             OH
           crystal meth,
          Your treating me bad. I've
         been up one week straight.
          Drugs talking to me,
           telling me to use.
         Chemical dependency
           I can't stop.
         ICE ICE CRYSTAL!
           Shut up
           CRYSTAL!
      I can't pay attention to you.
      It's driving me; Ice Ice Crazy.
        It's a done deal.
     The familiarity has been real!

53

BEAUTIFIED

By Roslyn OFlaherty

I dream of perfection. I'm a man with female body parts. I just want to be beautified. I'm trapped in a fucked-up face. My appearance identity and behavior; are not a gender norm. Morally unattractive by my standards. My worst nightmare is an obsession; which I have to be beautified. I'm a cross dressing transgender. Constantly changing my body parts. My plastic surgery's cost me. At least; two hundred and fifty thousand dollars or more.

I have an obsession with procedures. The purpose of using pain killers. Is to cure my pain. I have become an addict. With an addictive personality. I have a manipulating spirit. When it comes to prescription drugs for pain. I started out with 800mg of Motrin, Vicodin 5/300 3 or 4 tabs a day. I love taking OxyContin and being hospitalized to get Morphine. Prescription intervention is needed. I feel like I'm fighting the addiction. That has caused destruction against me.

I have breast and calf implants. The surgery on my face caused me. To be scared and disfigured. I put collagen in my lips. I thought I needed this filler. The extreme transformation; of cosmetic surgery caused infections. The doctors were board certified. I never thought I would turn out unattractive. I pressured myself to look perfect! And, became an addict to plastic surgery. My life is full of confusion.

The thought of a tummy tuck. Has crossed my mind. On more than a few occasions. My external appearance and complication. Was a horrifying nightmare. My body disorders made me question. Did I really need an image alteration? I was broke and still in debt to medical experts. I could not stop wanting to be beautified! My Adam's apple was removed.

I'm waiting to have a surgical procedure. To fix my latest scares. I plan on decreasing; the size of my far head. Alterations on my nose. With eyebrow implants to my fondness. A laser was used to eliminate my facial hairs. I am mortified about my disfigured body parts. I wonder what my ass would look like if I lifted it up? I need funds so I can be beautified. This has been a real hormonal experience. I could do without the hormonal occurrences. That I have endured; from some people in my life. It doesn't seem fear to me. I imaged I would be socially accepted. I wanted specified body-lifts so I could be a princess!

I decided to go shopping. To buy some new clothes. I could not find anything I liked on 3rd bx Avenue. So, I went to 125th street. I got out the cab on 125th and Lenox Avenue. I walked to the corner and saw my Mother. She did not know who I was. She had not seen me in years. I said, hello Mother. She looked at me and had to take a second glance. She was in shock, at my appearance. She grabbed me; receiving me in her arms with love. As she screamed my name Majhar, Majhar, my baby. She cried tears of joy.

We talked Ma had prayed every night. For the Lord to keep me safe. My mother was glad. Her prayers had been answered. She said she threw my dad out on the streets. The day I left. Family don't treat family like that! Your father was talking crazy... I apologize for his actions. Majhar he is in a nursing home. You must forgive him. Ma my dad was disrespectful towards me.

For him to say. Before I let another man fuck my son! I'll fuck him myself... I'll show you Majhar. I'll stick my dick so far up your ass! The penetration will; straighten you right the fuck out! So, you wanna be a fairy... I'll spread your mother fuckin wings! Ma! when dad went to take his dick out. I was done with him.

I explained to my mother. That before my operation. I thought genetic testing could tell me. Why I was stuck. Between being a male and knowing I was a female. Now that I have a mangina. I fight with myself sometimes. Because, I have changed God's image. When I had my gender reassignment surgery. I have female reproductive organs.

I lived as a woman for a year before I had my operation. It bothers me that I can't have a baby. Now I fight with the fact that. I will never have an offspring of my own. I need parental love from you Ma. Dad has disowned me. I'm having trouble finding a place in society. It's like I don't have civil rights or human rights. Is religion the law for transsexual people? Religious and political leaders made me feel

oppression. Like my life as a transsexual person, Is the initiation to hell!

Well I'm glad I still have you Ma. That will help keep me from being; in a state of despondency. I am not suicidal. I can't understand my life. This distressing situation, isn't good for my heart and soul? Who will accept the decision? I have made for myself; beside you Ma. My mother said we all are made in God's image. So, I was beautified at birth. I must love what God gave me. I am beautiful in mind and spirit. I must not live in shame. Ma People are cruel! I walk around hating them.

(PROVERBS 30 VERSE 12 SAYS- There is a generation that are pure in their own eyes, and yet is not washed from their filthiness.)

Me and Mama talked, I decided I have to 360 the self-pity. Revaluate my thinking and live in the now. I must not get depressed. To the point where I want to kill myself. I don't want to be on anti-depressant anymore. Society can be so cruel sometimes. "Mama says I'm an expression of love" I pray I will be set free by the hand of Lord... BIBLE KING JAMES VERSION HOLY BIBLE

Psalms 6 verse 2 says Have mercy upon me, O Lord;

For I am weak: O Lord heal me; for my bones are vexed.

MARK 12 VERSE 31 SAYS-
AND THE SECOND IS LIKE, NAMELY THIS, THOU SHALL LOVE THY NEIGHBOUR AS THYSELF. THERE IS NONE OTHER COMMANDMENT GREATER THAN THESE.

54

GROWN ADULTS

By Roslyn OFlaherty

My child, why are you aggravated; about not being a grown adult? You've not reached sexual maturity. Your intellect makes you believe it's alright to sneaking around in bars, So, grown men can rap to you. Physically developed from top to bottom. Looking grown entering a bar establishment name – THIRSTY POINT BAR... Wearing cut up shorts. That felt like they were cutting, your private area. With your ass hanging out the back. Thinking your tramp stamp. Was a style of a diva. Nipples stood up straight in your wife beater. Being bra less; with the rebellious look you were going for.

Still residing under Moms and Dads authority meant nothing. Living disrespectful - a rebel without a cause. Going through life with a false; sense of love, respect and happiness. Grown feelings come over you. While sitting on a bar stool almost passed out. Subsequently acting just like an actual drama queen. Now considering yourself as being a grown adult. You had a few Long Island Ice Tea's and became sloppy drunk.

One of the bars customers name; Cisco took you to his friend's crib. He desired your body. The thought never entered your mind. That Cisco only wanted to penetrate you. Living with a pregnancy or catching a disease. Never became a topic of discussion. Before he could get your shorts off, 10 inches was swinging in your face. Yes! That's what grown adults bring. Your naïve ass could not even holler back.

Now Cisco is ready to place; something in between your lips. Your throat was full of a nasty tasting. Wet substance making you choke while gagging for air. You let Cisco climb between your legs. For love and the bitch took your virginity. Banging you from the front and back causing severe pain. Which had you screaming an utterance sound of annoyance?

It would have been easier to get respect from a dog. Cisco took you to Murdock Park. Which had a lot of bushes in the area. The homeless lived in certain parts of the woods. You entered Murdock Park still smelling like sex still moist; wet from one end to the other. Feelings of embarrassment and hatred; entered your thoughts as, Cisco blindfolded you. A gun was placed to your head. Impairing your judgement along with Meth Amphetamines. Your new high was a twelve-hour experience.

Realizing now you gave away your virginity. Having confidence that what you were doing. Was part of love making. Cisco got paid-while you sucked dick all day. He kept you on the Meth, naked in the bushes. Your mind recognized the drug as making love. Which made you feel like a whore. Cisco collect the money; while you showed your tramp stamp. You believed he loved you. As long as you gave up the botty. You respected Cisco manhood more than being sexually assaulted. You knew you had become Cisco's Young Hooker...

Forcefully your hand entered a full-grown man's pants. Dude threated you despite the fact. You were already frightened. Slob-in the knob, with your hand wrapped around his 8 inches. Remembering this was the same man's private area from yesterday. The smell of his testicles gave away his identity; while massaging them in the palm of your hand.

An Insertion of fingers was in your virginal area. Occasionally the man would put his fingers in your mouth. So, you could taste your own juices. He started screaming at you; it tastes good doesn't it? You screamed yes; because he was hurting you! You pull his fingers out your twat; and started licking them automatically. You could no longer take the pain your pussy endured. Your mind started drifting away from the situation. Thinking grown folks are sexually disturbed. This can't be love. This man is a pervert.

Cisco is a thot and you feel like a thot in training. Low budget sex trafficking Cisco. Cisco was nickel and diming it. Just thirsty to sell ass for chump change. You've been corrupted by a grown ass; immature street park pussy peddler! You were stupid! Hungry for grown people's sex... Cisco had no regards to your sexual preference. And, you wound up in the bushes; with perverts eating out. Ass-up and turned-out!

There were two twin brothers; That were part of the Cisco clan. They would come to the park. Suck and fuck at the same time. Real tricksters! It turned out they were both brothers. That were into male masculine sex. The brothers laid head to foot; And, start sucking dick YUK... The brothers were moaning like bitches. You were shocked with all the muscles they had. Cum dripped out both their mouth's. You guessed they were keeping it in the family! If the bushes could talk... Whatever turns you on my brothers! They started eating out the anus. Sucking each other's ass. You never seen nothing like that in your life. They turned each other out!

Tear ran down your eyes; money wasn't come in right. Due to bad weather. Cisco made you turn tricks. In the last cars of the trains beating the shit out of you for refusing. You asked yourself how people. Could consider you to be trashy. The world was now an unpleasant place in your thoughts. You went on line on the computer. There you were in unfortunate quality. Laying there buck naked. In the bushes feeling dirty. High on Meth while drinking. Alcohol which was used for liquid courage. To keep your mind off. The previous sex memories that sickened you. Your mind was without expressive thoughts; just toxic views.

Sometime faith did not come easy. Actually, you were living a life style. Where half the time. Your mind and body needed a fix. Your concentration stayed; in survival mode as a junkie. Questions flowed through your mind. Were your parents looking for you? Wishing the police would pick you up. From this life of madness. Living in Murdock Park during the day. The park in which you use to; play on the swing as a child. Cisco taught you how to live. In many disgustingly dirty ass motel rooms at night. In which he brought strangers to ride you. On rainy days you were forced to have sex on trains. While you thanked God; you were still alive. Because, thoughts of suicide crossed your mind. In this miserable life as Cisco's sex slave.

Sentiments of being a prostitute. In an erotic web cam show made you cry. How could this excite people? The embarrassment of it made you feel. That Cisco had crossed the line. You still loved Cisco. His manipulating spirit was causing you. Low self-esteem, and emotional distress. Cisco's behavior as your ass hole pimp sickened you. Along with drinking and drugging. Which made you feel like you had a personality disorder. Being raped over and over again. Was this really rape? You never said NO STOP out of fear. Death sounded really good; right about now. Maybe Cisco should have shot you. Were you abducted from the bar? You left the bar drunk. As a minor leaving on your own free will.

Was your family and friend looking for you? The people in Thirsty Point Bar. Saw your grown ass leave with Cisco. Realizing now you're an immature minor. In sex acts with grown adults. Indecent behavior that went beyond. An erotic comfort zones. Is it possible to achieve what you truly; deserve happiness and love. With a peace of mind?

Time has passed you are now in a drug program. Trying to understand the reason. You never became a missing person? Just a whore and a drug addict. In love with Cisco! You told your parents about your awful circumstances. They said they did not care about your where about. Due to the fact they thought I ran away. You could not see beyond their bullshit! Your done with them: lesson learnt they could not even relate. To your pain and suffering. Considering yourself still in love with the stability Cisco showed you. This was the reason; he truly was your pimp for so long. He turned you out and, took away your humanity. Eternally grateful your life as a whore. Did not exist anymore. Your secret dark past made you understanding. It was unwise to over extend yourself. In erotic foolish sex with grown adults. As Cisco kept the money. To keep his ass out of debt. You were young and stupid. Surprisingly wild, evil and crazy thoughts. Kept entering your mind; contemplating revenge on Cisco's life. Really, he did not care if you over dosed on drugs. Caught a disease. Was killed by the men you engage with etc...

You are now aware that you must; keep your mouth shut and your legs closed! Feeling like a young lady. A spirit full of hope is what you needed! Every day you scrubbed your skin with disinfect. With thoughts of the men's hands all over you. Your skin started peeling off in your bath water.

Now you live with a self-esteem. That lets you believe. Thirsty Point Bar and Cisco. Should not have been more superior. Then your safety and wellbeing. Now knowledgeable to the fact; enticing men was not a good thing. Young and sexually exploited. There was truly no fun added in the process. The experiences in this dysfunctional lifecycle. Of being raped over and over again. Has made you feel like. A coward and; an emotional wreck. Being grown and stupid. Has made life mortifying. Nevertheless, you knew now. You were not a grown adult: Just Enslaved By Your Bitch Ass Pimp...

55

BEAT DOWN

By Roslyn OFlaherty

I can't take another beat down to the external punishment I live. Life as a battered woman with puffy eyes; fractured nose and a busted lip is not appealing. One incident my husband beat me so bad. I wound up with cracked ribs. Which he called an accident. I can't take no more. My husband's out of his mind. He has that killer swag. That's right! I like the bad boys. I think it's in my DNA...

I know my husband loves me. This controlling man is ridiculing me, With wrong improper obnoxious behavior. Which keeps me hospitalized. Cops don't even entertain my situation in their observance. I keep taking my husband back because he keeps stalking me. Making me a victim to his constant threats. It's easier to disregard the court order; lying in my dwelling. I belong in a battered woman's shelter under protective custody.

I fear for my life! I still take an ass whipping. Opposed to my husband being incarcerated. I can only live one day at a time. My hope is existing in fear of this condemnation to hell. I dread the day. I have to whip out my court order for protection. Due to my unmannerly husband battering me. I admit! I'm obsessed with his love and sex he gives me. To say he is rightly sorry. It enables me to forgive him at times.

I sacrifice my life with this lifespan of betrayal. I must stop hiding the improper abuse. Father God, please give me the strength. To walk away and not settle in this abusive situation. I wish to live in peace. Nevertheless,

I am truly scared of the brutal circumstances that occurs. My heart and soul are minutes away. From a beat down at the door.

> JEREMIAH 29 VERSE 11 SAYS
> FOR I KNOW THE THOUGHTS
> THAT I THINK TOWARDS
> YOU, SAITH THE LORD,
> THOUGHTS OF PEACE, AND
> NOT OF EVIL, TO GIVE YOU
> AN EXPECTED END.

56

I LIVE IN VIETNAM

By Roslyn OFlaherty

Vietnam, gang related turmoil existing without regard or feelings of others. Pit bulls were thrown off the roof for recreation. You could hear guns being shot. Through the hallway windows: as you walk out the building. People scared out of your wits. Are running or just hit the ground; because bullets are flying. Night and day folks had to concentrate. In staying alive from the stray bullets. Making its claim on the hood. Bodies left for dead are found in stair wells.

Gang morality are at an all-time high. As they take the law into their own hands. Upsetting the function and structure of neighborhoods. Is redemption possible! Poverty broken homes; with juveniles on probation engaging in turf wars. Captivating this as a form of love. Which they think are untouchable guidelines. To the law without justification. A period used to conquer their offensive actions?

Feeling successful despite of the fact. That they were looking for approval and security influences. For being a gang member could bring harm to them. As well as their family members. Not really understanding the unpleasant events to crime problems. That have become their lifestyle. You have friends whose Moms are gang leaders. The kids on the block are mean. Call gang Moms a handkerchief heads; the jargon that is a negative interpretation. Born into a life style that's recruiting another generation collectively. To wear colors and hand tattoos which may bring on facial tear drops. Straight from the park bench or school yard.

The gang leaders are given the utmost respect by their foot soldiers. Who sometimes have color head bandanna hanging from their back pockets; Worn with pride and respect to carrying out violence, hate crimes? In your community. which is called Vietnam. Sometimes juvenile gang members. Are considered little tyrants in the community. They grew up wanting to be a productive, citizens. And now have to do things. So, their single parent mom can feed and raise the family. Gangs became burdensome to social anxiety events. And, became the center of attention to bull shit. As the foot soldiers tries to be on their grind. They were forced to takes accountability for; the action of others and wind up incarcerated. Activities that make them guilty by association.

They are dead ass serious. When it comes to being loyal. While living in a fast pace life. Once a gang member, always a gang member is the mentality. Which can become threatening. To someone that loses their devotion to the cause. That is necessary to comply; with the understanding of loyalty. Life as a foot soldiers on the streets trapped in threats of death. Is this the basis to look guilt-ridden; in a life with obstruction of justice. That they want for our youth? Should they be ostracized from society? For throwing up gang signs; for status and protection? Are they wearing tattoos of recruitment? For what they think is patriotic to our neighborhood? Or, is this being used to identify juvenile gang members.

Walking with tattoo bill board identification; for the law or other rival gangs in society. To label or acknowledge them. Should parents be responsible for their child's. Lack of knowledge and direction in street life? That is not always the case spiritually. Can churches be held accountable to become a guide? For parents to justify the actions of their children? Should religion instruction prayer; be put back in the school system! Society has to take some of the blame. Especially for men and women who can't gain employment. After obtaining their degrees from colleges and universities. They are also in dept for collage loans. Many of them have child supports and court official stipulations. Threatening them to pay child support or they will be incarcerated.

A kid with a kid is forced to start slinging product in the streets. To avoid going to jail for child support wages. Causing these parents to be damaged emotionally and physically drained. Mentally due to the law's incidents forced upon them. That should be about mortal rights. Our youngsters are on the computers. Throwing up gang signs and they can't even pea straight. Minors half naked smoking refer on line. Not realizing jobs and legal official are monitoring. Their web page to determine the character and temperament. Of their personality while under observation. This may lower their chances to be hired for employment.

Public bureaucrat's lawlessness is ignored by terrorized civilians. Starting confusion that is leaving our state of the union in jeopardy. Of going back to the 1950's. In the era that could be consider the Wild-Wild West. Children with guns legally through gun control legislation. Which is classified as a punk bitch move as far as the hood is concerned. Lives are ended with a bang, funerals becoming the trend. with no real justification there will be less hope for our future how it could end. Protesters march in outrage without a wing and a pray. Marchers demonstrating for reconciliation; are putting their lives in harm's way. The dispute of who is guilty or innocent is not informative enough. So, who or what will save the nation's future security?

Our infants are being incarcerated at birth. Babies that are raised in jail for one year; with their moms after birth. Jails with nursery accommodations for pregnant mothers. There are some folks that treat the family composition in a derogatory way. What give anyone the right to put an impolite label on these babies. (Institutionalized infants –never that! Gang babies/ drug babies etc.) Really that's what we're doing now? They are innocent infants with parents. Babies that also belong to God Thy Father; TO Be All THE Glory.

Freedom in the air is not on my street. Vietnam is still here. Foot soldiers at a very young age are being incarcerated; given adult prison time. Is love the internal feelings that comes from their gang leader's code of silence. What happened to the village that raises the child? When is realism going to set in that Vietnams confrontations on the streets; is not common civility to becoming a war hero? All you get is categorized status and a gun. What they don't know is that society has to destroy many nationalities of color. In order to conquer the house poor and rich people of color. Folks need to watch what is going on with the government politically; and the supremacy pure color race. To divide and concur is what they want. Only because there is strength in numbers. So, the people of color can never unite as one... Why are people stuck in a financial crisis; or credit card debit which is just a burden. It's just a matter of time before people are picking cotton again. (Yah think???) Which brings on the family disorder. The trap to unoriginally cancellation of medical insurance Medicare / Medicaid etc. Benefits for rehab and hospital assistance or advice to services. Homelessness without food stamps. We can't go back to like were in the fifties. (Bail bond agent, Police brutality; and politician's with court judge's interference of justice.) Was at an all-time high. Junkies paradise was filled with dope fiends; laid out in the streets. Building owners burning down their property. To collect their insurance claims, as the policyholder. Bodegas robbed on the reg. This was part of poverty and homelessness... All this can bring (fraud, thief, and scams, white collar crime with a nonviolent status) to the street of Vietnam. Some Moms and Dads can't understand why young peers. That takes a life or cripples someone. Is glorified in their community called Vietnam. Violence started a long time ago. Parents feel the reality of this; will make people hit the streets marching. Looking for peace and justice for all. Ruthless is when someone tries to put a noose on your neck. Don't become incarcerate in the system; man can shackle your feet legally. Disrupting and holding back your future. With the intent to make you culture shock. A movement of empowerment designed to drive you to be criminally insane. By a deceitful authority. While you look for legal empowerment. Towards dignity, serenity and peace. God can redirect things in your life.

YOU CAN BE PRIVLEGED AND HAVE GOD REDIRECT. THE TROUBLE OR DANGER IN YOUR LIFE. STOP WAITING ON UNJUST INDIVIDUALS. WHO PLACE THEIR DISFUNTIONAL ACTIVITIES; FROM THE DIVERSE NEIGHBORHOOD OF VIETNAM? WHICH CAUSES RESENTMENT AND DRAMA IN YOUR PERSONAL SPACE. WHY SHOULD PEOPLE BE ALL UP IN YOUR EAR GATES. WITH SKEPTISIM OF A CHANGE OF MORALITY OR NONVIOLENCE. WHICH BRINGS ON A CONCISE MESSAGE; OVER YOUR LIFE WITH LIES AND DECIET. NOW YOU ARE A VICTIM OF CIRCUMSTANCES. LIVING IN POVERTY WITH CORRUPT CRIMES AND DEATH THREATS.

DON'T FIGHT A WAR THAT'S NOT YOURS. CLIMB UNDER GOD AND SIT STILL. TRANSFORM YOUR COMMUNITY AND CIVIL RIGHTS. INSTEAD OF BEING BEATEN AND TERRORIZED WITH LIFE. BELIEVE AND EXCEPT YOUR RELIGIOUS ACCORD. HAVE CONFIDENCE IN GOD AND ALLOW HIM TO BE WHO HE IS. YOUR LIFE HAS BEEN VIOLATED ON MANY LEVELS OF DISAPPIONTMENT. EXCEL BEYOND YOUR EXPECTATIONS OF CULTURAL MISHAPS. THAT HAS DISTROYED AND VIOLATED YOUR FAITH LEVEL.

EXTRA, EXTRA READ ALL ABOUT IT! Children are prey to the real world. Wanting them to bow down to freedom of correctness. Lured into violence OR raised into violence. To which are the systems and roots of self-destruction. With the killing on their mind inflamed with hostility. From leading them; from hallow to shallow. Rebels without a cause. To real life community activity. Step from their world to the real world.

BANG - BANG SHOOT EM UP; LEAVES FOLKS DEAD. A UNION FORMED WITH SOCIETY. TO THE STREETS AND JAIL PROTECTION. IS THIS CONSIDERED A TOXIC LIFE? TO NEGATIVE BLESSED POWER TO GLORY. IS IT RATIONAL TO LOSE VICTIMS AND GANG MEMBERS WITH PERMANENT ENDINGS. WHY DO WE FIGHT AMOUNST OURSELVES?

COULD THIS BE A SERIES OF PSYCHOTIC TENDENCIES? IS THIS A MOVEMENT OF GANG MEMBERS (A–G); YOUR DUDE, AND VICTIMS. PLEASE WILL YOU LISTEN TO OUR PRAYERS? OUR CHILDREN NEED THEIR PARENTS AND THEIRS PARENTS NEED THEIR KIDS.

WE MUST ALL FIGHT TO KEEP OUR FAMILIES TOGETHER. PLEASE LETS ALL GET CLOSER TO GOD TO BREAK THE CYCLES. JESUS ALREADY SHED HIS BLOOD FOR US. AND BLOOD IS BEING SHED ON OUR STREET IN VIETNAM. FOR THE LOVE OF GOD. WE CAN'T STAY SCORNED. WITH THE STAKES OF INCARCERATION BEING AN OPTION.

57

GOD'S CHILD

By Roslyn OFlaherty

God's Child
off to war,
Thou shall not kill!
Bill of rights
from the devil,
bombs ~ guns ~ casualties
and body bags.
Wars lost minds and soul. Families distorted, unpaid
bills left behind. Bended truths, wars billion-dollar
rate, making single parent households ruined damaged.
Who has the right to play God and send God's Child,
off to war?
THE FATHER OF OUR COUNTRY
                    VERSUS
OUR FATHER WHO ART IN HEAVEN
The thought of all this just blows me away.

58

CONVERT TO THE LORD
AND HIS KINGDOM

By Roslyn OFlaherty

Let us all give hope to those who live in disastrous conditions. Poverty stricken as they're struggling with what some call a recession with gentrification. The dollars asset value is eroding. The representation of the dollar; that is in circulation may change. Having a new distribution of currency; that some call the ditch dollar. This will be used in order to ruin the world.

Economics is crippling us. The recession is consumed with concentrating on foreclosure; lost wages that have made people homeless. World problems are getting bigger. Making people live in the moment. Escaping life with their center of attention on selling sex – porn, diamonds and the newest fashions? Should this be the encouragement of love relationships? This is being used to nurture our young who don't even believe in themselves.

Their minds are covered with thoughts of bling; with lust in their heart. It is important to realize that the launching of missiles. Could take place with the head of state consent; which could destroy the world. A cycle of drama that comes from; undesirable life styles of an evil journey. Deliverance from egotistical authorities is needed. "The tail can only be as strong as the head." Ignorance of the government defense keeps people from having faith. Tactics are being used through mind control.

Some individuals are walking around incapacitated. When it comes to discussing humanity being destroyed; politically and financially. Why is college education making our graduating students; over qualified for employment? They are forced to flip burgers for a living. College students are receiving credit cards. While attending college without descent employment or collateral. This is keeping them in a I.O.U. Bondage; which is murdering their spirits. Governments economics act of leadership. Allows Colleges – Jails/ penitentiaries; hospitals and pharmacies to be our billion-dollar industries. A monetary-end trap or productivity to death or homelessness.

Let's take a look at our health plans. We can't afford to go to the doctor. Why are we being forced to pay co-payments of 50$'s to the doctor to read a report that was generated from across the hall at (MRI) magnetic-resonance-imaging; scanner room. You just left 50$'s with the specialist office; who took the MRI test. A total of one hundred for a day's visit at a clinic. Some hospitals will bill you as much as $400.00. To use their hospital operating room. A bill your health coverage is not liable to pay. The pharmaceuticals industry prices are too high. You leave the doctor's visit unable to buy medication. The drug store pharmacy offers you 7 pills to help you until you can rectify the situation. People could die without their medication. Who will accept responsibility for that? You can live or die by the sword of health cares; catastrophic emergencies and rehabilitation service coverage. Many people are turning to naturopathic doctors. Others are turning to Holistic health care and medicine. Are these American Medical Association that have your best interest at heart? That is the Question to ask about many government health policies. Well we can all agree it is time to eat to live.

Senior citizens who have worked all their lives. Just to figure out how to little their Medicare part B kicks in for hospital coverage. This is considered your Medicaid at Human Resources. The Identification Number does not allow you a Medicaid Card. Many Soldier have served in the armed forces. They are on Social Security hungry with nutritional deficiencies. There are Mental Health patients; that should not have died from senseless deaths. Some individuals can't handle being locked up; in institutions or, living on the street in the homeless systems tents. Swept under the rug. With this unfortunate style of mental health incarceration. Due to the fact they may be ignorant to our man-made government.

Water bills are being paid by home owners. Their tenants are being forced to pay a water bill with rental agreements. Should they have to buy bottle water? In order for the family to have the adequate amount of fresh water; needed to drink in the household. Who would ever think, that the world could be taken over with water? Water that God provided us with! The filth and pollution in the water is not always a mistake... Man will drill for water one day as we, live in the land of the rich and thirsty! It might be time to consider catching rain water from the sky. Boiling it to drink and cook. Really is a plastic molded water bottle; healthy enough for our well-being. Are they toxic recycled products that disrupts the body?

The economy is in a financial turmoil. What is the tax code for the super-rich? They hide their money overseas. The rich should be willing to pay taxes. While they invest money to benefit themselves. It seems our government's cabinet will be the only ones undefeated. (Yah Think?) While using their political schizophrenia. A discrepancy that should be explained not ignored. Constitutionalism has become a political issue. Lies and fraud should be overthrown. In order to overturn the dishonor on policies / disagreed upon.

Climate disruption is making people struggle; to live through hurricane and tornadoes storms. Heat waves are killing people. Fires are destroying our land - households. Is the energy of the ozone layer a

danger to us? The earth is also being controlled with urban floods. Conditions that are impacting people's cultures. Leaving them in doubt an unsure future; as their homes slip downhill in the mud. Which becomes considered rubbish.

Lower levels of water spiraling into droughts. Many people are suffering and are thirsty. Corporations are selling water to the deprived. Times are coming - where only the rich will always have fresh water. There will be a water war all over the earth. Mosquitoes are giving humans viruses that are deadly. Who could ever visualize people suffering from bed bugs in their schools and dwellings? The epidemic of rats is taking over our neighborhoods and train stations. Animals are still becoming extinct throughout the world. Ours nations fight wars we don't understand! I wonder why we fight the same way in our neighborhood with racist ideology and police brutality. We struggle to live in our lost society as we look for world peace. People should never forget their past. In hopes not to let anyone replace it with a lost concept. Of our self-worth and new begging's. Burning and tearing down our neighborhoods. The danger of opening our hearts to others can cause disloyalty. We can't afford to walk backwards. And step on each other's toes. Turn around and concur a positive future and know your worth.

Our civilization is declining as we wait to see; past our dilemmas. We are all miracles deserving to live past our troubles. We have all sinned in one way or another... Some individuals are remorseful with feelings of being alone in life. Why can't some people have positive opportunities planned for themselves; without belittling anyone with their negative bitterness? There is no time to be petty. When we can love within our viewpoints in life expectations.

Turning our heads and sticking our nose up at each other. As we call ourselves people of God; with that stinking thinking. I hope one day we can live in a no judgement zone. Enabling us to fellowship with one another inside and, outside the house of the Lord. You grew up believing the saying. "It takes a village to raise a child." Do you have the right to give our discernment? On what love, truth and reality is for the lost souls? They have been casted away from the church. While fighting for strength to find something to accept as the power of true love with admiration in religion...

Is it of God for the church family to glorify themselves as; they look for gratification in Jesus name Amen? Is there really glory in this way of discriminating? Don't let our convictions be a dance with our enemies' dictatorship as; they feel they rule the world. The gift of life is truly forgiveness. Maliciousness at the expense of other: is not in the power of faith.

Lord I don't want to live in the wild wild West. With a dictator for a Government Leader. I'm not ready to be living like I am in the great depression. Where the meaning of existence as a human being; does not mean anything anymore. We as a people are living backward. The government with a broken congress in the white house. Will try to send us back 50 year in time. Earth will become an infernal region. A place where people will be living wretchedness while suffering.

VOCABULARY WORDS

rights, terror, judgmental, natural, morality, discovery, reality, ratchet, character, evil, compulsion, insanity, life, focus, condition, flaws, social-media, observation, traditionalist, demand, vengeful, legislation, lost, freedom, persecution, rules, controversial, extremists, pattern, world, maintain, brain, purpose, speech, ethical, potential, severance, nations, integrity, deterioration, worse, balance, suffering, aimed, persecute, cowards, knowledge, reason, restraints, inappropriate, subconscious, victimized, tolerate, laws, lies, corruption, negotiate, metaphor, independence, better, bargain #lol, keep it 100, fix, hurt, mistreated, hostile, suicidal, selfish, hostage, punished, predatory, consequences, treacherous, depression, anxiety, ending, biology, future, balance, destination, domain, worth, while, valuable, function, obsessed, best, wisdom, cure, past, emotions, suffering, pursue, responsibility, family, friends, marriage, compassion, reward, motivation, strength, hope, empathy, nice, commitment, dependency, choices, observed, teach, empathy, strategy's, sacrifices, encouragement, love, integrity, divine, guidance, structure true, salvation, function an change, ambition, mental balance.

We must watch out for people with controlling actions. An indefinite process of changes. That have no concerns for the poor or people who consider themselves; the middle class in this country. Money speaks with a currency policy. A processed action amongst the rich.

"That will determine the actions for the unfortunate."

KJV. Mathews 6:10 says-
Thy kingdom come. Thy will be done in earth, as it is in heaven.

REFERENCE

and modeled from The KJV OF THE BIBLE

THE TEN COMMANDMENTS

1. I AM THE LORD THY GOD
   THOU SHALT HAVE NO OTHER
   GOD BEFORE ME

2. THOU SHALT NOT MAKE UNTO THEE
   ANY GRAVEN IMAGE

3. THOU SHALT NOT TAKE THE NAME
   OF THE LORD IN VAIN

4. REMEMBER THE SABBATH DAY
   AND KEEP IT HOLY

5. HONOR THY FATHER AND THY MOTHER

6. THOU SHALT NOT KILL

7. THOU SHALT NOT COMMIT ADULTERY
8. THOU SHALT NOT STEAL
9. THOU SHALT NOT BEAR FALSE WITNESS
   AGAINST THY NEIGHBOUR
10. THOU SHALT NOT COVET

BIBLE KJV
THE TEN COMMANDMENTS
EXODUS 20 says-
20 And God spank all these words, saying
2. I am the LORD thy God, which
have brought thee out of the land of
E-gypt, out of the house of bondage.
3. Thou shall have no other gods before me.
4. Thou shalt not make unto thee
any graven image, or any likeness
of anything that is in heaven
above, or that is in the earth,
beneath, or that is in the water
under the earth.
5. Thou shalt not bow down
thyself to them, nor serve them: for I the
Lord the God am a jealous God

visiting the iniquity of the fathers
upon the children unto the third
and fourth generation of them that
hate me.
6. And shewing mercy unto thousands of them that love me, and keep my
commandments.
7. Thou shalt not take the name of
the Lord thy God in vain: For the Lord will
not hold him guiltless that taketh his name in vain.
8. Remember the sabbath day, to keep it holy.
9. Six days shalt thy labour, and do all thy work:
10. But the seventh day is the sab-
bath of the LORD thy God: in it thou
shalt not do any work, thou, nor thy
son nor thy daughter, the man servant
nor thy maidservant, nor thy cattle,
nor thy stranger that is within thy
gates:

11. For in six days the LORD made heaven
and earth, the sea, and all that in them
is, and rested the seventh day:
Wherefore the LORD blessed the sabbath
day, and hallowed it.
12. Honor thy father and thy mother;
that thy days maybe long upon the land
which the LORD thy God giveth thee.
13. Thou shalt not kill.
14. Thou shalt not commit adultery.
15. Thou shalt not steal.
16. Thou shalt not bear false witness
against thy neighbour.
17. Thou shalt not covet thy neighbour's
house, thou shalt covet thy wife,
nor thy manservant, nor his maidservant, nor
his ox, nor his ass, nor any thing that is thy
neighbour's.
18. And all the people saw the thundering, and
the lightning, and the noise of the trumpet,
and the mounting smoking: and when the
people saw it, they removed and stood afar off.
19. And they said unto Mo'-ses, speak thou
with us, and we will hear: but let not God
speak with us, lest we die.
20. And Mo'-ses said unto the people, Fear not;
For God is come to prove you, and that his fear
May be before your faces, that ye sin not.
21. And the people stood afar off, and Mo'-ses
Drew near unto the thick darkness where God was.
22. And the Lord said unto Mo'-ses, Thus
Thou shalt say unto the children of Is'-ra-el
Ye have seen that I have talked with you
from heaven.

23. Ye shall not make with me Gods of
silver, neither shall he make unto you
gods of gold.
24. A altar of earth thou shalt make
unto me, and shalt sacrifice thereon
thy burnt offerings, and thy peace
offerings, thy sheep, and thy oxen:
in all places where I record my name,
I will come unto thee, and I will bless thee.
25. And if thou wilt make me an altar
of stone, thou shalt not build it of hewn
stone: for if thou lift thy tool upon it,
thou hast polluted it.
26. Neither shalt thou. Go up by steps
Unto my alter, that thy nakedness be
Not discovered thereon.

ROSLYN OFLAHERTY
"THE FOUNDATION FOR THE LOST SOULS"
WE MUST DO MINISTRY

Shares Bible verses KJV
*****LET'S THANK THE LORD - FOR HE IS WORTHY*****

"For God so loved the world that he gave his only begotten Son, that whosoever believes in him should not perish, but have everlasting life.

John 3:16

Psalms 86 verse 1 thru 17

Verse 1 says - Bow down thine ear, Oh Lord, hear me: for I am poor and needy.

Verse 2 says – Preserve my soul: for I am holy: O thou my God, save thy servant that trusteth in thee.

Verse 3 says – Be merciful unto me, O Lord: For I cry unto thee daily.

Verse 4 says – Rejoice the soul of thy servant: for unto thee, O Lord, do I lift up my soul.

Verse 5 says – For thou, Lord, art good, and ready to forgive; and plenteous in mercy unto all them that call upon thee.

Verse 6 says – Give ear, O Lord, unto my prayer; and attend to the voice of my supplication.

Verse 7 says – In the day of my trouble I will call upon thee: for thou wilt answer me.

Verse 8 says – Among the gods there is none like unto thee, O Lord; neither are there any works like unto thy works.

Verse 9 says – All nations whom thou hast made shall come and worship before thee, O Lord; and shall glorify thy name.

Verse 10 says – For thou art great, and doest wondrous things: thou art God alone.

Verse 11 says – Teach me thy way, O Lord; I will walk in thy truth: unite my heart to fear thy name.

Verse 12 says – I will praise thee, Oh Lord thy God with all my heart: and I will glorify thy name for evermore.

Verse 13 says – For great is thy mercy towards me: * and thou hast delivered my soul from the lowest hell.

Verse 14 says – O God the proud are risen against me, and the assemblies of violent men have sought after my soul; and have not set thee before them.

Verse 15 says – But thou, O Lord, art a God full of compassion, and gracious, longsuffering, and plenteous in mercy and truth,

Verse 16 says – O turn unto me, and have mercy upon me; give thy strength unto thy servant, and save the son of thine handmaid.

Verse 17 says – Shew me a token for good; that they which hate me may see it, and be ashamed: because thou, Lord hast holpen me and comfort me.

This book SHADY RATCHETNESS TO GLORY is Roslyn Oflaherty's spiritual side. Her energy of empowerment to understand the beliefs in almighty God. Yet she is not a Minister or any kind of spiritual leader. Something within her wants to reach; out to the lost souls with encouragement and hope. In spite the fact that a small majority of people. May not appreciate some of her writings; her translations are explicitly stated; but not meant to be malicious. Grace was given with love because her heart was in the right place. Roslyn does not claim to be an Angel or a Biblical Scholar. Just a lost soul with a message to give people about faith in life. For those that consider her to be messy. TRANSFORMATION JESUS IS HER VINDICATOR; SHE HAS AGAPE LOVE TO BE BLESSED AND HIGHLY FAVORED! Remember- Ephesians 2:10 Holy Bible NLT says-

For we are God's masterpiece. He has created us anew in Christ Jesus, so we can do the good things he planned for us long ago.

HOLY BIBLE KJV

Roman 12:12 says - Rejoicing in hope; patient in tribulation; continuing instant in prayer; Luke 10:20 Rom. 5:2; 1Thess. 5:17

Luke 10:20 says – Not with understanding in this rejoice not, that the spirits are subject unto you: but rather rejoice, because your names are written in heaven.

Roman 5:2 says - By whom also we have access by faith into this grace wherein we stand, and rejoice in hope of the glory of God.

1 Thessalonians 5:17 says Pray without ceasing.

SHADY RATCHETNESS TO GLORY
ROSLYN OFLAHERTY
MOTAVATIONAL SUBJECTS
LET'S REINVENT OURSELVES
WRITER'S BLOG

───────

This book does not take the place of God's holy word!!!
All rights referenced and cited from the Holy Bible... Prayer works ALWAYS
Thank God ...
KING JAMES VERSION
KJV ~ pls. read Matthews Chapter 6
John Chapter 3 verse 16

References Continues:
AMAZING GRACE

A Christian hymn published in 1779 with words written by the English poet and Anglican Clergyman John Newton 1725 – thru 1807 Newton wrote words from personal experience. / found on line.

THE SONG- "JESUS LOVES ME LYRICS" Cited and reference from church...

(The follow information is referenced or modeled; or cited)

NAT TURNER AND ROSA PARKS INFORMATION FROM THE INTERNET, QUOTES. NAT TURNER =HISTORY.COM

ROSA PARKS =KNOWLEDGE, SEE MORE ON –BLACK HISTORY- HISTORY.COM – BIOGRAPHY.COM

DOCTOR MARTIN LUTHER KING INFORMATION ESSENCE VIDEO SOME INFO. FOUND ON LINE QUOTES DOCTOR MARTIN LUTHER KINGS – I HAD A DREAM=AVALON.LAW. YALE EDUCATION

PRESIDENT JOHN F. KENNEDYQUOTED FROM BIOGRAPHY. COM ON LINE

BECAUSE OF THE DYNAMIC NATURE OF THE INTERNET, ANY WEB ADDRESSES OR LINK CONTAINED IN THIS BOOK MAY HAVE CHANGED SINCE THE PUBLICATION AND MAY KNOW LONGER BE VALID.

BIBLE TEACHING AND REFRENCES: BIBLE KJV-

BIBLE STUDIES SISTER V. JACKSON BISHOP D. PERICE

GOD CAN'T BE BOXED OFF!

The Social order of some people; want to put God in a box. Their thinking is being used as a translator to righteousness. In which they maintain their personal stability. In this violent civilization of either the immortal or moral concepts; of humanities institutional racism.

We must help our children to see that their ambitions. While leading them successfully into a future. That enables them to survive. Faith will show you that; you have been released from bondage. We can be spiritual minded people with blessing. We don't have to live in the natural. Your walk with God is personal!!! We can put our sins on the Alter and give God the glory.

God uses people as vessels. He is not looking for perfection. You must be free in your mind state; to be able to love others. Humanity must matter without racism. With inferiority; on a political level of destruction. Towards people of color and other nationalities. That live as Americans. Human being is not a race. Gods created human beings and not a person or individuals as a race. That should be destroyed mentally and struggle in order to get a better quality of life...

Stop speaking on what is wrong with people, and know there are times. When you are a hot mess yourself. With Gutter Butt intensions. You must realize that Glory comes from Mess. Along with people's flaws. Well I want to ask you something. You as a human being. Can you say; Oh Lord I know I'm a mess. But God I'm going to need you to help me get it right. I wish to help people get through their weakness and defects. Without the intention of destroying them. No one has that right.

Every day I pray not to entertain behaviors. I have asked myself on many occasions; why I own people's shit. Which is their shit; their baggage. Have I become God! When I own their psychological garbage on how they perceive my mental status... Personally I don't even like them but I stay entertaining their crap. I'm trying not to hate them. And continue to try to let myself walk in love.

I tell God There are some folks I must leave behind. In order for me to grow as an individual. And through all the disrespect. I have learned to realize. Everybody's not going where I'm going. People are born alone and it's all right to learn how to be alone. I must not let anyone condemn me it's not their job. I must think smart and stay safe. In this world of justice.

SHADY RATCHETNESS TO GLORY
By Roslyn OFlaherty

There are circumstances in this book; stories are not to be emulated. There might be different entities in life cycles that may cause negative discrepancies. It contains sexual situations. For the readers who have any disagreements with this book. The author Roslyn O'Flaherty respects their judgement. This book may sometimes give many untruths to real matters; in hard core life along with facts of concerns. In order to explain life styles and human conducts; presented in life's reality of disagreement. NRA must correct the gun laws. Do you believe the laws on the right to bear arm should be evaluated? On mental health level. In order to protect people, and have a safe environment.

Guns control does not exist in my neighborhood. Hunters refiles and hand guns promotes a disastrous danger on so many harsh levels. We must understand that in life; we need more than just faith alone; to believe in our gun laws. Safety is needed in our environment of inappropriate racism. Many people are searching for leadership and better living conditions. Craving a route to unconditional love. We try to teach our youth to look away; from societies dreamland of negative expectations. Through acknowledging the lack of political peace amounts nations. Why are our next generation of young adults still losing their integrity through criminal fundamentals? They are only trying to live through poorly spoken American dream speeches. That sabotages human rights with empty promises.

Young minds are confused with the lifecycles of empowerment and repentance. Which teaches many to understand the reality of life's radical injustice that may cause drama. It is keeping people in bondage to the slavery of political science. Which is the worthless government's garbage. Open the Bible it shows you that this is God's Government. He can reform you. Devastation is caused by the enemy, used as a tactic of civil disobedience. Which may be considered deceitful self-gratification. Does our Government consider policy brutalities suitable for society? Yet it is a form of interference to cause; rejection with self-destruction and immoral mass destruction.

Should World Wars be presented upon us in the land of the so call free? Military conflict with an unhelpful impression. Which may cause nuclear death with a radiation illness.

The chains and shackles have been removed from our risks, ankles and necks physically. Psychologically it should have uplifted our spirits, minds and souls... To remain humiliated by unoccupied headed impartial individuals. Who are malicious and abusive making us wrongly accused? It sometimes causes a fight with many emotions for all people of this great nation. To have Black Lives Matters; painted on the ground of our neighborhood only shows where African Americans live. To single them out as a cult with other nationalities of the human race. Causing division through racism/segregation. God loves everybody Black Lives Matter is a global organization for peace. Sometimes he is not pleased with our action. But God is love. Even when we look for Social Justice.

Is social justice what is being called miscommunication or damnation? With dangerous privileges with rules. Which are used to dominate individual and situations. Do they realize racism is a spirit of depression; that needs deliverance. People should not entertain it and never become emotionally attached. They have to detach themselves; from the abusive people. There is no compensation for the sexually harassed and bullied persons who are clinically depressed. Do the countries' problems come from the voice of authority? Who is thought of as a Mobs Gangster Member; Donkey Donnie Dolittle? I was led to believe that he resided in a dwelling. That is painted a pure color. Dolittle wears a ceremony garment with tattoo #45. Have voter's rights brutally becoming a, form of disrespect. To free speech with blatant intent to harm people? Is it now used as the basis of selective permission for improvement to some? We must understand that we must join together for one purpose unity and respect.

It is time to acknowledge the rights of humankind in embarrassing circumstances. There are too many misinterpreted restrictions on people who are taught to compromise. (Life's old gift of manipulation and control.) Think for yourself! Trauma can sometimes come from not giving up one's dignity or pride, it often unsettles the enemy. Confrontation can be so bad that it puts someone on a destructive defense mode.

It is time for humankind to not let anyone put chains on their minds. In order to cast away spirits of hope. Don't try to put God in a box for your own subjective convenience... RATCHNESS WITH A SIDE OF SHADE - CAN BE SAVED BY GLORY... Fear cannot be the level of the upper hand anymore. It is time to assess our needs for being successful in order to attain opportunities! We must always remember God's Grace and move forward from there.

"One Nation under God"
Faith - Mercy- Grace and Glory…

KJV BIBLE verses-

Romans Chapter 5. Verse 2 and verse 6

Romans Chapter 5-Verse 2
By whom also we have access by faith into this grace wherein we stand
And rejoice in hope of the Glory of God.

Roman Chapter 5-verse 6
For when we were yet without strength, in due time. Christ died for the ungodly.

This book:
SHADY RATCHETNESS TO GLORY
BY ROSLYN O'FLAHERTY IS STORIES THAT ARE MY INTENSE
FICTION IMAGINATION OF NATURAL LIFE. WRITTEN TO
SHARE AND TEACH INFORMATION THAT IS NOT MEANT
TO DISCRIMINATE AS TO WHAT AN INDIVIDUAL MAY
EXPERIENCED IN LIFE. LEAVING A DRAMATIZED OUTLOOK
AND NEGATIVE OBJECTIONS. HOPING THE ENEVITABLE
BRINGS INDIVIDUALS TO THERE FULL PROTENTIAL
OF THEIR HOPES AND DREAMS TO REACH FORTH TO
RIGHTOUSNESS

WRITTEN IN HOPES TO OPEN ONES MINDS AND HEART
SO WE DON'T DESTROY UNCERTAINTIES. IT IS NOT
THE INTENTION TO INCORROUAGE TRAMA OR TO BE
DISRESPECTFUL TO ANYONE. WARNING ANY NEGATIVE
DRAMATAZATION GIVEN SHOULD NOT BE COPYED IN
REAL LIFE. IT HAS BEEN WRITTEN TO GIVE WISDOM AND
POSITIVE DIRECTION IN LIFE.

MANY OF US LIVE A STRESSFUL LIFE WITH LOW SELF ESTEEM.
YET WE ARE READY TO ALWAYS BETTER OURSELVES.
DON'T LET YOUR CONVICTIONS BE A DANCE WITH THE
DEVIL AND HIS DICTATORSHIP. SOME FOLKS HAVE NEVER
EXPERIENCED HARD TIMES.

SOME PEOPLE NEVER ACKNOWLEDGED THINGS THAT HAVE
BEEN DENTRAMENTAL TO THEMSELVES AND OTHERS.
BECAUSE THEY FEEL OFFENDED AND DISHONOR FROM
OTHERS JUDGING THEM BY THEIR PAST REPUTATIONS.
THAT IS KNOW LONGER ACKNOWLEDGED TO BE IN
EXSISTENCE AS A BELIEF. THIS BOOK IS NOT MENT TO
BELITTLE ANYONE. OUR CIVILATION IS DECLINING IN
ABSTRACT TRUTHS. ALONG WITH SOME INDIVIUALS LACK
OF KNOWLEDGE OF THIS EARTH DECLINING. IT IS TIME TO

GO OUT AND SAVE SOULS. MIND INSPIRATIONAL WORDS
FROM THE HEART WITH A MESSAGE FROM THE SOUL...

*****ALL BIBLE VERSES IN THIS BOOK SHADY RATCHNESS
TO GLORY BY ROSLYN OFLAHERTY ARE FROM THE KING
JAMES VERSION OF THE HOLY BIBLE... referenced modeled and
cited information...

Roslyn OFlaherty is from New York, NY. She was raised in the City
that never sleeps. Edenwald / Throggs Neck / and Boston Road is where
Roslyn learned no one could walk in her shoes; better than her. In the
struggles of hard times... No regrets; she was taught and the outcome
of her family shows it. All of her immediate family can hold their own.
Which sometimes makes her know; she is not needed as a care giver
anymore. But she stepped into two new generations. That touched her
heart with felt love. She Thanks God for letting her be Ma, Grand-Ma and
Grand Ma GG. Praying for direction and guidance. Through her willing
participation that brings a pleasant advantage; over her heart felt love...
Roslyn's assignment is to help others... Which comes pure from her heart.
All her life she has been a care giver to many individuals. When she gets
blessing. She tries to Bless others.

By reading SHADY RATCHETNESS TO GLORY BY ROSLYN
OFLAHERTY you will find the writer's book contains a mentality that
is often hushed because of people's condescending attitudes. We must all
look for God's Government and pray against deception and fear. The Holy
Spirit comes to us. To break the spirits of shady tactics and ratchetness. So,
we can except God's Glory to experience and acknowledge his son with
gracefulness...

Frequently many people lived religious slavery. Racial consciousness
comes along with poverty. Families structures looking good on the outside.
Truthfully told it was horrific; mentally on the inside. Silenced in this
dangerous world concept. Of making it to heaven from earth. While the
global government's politicians wish to bring cotton; cheap labor and
enslavement back. Or, do you think they want us to; have us living like we
are back in the Fifties. (1950's). African Americans back then were called
colored people. Political Liars Sipping Tea - with racial laws that allows

them to throw shade. This stops unity and peace for productive citizens. While bringing out agony to the cultural concepts nationwide. We hear about organized religion with rapes and riches that prospered through deception. Murder and children's deaths unexplained. Some deaths in streets, prison hospitals and churches; are swept under the rug. Like they never existed. Is this considered a form of assignation. With no morals towards negative behavior; in this imperfect life. Many individuals' worries are on voting ballots going to be controlled unfairly. Government puppets full of political liability and the ultimate evil. Still play with their nuts. While figuring out their pass X-rated exploitations A menace trying to bring on the center of attention mass destruction to our nation. While trying to keep people calm and relaxed. The stage has already been set; while you wait on justice the american way. Do people still believe prayer works anymore?

Voting can't be the ploy to keep people from rising up. while dealing with theses tyrants. We can't become prisoners of our pass ancestors history. Women raped in cotton fields. As they are forced to pick cotton. Our men becoming the deceased. In wars conflict regime that brings on suffering. That have nothing to do with them. Know regards to children and families; just a life of exertion to pain with no justice. We can't afford to rip and run. Through this dysfunctional journey. The future must change. Time to rise up to their stupidity; to harming our young adults while they try to become successful. Culture leadership and organization are becoming a hilarious shadow to life. Is this the time to hit the street people? Without getting caught up. In shameless immoral psychotic behavior of government murders. Independence of true godly relationships has been destroyed. It is time to get close to the true Father God. He is special... The Bible is your weapon. For a Nation of brotherhood around the world. An assignment to plunge into with love. That should not be threatened with trauma.

BIBLE KJV Proverbs 30 says-
Every word of God is pure: He is a shield
Unto them that put their trust in him.

Occasionally:
THE FLESH
IS
WEAK?

WHO IS HE THAT OVERCOMETH THE WORLD, BUT HE THAT BELIEVETH THAT JESUS IS THE SON OF GOD?

1ST JOHN 5:5
CITED FROM; Holy Bible KJV

THE SINNERS PRAYER
BY DR. RAY PRITCHARD

(referenced and modeled /cited from)
FOUND ON / crosswalk.com

LORD JESUS, for too long I've kept you out of my life. I know that I am a sinner and I cannot save myself. No longer will I close the door when I hear you knocking. By faith I gratefully receive your gift of salvation. I am ready to trust you as my Lord and savior. Thank you, Lord Jesus, for coming to earth. I believe you are the Son of God who died on the cross for my sins and rose from the dead on the third day. Thank you for bearing my sins. _____ _____ ...

If you have prayed this prayer in sincere faith, you may want to put your initials by the prayer. Along with today's date as a reminder that you, have come to Christ in faith. Trusting him as your Lord and Savior.

Referenced and cited- Reinhold Niebuhr

THE SERINITY PRAYER

God grant me the serenity
to accept the things I cannot change,
courage to change the things I can,
And wisdom to know the difference.
Prayer authored by Reinhold Niebuhr
Living one day at a time;
enjoying one moment at a time.
Accepting hardships as the pathway to peace;
Taking, as he did, this sinful world
as it is, not as I would have it;
Trusting as he would make all things right
if I surrender to His will;
That I may be reasonably happy in this life
and supremely happy with Him Forever in the next. Amen.

Reinhold Niebuhr 1892 –1971 Serenity Prayer reference and cited - found
on beief net.com

"For God so loved the world,
That he gave his only begotten
Son, that whosoever believeth
in him should not perish but have
everlasting life."

John 3:16

Reference Thomas Nelson – The Holy Bible
King James Version, Revised 1987

"Jesus was beat on your behalf"

THE FIRST EPISTLE OF JOHN KJV - 1 JOHN

1. That which was from the beginning, which we have heard, which we have seen with our eyes, which we have looked upon, and our hands have handled, of the word of life;

2. (For the life was manifested, and we have seen it, and bear witness, and shew unto you that eternal life, which was with the father, and was manifested unto us ;)

3. That which we have seen and heard declared we unto you, that ye also may have fellowship with us: and truly our fellowship is with the father and with his son Je'-sus Christ.

4. And these things write we unto you, that your joy may be full.

5. This then is the message which we have heard of him, and declare unto you, that God is light, and in him is no darkness at all.

6. If we say that we have fellowship with him, and walk in darkness, we lie, and do not the truth.

*7. But if we walk in the light, as he is light, we have fellowship one with another and the blood of Je'-sus Christ his son clean Seth us from all sins.

8. If we say we have no sin, we deceive ourselves, and the truth is not in us.

*9. If we confess our sins. He is faithful and just to forgive us our sins, and to cleanse us from all unrighteousness.

10. If we say that we have not sinned, we make him a liar, and his word is not in us.

Shady ratchetness to glory... by Roslyn OFlaherty... She is Dedicating this book to those who left us too soon: and the lost souls.

A-men

John 10:10 KJV in the bible says: The thief cometh not, but for to steal and To kill, and to destroy: I am come that they May have life, and that they have it more abundantly...

"LOVE THY FATHER"... "JESUS IS THE LIVING WORD"... A-men... For those of us who have sinned and it's eating you alive. It's time for you to tell what you did. You know what you did... So speak up... God knows that you sinned. Your sins have been washed away in the blood of Jesus: so you can walk in righteousness. We have all sinned in one way or another. So it's time to give your true testimony. You see, you were forgiven a long time ago. It's you who wishes to carry all that baggage in your mind. You ought to know that your soul can't be truly free; until you release the confessions imprisoned within yourself...

All this is turning you into a vagabond. Which is a façade, immoral ratchetness altering your state of concentration. It is bothersome to your state of existence. Save your soul; be released from this trouble. Which has turned your consciousness upside down... Free your soul, and be delivered from your devastating psyche; bottled up inside of you. It is a blessing to be sane. Accept the gift of the Holy Spirit.

> "Walk in love with grace, mercy with the hearing of faith in Gods laws. Be restored and Experience God's glory. Look for God's righteousness to stay prayed up in your heart. Confess your sins to Jesus who died on the cross and opened his arms to you... God Knows your sins so; don't stay under attack with hate and evilness...

> Stay Blessed with forgiveness..."

Roslyn OFlaherty

Mark 11:25 says – and when ye stand praying, forgive, if ye have ought against any: that your Father also which is in heaven may forgive you your trespasses.

"THERE IS A FATHER TO THE FATHERLESS" ... "FATHER GOD" ...

Holy Bible KJV
REVELATION 20: 10 thru 15

10 And the devil that deceived them was cast into the lake of fire and brimstone, where the beast and the false prophet are, and shall be tormented day and night for ever and ever.

11 And I saw a great white throne, and him that sat on it, from whose face the earth and the heaven fled away; and there was found no place for them.

12 And I saw the dead, small and great, stand before God; and the books were opened: and another book was opened, which is the book of life: and the dead were judged out of those things which were written in the books, according to their works.

13 And the sea gave up the dead which were in it; and death and hell delivered up the dead which were in them: and they were judged every man according to their works.

14 And death and hell were cast into the lake of fire. This is the second death.

15 And whosoever was not found written in the book of life was cast into the lake of fire.

"JESUS SAID FOLLOW ME"...

This book does not take the place of the holy bible…

BIBLE – KJV

JESUS WAS BEATEN ON YOUR BEHALF

PSALMS: Chapter 144 VERSES 11 THRU 15

11. Rid me, and deliver from the hand of strange children, whose mouths speaketh vanity and their right hand of false hood:

12. That our son may be as plants grown up in their youth: that our daughters may be as corner stones, polished after the similitude of a palace.

13. That our garners may be full, affording all manner of store: that our sheep may bring fourth thousands and ten thousand in our streets:

14. That our oxen will be strong to labour, there be no complaining in our streets.

15. Happy is that people that is in such a case yea, happy is that people, whose God is Lord:

PSALMS: 144:7

7. Send thine hand from above rid me, and deliver me out of the great waters, from the hands of strange children.

PSALMS 18: 11

11. We love thee O Lord my strength.

PSALMS 144:1

1. Be the Lord my strength which teachth my hand to war and thy fingers to fight.

MALICHI 2:11

11. Ju-dah hath dealth treacherously, and abomination is committed in Is-ra-el and in Je-ru-sa-lem: for Ju-dah hath profaned the holiness of the Lord which he loved, and hath married the daughter of a strange God.

PSALMS 128:3

3. The wife shall be like a fruitful vine by the sides of thine house: the children like olive plants round about thy table.

DEUTERONOMY 33:4

4. Mo'-ses commanded us a law, even the inheritance of the congregation of Ja'-cob.

ISAIAH 53:10

10. Yet it pleased the Lord to bruise him; he hath put him to grief: when thou shalt make his soul an offering for, he shall see his seed, he shall prolong his days, and the pleasure of the Lord shall prosper in his name.

ISAIAH 54: 9

9. For this is like the water of Noah unto me: for I have sworn that the water of No'-ah should no more go over the earth; so have I sworn that I would not be worth be wroth with thee, nor rebuke thee.

REVELATION 4: 3

3. And he that sat was to look upon like a jasper and a sardine stone: and there was a rainbow round about the throne, in sight like unto an emerald.

"THE FATHER TRUELY LOVES YOU"

Gods Law- Given by Moses the Servant.
Grace- Given by Jesus Christ his son.
GRACE SHALL MAKE YOU WHOLE...

HOLY BIBLE KJV-
PSALM 46 VERSE 10

BE STILL, AND KNOW THAT I AM GOD: I WILL BE
EXHALTED AMONG THE HEATHEN. I WILL BE EXALTED
IN THE EARTH.

THE GOSPEL ACCORDING TO JOHN
JOHN 1: VERSE 14

AND THE WORD WAS MADE FLESH, AND DWELT AMOUNG
US, (AND WE BEHELD HIS GLORY, THE GLORY AS OF THE
ONLY BEGOTTEN OF THE FATHER,) FULL OF GRACE AND
TRUTH.
THE HOLY BIBLE KJV

"Roman 8:31"

What shall we then say to these things? If God be
for us, who can be against us?

HE THAT WALKETH
WITH WISE MEN SHALL
BE WISE.
BUT A COMPANION OF
FOOLS SHALL BE DESTROYED.

PROVERBS 13:20 KJV

Glory
Is who You are!

Shady ratchetness
To
Glory

BY ROSLYN OFLAHERTY

HOLY BIBLE KJV 1ˢᵗ Corinthians 1 verse 27
But God hath chosen the foolish
things of the world to confound the
wise: and God hath chosen the weak
things of the world to confound the
things which are mighty Ps. 8;2

The author of SHADY RATCHETNESS TO GLORY. Roslyn Oflaherty was not raised in the church. (She never had a church family) Yet feeling of church is in her. Religious people spoke over her life. Stating she will never enter the kingdom of God. They felt she did not have a personal relationship with God. Due to the fact she did not follow any religion. Roslyn was a lost soul; raised in the streets of New York City. As an Uptown girl from the Boogie Down Bronx.

This book is considered her ministry. Roslyn is on assignment to help others; because it came from a pure heart. She believes the church was in the streets. A real togetherness of the families with children in her community. Detering the struggles of hard times. Yet the struggle of hard times came; later on, in life as a battle. Which identified her as true lost soul. She would always ask God. How she people would stop; killing her with kindness. As they sabotaged her aspirations. Some people have to hit rock bottom. In order to seek God. Then they were grateful enough to honor God. Jesus was the foundation that was needed. (The body of Christ.) The Father, the son and the holy spirit. The people crucified Jesus and he died for our sins.

Some passages in the book, SHADY RATCHETNESS TO GLORY. May have seem to identified; with many people's life's history. Which is shared with optimism or a history. With no entitlement to freedom. We can't conform to what people say. We should try to love them. There are missing conclusions of attributes to the soul's energy. Which is in the need of balance. To mental and social factors with gratitude. Let the holy spirit speak to you. The communities must speak up for each other. Live pass poverty with kindness and spirituality. Life also shows us a modern-day oppression. Mostly because some of us live in the land of shade. We all carry the name of God. A merciful God. Who wants you to come as you are? You must believe that he will clean you up.

God is a relationship. Everyone's relationship is different. Jesus died for our sins. Sin is the government, oppression, injustice etc. Family is a ministry. Our lives are off the chain. It's time for the chains to come off our necks. We are not enslaved. Share and respect everybody with love. You don't have to entertain certain people. Most People can cut the generational curses; that are so ratchet. Some people are not going to change. All this can take time and growth. We must not act on our emotions. Upstand who you are. Church has become a hospital with wisdom that should be a foundation. An open book. Like the Bible. The people should be converted by grace. Grace is what is used to cover sin.

The author has learned; God answers prayers. We don't have to be messy to comply with church. Church is a community. Not man-made denominations. We must be able to be effective for God; and the body of Christ without being convicted. Remember to understand your identity.

Bible King James Version Acts 17 verses 22 thru 28
Acts Verse 22 says- Then Paul stood in the midst of
Mars' hill, and said, Ye men of all Athens, I perceive
that in all things ye are too superstitious.
Acts vs 23 says- For as I pass by, and be held your
devotions, I found a alter with this inscription,
TO THE UNKNOWN GOD. Whom therefore Ye
ignorantly worship him.
Acts vs 24 says- God that made the world and all
things therein, seeing that he is Lord of heaven and
earth, dwelleth not in temples made with hands.
Acts vs 25 says- Neither is worshipped with men's
hands, as though he needed any breath, and all things.
Acts vs 26 says- And hath made of one blood all nations
of men for to dwell on all the face of the earth, and hath
Determined the times before appointed, and the bounds
of their habitation;
Acts vs 27 says- That they should seek the Lord if haply
They might feel after him, though he be not far from
every one of us.
Acts 28 says- For in him we live, and more, and have our
being; as certain also of your own poets have said, For we
Are also his offspring.

Bible KJV
Titus 2 verse 11 says
For the grace of God
That bringeth salvation
Hath appeared to all men.

WHY MUST WE ALWAYS BE POLITICALLY CORRECT?

Printed in the United States
by Baker & Taylor Publisher Services